D0051644

Judith Cook was born and brought up in Manchester. She began her career as a journalist for the *Guardian* and went on to become a freelance writer, winning awards for investigative journalism and having several highly acclaimed works of fiction and non-fiction published. Judith Cook lives in the fishing port of Newlyn, Cornwall, with her partner and two cats.

The first four entries in the Casebook of Dr Simon Forman, *Death of a Lady's Maid*, *Murder at the Rose*, *Blood on the Borders* and *Kill the Witch*, are also available from Headline.

Praise for Judith Cook's work:

'Among the pleasures of Cook's Elizabethan series are the beautifully researched period settings . . . Forman is a cleverly characterised hero, with just enough modern sensibility to give him a fascinating edge'   *The Times*

'[Cook] spins a fast and entertaining tale'   *Guardian*

'A good, pacy read . . . Cook is keen on fine historical detail and has obviously mastered her subject'
Evening Standard

'A well-balanced thriller . . . intelligent and entertaining'
TLS

School of the Night

Judith Cook

HEADLINE

Copyright © 2000 Judith Cook

The right of Judith Cook to be identified as the Author of
the Work has been asserted by her in accordance with the
Copyright, Designs and Patents Act 1988.

First published in 2000
by HEADLINE BOOK PUBLISHING

First published in paperback in 2000
by HEADLINE BOOK PUBLISHING

10 9 8 7 6 5 4 3 2 1

All rights reserved. No part of this publication may be
reproduced, stored in a retrieval system, or transmitted
in any form or by any means without the prior written
permission of the publisher, nor be otherwise circulated
in any form of binding or cover other than that in which
it is published and without a similar condition being
imposed on the subsequent purchaser.

All characters in this publication are fictitious
and any resemblance to real persons, living or dead,
is purely coincidental.

ISBN 0 7472 6174 1

Typeset by
Letterpart Limited, Reigate, Surrey

Printed and bound in Great Britain by
Clays Ltd, St Ives plc

HEADLINE BOOK PUBLISHING
A division of Hodder Headline
338 Euston Road
London NW1 3BH

www.headline.co.uk
www.hodderheadline.com

To my splendid copy-editor, Joan Deitch.

Acknowledgements

General sources used include Forman manuscripts in the Bodleian Library, Oxford and King's College, Cambridge; the medical information comes from *Simon Forman's Casebooks* (ed. A. L. Rowse), *Dr Hall's Casebook* (ed. Joan Lane) and *Culpeper's Herbal*. More about the real School of the Night can be found in *The Search for Christopher Marlowe* (ed. Wraight and Stern), and *The Elizabethan Underworld* by Gamini Salgado. I feel there should also be a special mention for that great Elizabethan dramatist and character, 'rare' Ben Jonson, described by one who spent time with him when he was in tavern mode that it was like listening to a big drum being beaten in a small room. His poem *The Voyage* was the inspiration for the dénouement of the book.

Chapter 1

Candied Sea Holly

'Candied sea holly!' Actor Tom Pope threw back his head and roared with laughter. His friend, Dr Simon Forman, looked aggrieved. The two men were sitting in Tom's comfortable kitchen in his small, neat house on the Bankside, close to the Rose Theatre. They had sat long over their wine, the hour was late and Tom's wife Jenny had left them to it and gone to bed since she would have to be up betimes to see their sons off to school.

'You're actually trying to make me believe that sugared sea holly works as an aphrodisiac?' Tom persisted.

'So I'm reliably informed,' replied Simon. He had drunk enough to feel somewhat slighted. 'It's long been considered so in the Eastern counties, most especially around Colchester, where it is picked in quantity and much shipped over to France. Anyway,' he continued triumphantly, 'the School are going to experiment and test it for themselves, and to that end I have sent away for a box.'

Tom shook his head. 'And I thought your "School of the Night" was a sober gathering of mathematicians and practitioners of the New Science under the leadership of no lesser person than the great Sir Walter Ralegh. Though, I suppose if it were that sober, Kit Marlowe would hardly be a regular attender.'

1

'It *is* a serious gathering,' insisted Simon. 'I admit I've only been to three meetings up there in Ralegh's Tower, but two have dealt with navigation and the question of longitude, and the third with the true date of the events in the Old Testament.'

'So where does your aphrodisiac fit in?' enquired Tom. 'Do you intend trying to discover what wiles the Queen of Sheba used on King Solomon or Salome on King Herod?'

Simon shook his head. 'It is to be a properly conducted scientific experiment. Once the sea holly has arrived, we are all going down to Sir Walter's country mansion near Sherborne in Dorset where some of us intend to partake of different amounts of it and then record the result.'

'On your own?' asked Tom with mock seriousness. 'With each other? That would suit Kit Marlowe, I suppose. Or do you intend inviting ladies along with you? Then again, I suppose you might follow the example of the Ancient Romans with the Sabine women and round up half a dozen lusty local wenches!'

Simon rose to his feet with a certain amount of drunken dignity. 'I see you are determined not to take me seriously.'

Tom shook his head. 'No, old friend, I must admit I'm not.' He paused for a moment before continuing with some difficulty. 'How is Avisa?' Only to Tom had Simon fully confided the truth about his relationship with Avisa Allen, his mistress and the love of his heart. There was little hope for the future, for by the time they met she was already the wife of a City merchant and had been for some years. Now she was expecting a child – *his* child, although her husband was unaware of it. The question partly sobered him up.

He sighed. 'Not very well. She's carrying after a sickly fashion though I've cast her horoscope several times and it assures me there will be a happy outcome. But it is making her fretful and whenever we meet now, which is rarely enough, we seem to quarrel.'

'I've every sympathy for how you feel about her,' said Tom, 'but you know my own opinion. It would be better for both of you if you could part friends, then you could find yourself a woman with no such ties and make her your wife – one who would be a proper helpmeet to you, like my Jenny is to me.'

'Your Jenny is a rare soul,' agreed Simon.

'She is indeed. And scarcely a day passes when I don't count my blessings, though even we quarrel from time to time. But I believe in the old adage, never let the sun go down on your wrath.'

The two men went to the door and Tom followed Simon on to the path outside, drawing in great breaths of air in an attempt to clear his head. It was a wet winter and there was an unpleasant dank chill in the air. A brackish smell came to them from the river.

'I wish I too was going home to a warm woman in a warm bed,' said Simon. 'I've always found enforced celibacy hard to bear.'

'Then surely trying out aphrodisiacs will only make it worse,' commented his friend, shivering a little.

Simon looked somewhat sheepish. 'From what I gather, although Sir Walter does not altogether approve, there will be willing ladies provided for those who find it necessary.'

Tom looked grim. 'Then you'd better take care, Simon. The last time you attended some sort of erotic show, when you were up in the wilds in Edinburgh, you ended up being arrested and accused of murder!'

'But the circumstances, as you well know, were exceptional. It can't happen this time,' Simon retorted.

'When do you leave London?' asked his friend.

'It depends on when the sea holly reaches me. I'm expecting it any day. Then I shall be off to Ralegh's country house at Cerne Abbas.'

'Cerne Abbas?' queried Tom, then started to chuckle again.

Simon sighed. '*Now* what?'

'The name means nothing to you?' Simon shook his head. 'Then all I can say is that you're in for a surprise. We passed through the village on our way to play in Dorchester some years back. I remember it well. Good luck!'

He clapped Simon on the back and retreated indoors while Simon made his way somewhat uncertainly into the night. He let himself into his quiet house and made his way upstairs to his bed. A constant and monotonous snoring came from behind the door to the back bedroom where his servant, John Bradedge, slept with his wife Anna and their small son. He smiled with some relief, remembering the times on their various adventures when he had been forced to share a room with John and had been driven to distraction by the noise. On the other hand, John had made himself invaluable to him since he and his family had joined Simon's household.

He slept uneasily as is often the case after too much red wine and awoke some time in the dark small hours with a kaleidoscope of thoughts going round and round in his head. Professionally things were going extremely well. The Royal College of Physicians had been forced to give him back his licence to practise some time ago by order of no lesser personage than the great Sir Robert Cecil, Acting Secretary to the Privy Council, though his relationship with that gentleman was one which still made him shudder. Still, it was no longer only the actors, the local artisans and the Bankside poor who wanted his services but wealthy City merchants, men of the professional classes and their wives, even a bishop.

Yet there was a considerable hole in his personal life. He had always been susceptible to women and there was no shortage of those happy to make themselves available to him – even, though he preferred not to think about it too much, some of his patients.

Years ago, when he was in Europe, Simon had found a woman he wanted to make his wife, only to lose her in a fever epidemic. Since then he had never been moved emotionally until he met Avisa. It seemed so unfair. They had so much in common, for she was almost as skilled a distiller of strong waters and maker of salves as a trained apothecary. She shared his interests and his sense of humour and there she was, married to a man twenty years her senior, a fellow who seemed set to live until he was a hundred. Against all his own rules in matters astrological, Simon had actually cast Allen's horoscope in an attempt to discover if he was likely to be carried off in the foreseeable future, but the answer seemed to be that his rival was destined for long life.

He came down for breakfast the next morning in a poor humour and with a thick head. 'This came for you yesterday evening, doctor,' said Anna as he slumped at the kitchen table, 'brought by a man who said he had come from Essex.' She handed him a letter fastened with a seal.

Dear Doctor Forman, he read, *this from apothecary Beck. I fear I am unable to send you the 'eringo' (or 'oringoe' as it is sometimes known), the candied sea holly, for which you asked since suddenly I am quite out of it. However, I am enquiring around others in my trade including a colleague in Manningtree and another as far away as Norwich and am hopeful that one or other of them will be able to assist you. I will, of course, pass on to them the money you sent me. I trust that it will not be too long before I am successful. Your obedient servant, Joseph Beck.*

Simon screwed up the paper and threw it across the kitchen. John and Anna exchanged looks. It was obviously going to be one of those days. Simon finished his morning ale, pushed away the bread and honey Anna had prepared for him and rose from the table, growling that he was away to his study and he hoped the people of the Bankside Southwark were feeling fit and well, for he was not! Fortunately he was in luck, for apart from a young man wanting his horoscope cast to discover if the merchant venture in which he had a share would succeed, a carter with an abscess on his neck which required the lance, and an elderly woman unable to shake off a nasty cough, he was left to his own devices.

The noise of an arrival at his front door caused Simon to raise his head from trying to catch up with recording his case notes. He heard the door close again and Anna's footsteps cross the hall. She knocked on his door and opened it. 'This has just come for you, doctor,' she said and handed him a box made of thin wood, some twelve inches square by about four inches deep.

Simon took it from her and examined it. 'Was there no note?'

'No, sir. It was brought by a carrier who said he came from Colchester. I asked him who had sent it and he told me the man who gave it to him said he was an apothecary.'

So, thought Simon, Joseph Beck must have been immediately successful and found me another supplier of candied sea holly as soon as he had sent word to me that he had none himself. He thanked Anna and took the box over to his desk. The lid was secured with small tacks and it took him only a moment to prise it open. Whatever lay inside was covered with a small piece of cloth which he removed. Although he knew the plant's properties lay in its extremely long root, Simon had somehow expected to find pale turquoise blooms and silver-grey spiky leaves. Instead what met his gaze were small pieces of something resembling very white parsnip or horseradish, but smoother. Yes, indeed, it was the sea holly.

Riffling through some papers, he quickly found the note he had received from a physician in Norwich. It began with a description of the plant and where it could be found: sand dunes and fine shingle beaches. The root, he read, could sometimes grow as long as eight or ten feet and quite straight. *The plant is venereal,* the writer continued, *and breeds seeds exceedingly, strengthening the spirit procreative; it is hot and moist and under the celestial sign of the Balance. It is of much benefit to men of middle years or older.* The physician went on to list the plant's many other uses – for curing the stone, cleaning the liver, curing defects in the reins (kidneys) and most especially as a palliative 'for the French pox'. Bruised and applied as a poultice, it also aided sufferers of sore throats. The distilled water of the plant with its flowers apparently cured everything from ear-ache to 'melancholy of the heart.'

Simon smiled, returned to his desk and penned two notes, one to be sent to Joseph Beck thanking him for finding him the sea holly so soon, and the second to Sir Walter Ralegh informing him of its arrival. He called for John Bradedge and asked him to find a carrier going to Colchester who would take the first letter to Beck and to deliver the second one to Sir Walter's house himself.

He was still admiring the sea holly in its sugary coat when Anna tapped on his door to inform him he had another patient, a gentleman who needed his advice most urgently. Feeling now in much better spirits, Simon put the box aside and asked her to send him in.

The gentleman informed Simon that he was one Master James Tapworth, a silversmith whose shop was on the Cheapside but who now lived much of the time at his substantial country property near Chelsea. His wealth was evident, from his fine long furred gown of dark velvet, to the handsome gold chain across his chest, while on his fingers he wore a number of expensive rings. Simon put his age at about sixty.

'So, sir, how might I help you?' he enquired, adding with a smile, 'Though you look fine and healthy enough.'

Master Tapworth did not return his smile. 'So I too would have thought,' he replied heavily, 'but it appears it is not so.' Simon motioned him to sit down. Before doing so the man looked behind him as if he suspected someone might be lurking at his back or inside a cupboard. 'You are sure – quite sure – that we cannot be overheard?' he demanded.

Oh no, thought Simon, here is yet another of these obsessive old fellows with a bee in his bonnet. Presumably this one's convinced that such is his importance he's followed everywhere by would-be murderers. 'Quite sure,' he promised the man in his most soothing manner, 'All that passes between you and me in this room is privy only to us two. My servant Anna is absolutely trustworthy and would not, under any circumstances, enter the room without knocking first. She is well trained.'

The man grunted, mumbled something inaudible, and eventually sat down.

'Well?' queried Simon patiently.

Tapworth ran his tongue over his lips then finally made a start. 'You must know, Dr Forman, that a month ago I remarried. My first wife, a good pious woman, died some two years ago leaving me without an heir. Unhappily she proved barren.'

Ah, thought Simon, and now he wants me to cast his horoscope to discover if his new wife is already with child or, if not, how soon she will be.

'How old is your wife?'

'Sixteen,' replied Tapworth.

Simon's eyes widened. 'Er . . . so young?' Then, seeing the expression on his client's face added quickly, 'Young, I mean, for running a large and established household.'

Tapworth dismissed this. 'That's of no account. I have an excellent housekeeper, a steward and a pack of servants to see to all that. Lavinia's task is to provide me with a child – preferably several.'

'Well, it's very early days if you've only been married a month,' Simon reassured him. 'I take it that's what you have come to me about? Though it would be more useful if I saw your wife. Is she a robust girl? In good health?'

'Oh, she's as fit as a flea,' Tapworth informed him. Then he hunched his shoulders and slumped in his chair. 'That's not the problem.'

'What is it then?' asked Simon, becoming somewhat impatient.

'You must know I spent some time and took great care in choosing the woman who would be my second wife. After much thought I decided it would suit my situation best to take a young one, on the grounds that a docile girl would accept me meekly and unquestioningly as her lord and master. This was important but not the prime reason which was that, being young and strong and in sound health, she would have no difficulty conceiving and bearing children. It took me some time to fix on the right girl but eventually I found what I was looking for. Lavinia's father is a coachmaker in Smithfield, a wealthy man, and she an only child who would bring with her a substantial dowry. So her father and I agreed and the match was concluded.'

Simon began to wonder where all this was leading. The thought crossed his mind that perhaps this Lavinia was not as meek and docile as Tapworth had hoped.

Tapworth hesitated for a moment, then continued. 'My wife is . . . very pretty. Some might even say beautiful, with a shapely – er – full-bosomed figure.' He ran his tongue over his lips again.

The old lecher's positively drooling, thought Simon.

'Maud, that was my first wife, was nothing like that. As I said, she was a good and pious woman; very pious.' He stared into space for a moment then recovered himself. 'So I will admit that the wedding day could hardly come quickly enough for me. The festivities seemed never-ending before we were finally put to bed and left alone together. It was then that the problem arose. There was a difficulty . . .'

'Ah,' smiled Simon. 'So young and inexperienced a maid was fearful, I suppose?'

Tapworth glumly shook his head. 'Fearful! God's Blood, she couldn't wait for it! Where she'd heard or learned of such matters ... Anyway, scarce had I started to take off my bedgown when she flung off her shift, lay back on the pillows and urged me on.'

'Then I'm still at a loss to understand your concerns. Most men would think themselves in heaven in such circumstances,' commented Simon, wondering who had been tutoring the young woman beforehand. He doubted it was some old wife.

'My concern is that I could not ... it was impossible ...' Tapworth rose to his feet and banged on the desk. 'Isn't it obvious, man?'

So that was it! Simon put on his most reassuring expression. 'Do I take it then that on this first occasion you were impotent? That is not unusual in the circumstances, following a formal and prolonged festivity – and no doubt you'd drunk much wine?'

Tapworth shook his head. 'It was not only on the wedding night. I have not been able to ... to rise to the occasion since. And as for Lavinia, who I'd thought so modest and unknowing a maid, she has given me an ultimatum. If she is not to be my wife in the true sense of the word, she will tell her family everything and ask them to set about getting our marriage annulled and see that her dowry is repaid in full. She is quite brazen about it. She says she agreed to marry me, an old man who wouldn't last long, to please her father so long as her second husband was entirely of her choice!' He sat down again. 'So, Dr Forman, I want some medicine – some drug which will put matters right.'

'I wish it were so simple,' Simon told him. 'There are many supposed aids, such as the powdered horn of a unicorn which I can tell you now I do not have and nor, so far as I know, does anyone else: what they pass folk off with are powders made from the ground horns of common cattle! Some physicians suggest roasted tamarind seed in eau-de-vie, and I could make you up such a draught, though personally I believe you might do better with the specific much lauded in this neighbourhood: that a plate of seafood, oysters, whelks and shrimps (especially shrimps) taken before bedtime is most effective. Then again, some wise women use mandrake root.'

'Tamarind seed? Mandrake root? *Shrimps?*' The silversmith drew breath. 'Is that the best you have to offer?'

It was then Simon had an idea. 'Do you know, Master Tapworth, I think you might be in luck, coming to me as you have today. For there is one other thing. I have recently learned that the candied root of the *eringo* plant is said to be very effective in curing this problem and to that end I ordered some from an apothecary in Colchester. As it happens, it arrived this very morning.'

'Well then,' broke in Tapworth, 'why didn't you tell me this before? What have you been waiting for?'

'Because so far as I am concerned it is quite untried and untested. Indeed, I sent away for it so that it could be examined by a group of learned men in careful circumstances and the results recorded. However, if you are willing to take the risk – though I understand it has long been used as a specific in the Eastern counties both for your problem and a variety of ailments – I will give you a little to try.'

Tapworth slapped his hand on the table and smiled for the first time. 'Then I can't see there's any real risk.' He drew a large purse from his doublet, which clanked with coins and drew out five guineas. 'Sell me some of your *eringo*, Dr Forman, and it will be worth every penny.'

Simon took the money. Even if the sea holly did not really have the properties attributed to it, all might be well if Tapworth believed that it did. He opened up the box and took out four pieces of the sugared white root which he then put into a parchment packet and handed to Tapworth. 'The best of luck, Master Tapworth. And when your bride conceives, bring her to me and I will cast her horoscope and so do my best to tell you the outcome.'

Chapter 2

The Conducting of an Experiment

The following morning Simon received a courteous note from Sir Walter Ralegh to the effect that now the *eringo* had arrived he was inviting those interested to Dorset in a week's time. Until the recent upset over his marriage to one of the Queen's maids of honour, Bess Throckmorton, Sir Walter had been so much the Queen's favourite that she had loaded him with honours and property. The Bishop of Durham had been smartly evicted from his house on the Strand to make way for the handsome young man from Devon, and Her Majesty had also given him the right to live in the Old Castle on the outskirts of Sherborne, with sufficient land to go with it to enable him to build a lodge in the countryside near Cerne Abbas.

The gathering would be housed in the castle but it was proposed that meetings and scientific discussions would take place in the lodge away from any other distractions. The new Mistress Ralegh was already at the castle, keeping well out of the way of the Queen, who had been so enraged at the secret marriage of her handsome favourite to one of her maids that she had sent both of them to cool their heels in the Tower of London for several weeks.

Not long after reading Sir Walter's note, Simon received a

visitor. He and the Rose Theatre's famous poet, Kit Marlowe, had been thrown together during his dramatic sojourn in Edinburgh* but since returning to London, Simon had seen little of him. He had, however, heard a good deal and none of it comforting. Marlowe's behaviour was at best erratic and when he was, as now, drinking heavily it could be wild to a degree. The deaths of his two closest friends, Robin Greene and the poet Tom Watson, had not helped nor, it seemed, was he able to find solace in his work. There had been no new play at the Rose Theatre since the notorious *Doctor Faustus*.

A whole series of unfortunate incidents had culminated, according to Tom Pope, in a frightful scene at the wedding breakfast held by Philip Henslowe to celebrate the marriage of his step-daughter, Joan, to his great actor, Ned Alleyn. Marlowe had arrived drunk, dishevelled and determined to pick quarrels with everyone in sight. At the end of this display, he had poured out a torrent of arrogant – indeed, blasphemous – abuse which had sent shivers down the spines not only of the pious but of all who heard it.

Certainly, thought Simon, he did not look well. His eyes were bloodshot and puffy, his skin pasty. A bruise on one cheek suggested that he had recently been in a fight and, unusual for one normally so immaculate in appearance, his shirt was grubby and his doublet stained. He strode into Simon's study and prowled around the room refusing an invitation to sit down.

'So this is your inner sanctum where you dispense physic, part credulous folk from their money by casting their horoscopes, and seduce women,' he remarked with some of his old spirit.

Simon smiled. 'Certainly I dispense physic and, as you well know, I truly believe in the powers of the planets. As to seducing women . . . there's been precious little of that of late and at the

*see *Blood on the Borders*

very least I would offer them my day bed in the next room rather than the floor.' He cast a critical eye over Marlowe. 'You look as if you could well use some of my physic to good effect. I can give you some Solomon's Seal boiled in white wine to apply to that bruise, and I imagine something to clear the blood wouldn't come amiss. Nettle juice is an excellent specific, along with syrup of hops. Don't brush me aside! I treated your late friend Robin Greene with it enough times.'

'And look what use that was,' retorted Marlowe. 'He's dead and in his grave.'

'Neither nettle juice nor syrup of hops will cure a man of the French pox, especially when coupled with a ruined liver,' said Simon, 'but he wouldn't be told.'

'Very well then,' said Marlowe, 'make me up your potion or potions. Don't worry, I can pay you for them! But that's not why I'm here. I had a note from Ralegh this morning about a meeting of the School of the Night at his place in Dorset. I understand you are to provide us with an aphrodisiac in the shape of candied sea holly. He does not say whether or not he intends to provide partners in order to try out its efficacy . . . perhaps he expects us all to be so overwhelmed with lust that we fall on each other! An interesting thought. I came to suggest that we might travel down to Dorset together. If we leave London early on Thursday, we should manage two-thirds of the journey before nightfall and arrive in Sherborne by noon the following day.'

'Company would certainly be welcome,' replied Simon some-what cautiously as visions passed in front of him of having to extricate his companion, fighting drunk, from every sizeable inn between London and Sherborne.

'Don't fret,' said Marlowe, reading his mind. 'I intend to save any debauchery for your experiment. Do you really believe it works?'

Simon shrugged. 'I don't honestly know. Certainly they swear by it in the Eastern counties, and I admit to having actually prescribed some yesterday to a man who came to me in most dire straits.'

'Fascinating. And what were they?'

'He is wealthy and fat and all of sixty and, being widowed, has married a lusty wench of some sixteen summers. At first I thought he might intend giving it to his bride, to help her over her maidenly modesty but finally, through gritted teeth, he informed me that she was only too apt at the sport while he . . . you can guess the rest.'

Marlowe laughed and Simon measured him out the potion for his bruised face ('I was stupid enough to go home to Canterbury and was insulted by some lewd fellow in a tavern') and the draught for clearing the blood. Marlowe threw some coins on Simon's desk, pocketed the phials and, with an airy wave of his hand, arranged to meet Simon outside his house by six o'clock on Thursday morning.

Having closed the front door behind him, Simon sought out John Bradedge to inform him of the plan and warn him to make ready for the journey. His man received the news with a good deal less than enthusiasm. He had been very alarmed at Kit Marlowe's involvement with the good doctor in Edinburgh, being fully aware of the poet's dangerous reputation which lost nothing in the telling, and he had only managed to rescue his master from being hanged for murder by the skin of his teeth. Admittedly that had not been Marlowe's fault, but John remained deeply suspicious. As to cavorting down to Dorset with some kind of love potion to meet up with a crew of blasphemers, sorcerers and so-called scientists, led by a Wizard Earl, nothing good could possibly come of it.

'Those who belong to the School of the Night are none such as you describe, whatever you might have heard to the contrary,' returned Simon exasperatedly on hearing these doubts. 'Some are mathematicians, others knowledgable in the New Science and geography, and as for your "Wizard Earl", Henry Percy, the great Earl of Northumberland, is one of the finest scholars of the age and patron to many good men.'

John shook his head. 'Mark my words,' he warned as he had on other, previous occasions, 'no good will come of this.'

'This time you're quite wrong,' replied his master. 'Nothing *but* good can come from a meeting of such fine minds,' at which he left the kitchen. John watched him go with a heavy heart – though even he could not have foreseen how soon he was to be proved right.

It was still dark when the three men rode away from the Bankside and began making their way across country to the road running west to Salisbury and Exeter. They planned only a brief stop around noon for sustenance since night fell so early, but at least the weather was kind – cold but not freezing.

Simon and Kit Marlowe, who was looking considerably better, chatted to each other when it was possible, given their need to press on. Marlowe was full of the latest gossip concerning Ralegh's standing with the Queen following his marriage. 'Of course, she's always desperately jealous if a favourite has the gall to marry and, as you must know, the maids of honour are supposed to ask her permission – which she rarely wants to give – so she saw it as a double wrong.'

'What will Sir Walter's new wife make of our meeting and of our experiment with the *eringo*?' Simon wondered, 'I hardly think it likely that either she or Ralegh would need such an aid, being so newly wed.'

'I imagine she will play the pleasant hostess and be kept well away from anything considered in the least doubtful,' said Marlowe. 'Anyway, I think it unlikely that Ralegh will participate, though I've no doubt that at one time he would have done so. Have you heard the story of his being surprised *in flagrante delicto* with another of the Queen's maids? No? The event took place some years back in the gardens of Nonesuch Palace. Apparently the couple couldn't restrain themselves, though at first the girl affected modesty when Ralegh made his proposition, saying, "Oh, sweet Sir Walter, what are you asking of me?" However, within minutes she was up against a convenient tree, cooing, "Nay, sweet Sir Walter . . . sweet Sir Walter," until at last, both the danger of their predicament and her ecstasy was such that she was crying out – to the interest of the small crowd that had by this time gathered to watch the event – something that sounded like "swisser, swasser, swisser swasser" and finally, "Ooooh, Sir *Walter*!" He was fortunate not to have been in trouble with the Queen then, for I'm told he got the wench with child.'

It was past noon before they finally broke their journey in the market town of Andover. During a meal of bread and cheese and ale, they discussed where best to put up for the night.

'Surely it must be Salisbury, Simon,' said Marlowe. 'Weren't you born there?'

'In Quidhampton village, nearby,' replied Simon, without enthusiasm, 'but I haven't been home for some time. My father's long dead, I'm estranged from my mother, and my brothers and sister are married and busy with their own lives. I have no other ties.'

'So which inn in the city do you recommend for tonight?' continued Marlowe, then finally became aware of his companion's reluctance. 'Do I take it you want to go elsewhere?'

'I'd prefer it if we found somewhere on the road the other side of Salisbury,' Simon told him firmly. 'I have my reasons.'

'And they are?' Marlowe persisted, determined not to let the matter rest.

Simon sighed. He might as well explain, since it was clear Marlowe wasn't going to leave him alone. 'Well, if you must know, there are at least two. I left Salisbury under a cloud, firstly for having crossed a highly unpleasant landowner by the name of Sir Giles Escourt who had me put in prison for the best part of a year, and secondly – well, that was a different matter. I fell in love, a boy and girl affair, with a maid of the name of Anne Young. We considered ourselves handfasted to each other and at that time I had every intention of marrying her. Anyway, not to put too fine a point on it, I bedded her with her willing consent, but well before I had the wherewithal to wed, she bore me a son. The scandal, coming as it did on top of my imprisonment, proved too much both for me and my family and so I fled first to London then to the Low Countries.'

'And the child?'

'My brother tells me he's a sturdy lad and that Anne is now safely married. But you can see why I've little enthusiasm to visit my old haunts.'

Marlowe gulped the rest of his ale, slapped his thigh and laughed. 'What a dark horse you are, Simon Forman! I'd no idea we shared time in gaol in common or that you had a bastard son. Well, well.'

From John Bradedge's face it had obviously been news to him as well, but Simon thought it unlikely he would make much comment. While his man was now a faithful servant and an excellent husband, he too had fled into the army in the Low Countries leaving behind a reputation for idleness, gambling and ruining young women. Marlowe said no more about staying the night in Salisbury and they passed swiftly through the town, pausing only to admire the splendid cathedral before moving on and resting for the night at a wayside inn some few miles down the Exeter road.

By noon next day they reached Sherborne Old Castle, riding in under a fine gatehouse. The scene that greeted them was a busy one as most of the visitors appeared to have arrived at about the same time. Two very fine carriages were drawn up in the courtyard, one bearing the arms of the Percies of Northumberland and the other a similarly elaborate crest which was unknown to Simon.

'Very interesting,' remarked Marlowe on seeing it. 'It seems the Countess of Pembroke is to be part of our company. It's not all that surprising, as her younger brother is married to one of Ralegh's family and you must know her elder brother, Sir Philip Sidney, at least by reputation.'

'Indeed I do,' replied Simon, 'though I've never had the honour of meeting him. Do you know the lady?'

'A little. Tom Walsingham first introduced me to her at Court, then last year she spent some time with Tom at Scadbury when I was visiting him.'

'You seem to know everyone through your grand connections,' remarked Simon.

'Not quite everyone, but it's a small and intermarried world. Philip Sidney is husband to Tom's Cousin Frances.' Marlowe eyed Simon. 'You'll be most struck. Although women have no fleshly attraction for me, I have to admit the countess is strikingly beautiful. Clever too. She writes poetry, acts as a critic for that of her brother and, I'm told, conducts scientific experiments aided by her *laborator*, Adrian Gilbert. They say too . . .' He paused.

'What?'

'No matter.' He shook his head and gave Simon what could only be described as a leer. 'Also, her husband, the Earl, is four and thirty years older than she, so you might well find her taking an interest in your candied sweetmeats.'

'You mean for her husband, of course?' asked Simon with assumed innocence as a groom appeared to take their horses.

'Of course,' replied Marlowe, demurely. 'What else?'

They dismounted and handed their horses to the groom, whereupon an impressive-looking steward appeared from the doorway to ask who they were. Having ascertained the information, he called peremptorily for a maid to show the gentlemen to their rooms and Dr Forman's servant to his quarters. The Old Castle was a rambling affair and after being taken up a fine staircase they were led along seemingly endless corridors, up two steps here, down three there, until they were shown into two well-appointed small rooms, both with windows overlooking fine rolling parkland. The girl then curtsied and informed them that Sir Walter would be hosting a late dinner very shortly.

After tidying himself and washing his face and hands in the bowl of clean water provided, Simon collected Marlowe and they attempted to return the way they had come. It proved difficult, for there seemed to be several staircases, and while two at least looked as if they were rarely used, the one they chose brought them out not into the hall but into the kitchen quarters where a host of cooks, potboys and serving girls were rushing about in clouds of steam.

'Sweet Jesu, I can't see how I can possibly tell John where my room is,' commented Simon, 'let alone find my own way back to it, even with a clear head. And if I've been drinking . . .' but before he could say any more they reached the great dining room where they were greeted by Sir Walter in person. He was, as ever, charming, expressing his hope that their journey had not been too tedious and his pleasure that they had accepted his invitation.

'You have the *eringo* with you, Dr Forman?' he enquired.

'It's safe in my room,' Simon assured him, trusting he would be able to discover it again.

Ralegh smiled. 'I don't think I will be joining in *that* particular experiment, although I know some of the younger men are enthusiastic. However, I've made it quite clear to them that I will not have the maids pestered to assist them, nor have I sent to the Bankside for a carriage-load of Winchester geese! It is to be strictly a scientific study which I have suggested takes place tomorrow evening after supper. Before that, we will have talks and discussions on a number of fascinating topics.'

At this point several ladies entered the room, among them Lady Ralegh, she who had been Bess Throckmorton. Sir Walter introduced Simon and Marlowe to her. She was indeed a very pretty young woman but she was quite overshadowed by her companion. It must be the Countess of Pembroke, thought Simon.

'And this is Mary Herbert,' Ralegh confirmed, 'a kinswoman and friend of the family, also sister, as no doubt you know, to the peerless Sir Philip Sidney.'

Mary Herbert was of middle height for a woman, with a shapely figure. Simon had to agree with Marlowe, that here indeed was true beauty. Her face had the fine bones that would see her through with distinction into old age, and her reddish-gold hair was arranged in a way that looked as if it had been left to fall naturally but had no doubt taken her maid no small time to achieve. She was dressed plainly but with exquisite taste. She greeted Marlowe as if he were an old friend, enquired after the health of Tom Walsingham, then turned her attention to Simon, giving him a frank and appraising look.

'This is my friend, Dr Simon Forman,' Marlowe told her.

'Dr Forman? Why, I've heard of you,' responded the lady as Simon bowed.

'I find that hard to believe,' he replied.

She smiled. 'You do yourself an injustice. From what I've been told, you are not only a good physician and caster of horoscopes, but one who is interested in many aspects of scientific study, as I am myself.' At this there was a general move into the dining room to sit at table. 'We must talk of such matters later,' said the countess. 'There will be plenty of opportunity.' With that she smiled, passed on before them and went to a seat near Ralegh at the head of the table.

'Well, well, so soon, so soon,' mocked Marlowe, causing Simon to dig him sharply in the ribs. 'Does she yet know, I wonder, that the use of candied sea holly features on the list of events?'

After dinner their host led the way into a large room set about with chairs and where a fire burned brightly in the grate. It was a distinguished gathering. As well as the handsome Wizard Earl, Simon noted the brilliant mathematician and astronomer, Thomas Hariot, the geographer, Robert Hues, a noted scholar called Thomas Allen, and a minor poet by the name of Matthew Roydon. There were others present that he did not know, some relatives or friends of his host rather than members of the School of the Night, he guessed. He was amused to note that while Bess Ralegh and the other women had not joined them, Mary Herbert took her place among the men without a qualm.

Over wine, the talk turned to many topics, Ralegh encouraging each of his guests to say something of what interested them. It was hardly surprising that Simon soon found himself the centre of a good deal of attention, closely questioned as to the possible properties of the sea holly.

'Can't we try it now?' enquired a young man called Spenser Carew, his face already flushed with wine.

'Most certainly not,' replied Sir Walter. 'That is for tomorrow, after a day spent discussing higher matters.'

'I've heard it said you practise necromancy, Dr Forman,' persisted Carew. 'Is that true?'

'It is not,' replied Simon. 'I consider myself to be a seeker after truth, not a meddler in Black Arts. I study the courses of the planets in their spheres as well as medicine, and also have some interest in alchemy although I have neither the time nor the necessary space to pursue it very vigorously.'

Mary Herbert leaned across and smiled at him. 'Have you ever met Dr Dee?'

Simon had to confess he had not. 'No one in my profession could fail to know *of* him and his work, but when I first came to London he was in foreign parts and now lives, I understand, in the North Country, but I doubt I'd have the temerity to approach him if he were here.'

'I'm sure he would be most happy to make your acquaintance. He taught my brother Philip and me when we were young. I'm proud to consider myself one of his pupils.' Simon found this fascinating. For such a great lady the countess had the most unusual interests.

'How about Edward Kelley?' enquired Ralegh. 'Did you ever cross his path?'

Simon frowned. 'Kelley? The name means nothing. Should it?'

'There's no real reason why it should unless you were in London in the 1580s,' Hariot informed him. 'In his own opinion he was the greatest physician, astrologer and alchemist in England, and called himself "Doctor", but he was none of these, only a dangerous trickster. Fraud, coining, supposed "Black Magic" – he tried them all.'

'He had his ears cropped for necromancy,' commented Marlowe, 'and was branded on the hand for coining, or so I'm told.'

'Yet they say Lord Strange made much of him,' commented Ralegh. He turned to the Wizard Earl. 'Is that right, Henry?'

'So it seems, but then Ferdinand – Lord Strange – has always been most superstitious and credulous, and Kelley had great

24

charisma and could be very convincing. Indeed, he even convinced Dr Dee that such were his powers he could "scrie" for him.'

'What does scrie mean?' enquired Carew, who seemed determined to put himself in the forefront of any discussion.

'It comes from the ancients,' Hariot told him. ' "Scriers", of which Kelley said he was one, claimed they could see the future in pools of ink and mirrors or, in the case of Kelley, in Dr Dee's crystal globe.' He sighed. 'But I still find it hard to understand how he could have so fooled Dr Dee.'

'From what you say, I take it this Kelley's dead,' commented Simon.

'Oh yes,' the Earl assured him. 'He fled from the country some three or four years ago after being involved in the murder of a man called Houghton. He escaped justice because Dee had been invited to a number of European courts and Kelley was able to persuade the good doctor to take him with him. What would have happened when they came back to England I don't know, but fortunately Kelley died abroad, thus defeating the Tyburn hangman.'

The talk then turned to other matters until the evening, when Ralegh hosted a fine supper followed by music from a consort of musicians. After this the company took to their beds, having been asked to be up betimes and with clear heads, since after breaking their fast they would ride over to spend the day at Ralegh's lodge near the village of Cerne Abbas.

As soon as Simon came in sight of the hill above Cerne Abbas the next morning, he broke into a great laugh as he looked up at the mighty figure cut in the turf.

'I see what Tom Pope meant when he told me I'd come across a fellow who had no need of my *eringo*!'

Marlowe laughed too. 'Indeed not. Dear me, did all men in

ancient days have such mighty members? If so, then while, as you know, I fail to be convinced of the truth of many of the tales in the Old Testament, I will now accept the word of the prophet who wrote "there were giants in those days".'

The day was passed in much lively discussion. Thomas Hariot spoke of the moons he had seen circling the planet Jupiter, by means of his great new telescope; Robert Hues, the geographer, told of his recent visit to the New World, while in the afternoon, prompted by Marlowe, there was much debate as to the truth of the early books of the Old Testament. Marlowe's view was that they were little more than legends. 'For instance, Moses led the Children of Israel around the desert for forty years before reaching the Promised Land when any competent fellow could have done it quite easily in less than one. And most damning of all is that the Jews claim the world was begun six thousand years ago, when we now know from the Indians and many authors of antiquity that it has been spinning here for at least sixteen thousand.'

As dusk began to fall and the party set off on their return journey, Mary Herbert fell in beside Simon and the two chatted to each other until they reached the castle. When he helped the lady dismount, she smiled up at him. 'What an unusual and interesting man you are, Dr Forman,' she told him, giving him a look which in a less august personage Simon would definitely have considered to be of a coming-on nature. 'We must improve our acquaintance further.'

But surely not, he told himself, as he washed his face and changed into a clean shirt. Surely she wasn't hinting at . . . Well, time would tell. The evening was before him and, of course, the experiment. But there was no doubt over supper that the countess was treating him with growing familiarity, sufficiently noticeable for Marlowe to pick it up and treat Simon to some coarse asides and whispered enquiries as to whether he intended to hog the whole box of sea holly for himself. Finally the time came when Ralegh returned to the matter in hand.

'As you all know,' he said, 'Dr Forman has with him a box of *eringo*, the candied root of the sea holly, which is grown in the Eastern counties as an aphrodisiac. Whether it is or not, we have no means at present of knowing, so the experiment I propose is that all who wish to partake of it may take a little and see what effect it has on them, if any, and note it down. I must also remind you that I will not have any of the maids pestered to join you in the experiment.'

'Does that include lads?' murmured Marlowe to Simon. 'I noted a most handsome young groom when we arrived.'

'Or anyone else in my house,' continued Ralegh, whether or not he had heard this.

'I sent for my mistress to come to me,' boasted Carew, 'and she arrived while we were at Cerne Abbas. I trust you have no objections?'

'None at all,' replied Ralegh with a smile. 'No doubt some of the company here will consider you fortunate.'

'And you, Dr Forman?' murmured Mary Herbert, when she had the opportunity. 'Do you feel in need of this *eringo*?'

'I can't say I do. It's not hitherto been a problem,' he assured her.

'Ah, but surely you must try your own experiment? It seems only right.'

He was about to make some reply but with a wave of her hand she crossed the room, said good-night to her host, and disappeared through the door.

'Come on then, Dr Forman,' urged the wearisome Carew. 'Where is this stuff?'

'I have the box here,' Simon replied. He placed it on the table and opened the lid. The company gathered around and inspected its contents.

'It doesn't look very impressive,' commented Carew. There was a murmur of agreement. 'Are you sure they haven't sent you pieces of parsnip?'

'The apothecary in Colchester from whom I bought it is a most honest fellow. I've known him for years,' Simon said. 'I often buy from him.'

'What I am suggesting,' said Ralegh, 'is that Simon leaves the box here on the table and that anyone who wants to try the *eringo* can do so at his leisure.'

At first there was no move then Carew put his hand into the box and scooped up a handful of the candied pieces. 'I still think you've been gulled, Dr Forman, but here goes.'

'Not that many, I beg you,' said Simon. 'Two or three pieces at most. Not only are there others who may be wanting to try it, but more importantly, I've no idea what effect it might have.' Carew pulled a face but dropped several pieces back, then smirked and left the room. One or two others followed suit while the rest hung back.

'And you, Simon?' mocked Marlowe. 'Surely you must take part in your own experiment?'

By now Simon had lost most of his enthusiasm for it but Marlowe was right. If there was any risk then he must be seen to take it too. Reluctantly he picked up two pieces of the root, bade everyone good-night, and took them up to his room. He should have felt tired, he thought, as he sat on the bed and pulled off his boots. The ride to Cerne Abbas had not been a long one but it was at least exercise, and the intense discussions which had gone on all day had required much concentration, and that in itself should have made him sleepy, especially after a fair amount of wine. But instead his mind ranged around the events of the day, the subjects discussed, even the elderly husband who had seized on *eringo* as the answer to his desperate need. Then, of course, there was the countess . . .

He got into bed, blew out his candle and tried to settle to sleep. He must have dozed off for he awoke with a start at the sound of feet padding softly across his room. He sat up at once. A shaft of moonlight came through the casement and picked out the figure of Mary Herbert wrapped in a silk bedgown. She put her finger to her lips to stop any exclamation then, with all the confidence in the world, she shed the bedgown and climbed into his bed.

'Well,' she said, with a wide smile, 'shall we conduct this experiment?'

Sometime before the late dawn she left as silently as she had arrived. It was almost as if he had dreamed the whole thing, thought Simon. Well, the *eringo* had certainly worked for him, or possibly for them both. Truly it had been a night to remember. He yawned. Now it was almost time to get up, he really did feel tired and in spite of himself fell into a heavy doze.

He was woken what seemed like only minutes later by a banging on the door. Then, without warning, it was thrown open and Bess Ralegh rushed in followed by a weeping maid. Still feeling dazed, for one moment Simon thought that perhaps everyone in the castle had eaten *eringo* and were now running madly about leaping in and out of each other's beds but he was soon disabused of the notion.

'Forgive my bursting in on you like this, Dr Forman,' said Bess Ralegh, catching her breath, 'but one of the servants has been taken desperately ill.'

'What's wrong with him?' asked Simon, wondering at what point he could decently get out of bed and dress.

The girl burst out howling again. 'It seems,' Bess told him, 'that one of the potboys, Jack, who Lizzie here now tells me is her lover, knowing of your experiment, went and helped himself from your box when all others were abed – though it is most likely that is *not* the cause, for no one else appears to have been taken sick.'

'I can vouch for it not affecting me, at least not in that way,' Simon replied. 'Now, if you'll allow me to dress, I'll be with you straight away and see if there's anything I can do.'

Once they had gone he dressed as quickly as he could, splashed his face in the bowl of water which had been left for him then went over to the table by the bed where he had left his rings and other small items. He smiled. Certainly *he* had no complaints about the candied sea holly.

Chapter 3

Poison

The potboy lay in the corner of one of the large attics in which the servants slept, having staggered back to his own bed from that of Lizzie in the early hours of the morning. His face was white and glistening with sweat and he groaned, drawing his knees up in paroxysms of pain. Simon knelt by the straw mattress and felt the boy's forehead.

'He's certainly taken something to cause this,' he commented, 'and there is little time to lose. First, he needs salt and water to make him vomit and then he must have a purge.' He turned to his hostess. 'Have you dried rue in your stillroom?' She nodded. 'Fresh is better but we must do the best we can. You, girl, stop bawling if you want to save your lad's life. Go at once and bring back a pint of salt and water and a wine cup in which you must put a good few pinches of rue, some honey and then wine.'

'I'd best go with her,' said Bess Ralegh, 'if speed is of the essence. I can hardly trust her to do as she's told in the state she's in. Come along, Lizzie, at least you can carry the tray for me.'

Simon bent over the boy again. 'Come now, we hope soon to have you right. Tell me, how much of the candied sea holly did you take?' Jack howled as another spasm seized him and turned

31

his head away. 'This won't do, you must tell me. It could be a matter of life and death.'

'Three pieces,' gasped the boy at length. 'Three pieces. That was all that was left in the box. Aaah!' He writhed again.

'What else did you eat last night?' Simon urged. 'I must know that too.'

'We had . . . what was left over . . . from . . . the big supper. Game, pieces of capon and pigeon . . . what you gentlemen ate.'

There was the sound of footsteps on the attic stairs and Bess Throckmorton reappeared followed by Lizzie bearing a tray and a lad with a pail. Simon thanked them. 'I think you can leave us now, Mistress Ralegh,' he told her, 'for what is to come will be far from pleasant. Make my apologies to the rest of the guests and tell them I'll be with them as soon as possible. I presume no one else has been taken in such a fashion?'

Bess looked grave. 'There is one other, but nothing like so severe. Young Spenser Carew from Cornwall is also unwell. He complains of stomach cramps and has been very sick, but then Walter tells me he ate most greedily and drank much as well as eating the *eringo*. But there are no others suffering in such a fashion and after all, you yourself are not sick and I'm told you also took it, did you not?'

Simon agreed that he had. In spite of the circumstances in which he found himself he had to smile at the memory of the night's pleasure. Given the expertise of the countess he had no doubt that the result would have been the same without the need of any aphrodisiac. Left alone apart from Lizzie, Simon applied himself to the task in hand, first forcing Jack to drink the salt water (with the expected result) then to take the rue and honey in wine as a purge. The emetic did seem to bring some relief, for the spasms eased and some colour began to return to the patient's face. Finally, Simon rose to his feet.

'Stay with him,' he said to the girl, 'and see how he progresses. It looks as if we've saved him, although he is very weak. The rue, as well as purging him, will help strengthen his heart. Now I'd best go and see to the other sufferer.'

As might be expected, Carew was quick to blame Simon for his sickness. He was still in his bed but looked very much better than the potboy, for although he was pale he was alert and obviously not in pain. 'I told you I didn't reckon much to your sea holly,' he began as soon as Simon entered his room. 'What were you trying to do? Kill us all? Annie here feared for my life, didn't you?' The sultry-looking girl, still dressed only in a somewhat inadequate shift, nodded.

'And I told you from the beginning that taking the *eringo* was an experiment,' Simon reminded him firmly, 'though I didn't think it would do you any harm for I've no reason to believe my apothecary friend would have sent me something about which he might have serious doubts. Bear in mind *eringo* has been taken for years in some parts of the country.' He paused. 'And if you really do believe that's what has caused your trouble, then you should be pleased I prevented you from eating twice as much. I don't know what has caused this sickness in you and the kitchen boy but I simply cannot think it was the sea holly, or many more of us would have been sick, myself included.'

Carew seemed unconvinced but finally agreed, with some reluctance, to take a dose of rue from Simon 'so that we can be sure whatever gave you this sickness is purged from the body'. Simon watched him drain the cup then left him to the ministrations of his slatternly mistress. He really did believe the sea holly to be intrinsically harmless, but it was now essential to discover if anyone else had suffered any ill effects, however minor.

He was soon reassured on that front for there had been no other victims of the strange sickness, rather the reverse. A couple of the younger men admitted to having had most remarkable sensual delights in bed, but then one was newly-married and the other, like Carew, had brought his young mistress with him, though no doubt suggestion had also played its part. The poet Matthew Roydon admitted to suffering salacious thoughts of a nature which made him curse himself for not having had the forethought to provide himself with a suitable companion. Marlowe, when pressed, smiled and said little except to confirm that he had suffered no ill effects from the experiment, causing Simon to wonder where the handsome young groom had spent the previous evening. The poet then asked that the company excuse him as he intended to settle down to work on his epic poem, *Hero and Leander*. He had been having trouble completing it, but the night's experiences had suggested ways in which it might now progress.

In view of all that had happened, Sir Walter suggested that instead of riding over to his lodge, the party might remain at the castle since no doubt Dr Forman would prefer to be near his patients. He then put his own forthright view. 'I do not think myself that the *eringo* was to blame for these misfortunes – unless Carew and the potboy were particularly susceptible to some aspect of it. Certainly in the case of Carew I would put his sickness down to excess food and wine followed, no doubt, by strenuous activity! So, shall we adjourn elsewhere? I have provided paper, pens and ink for you to make your notes on the effects of *eringo*.'

Simon thanked Sir Walter for his thoughtfulness and excused himself briefly as he wanted to reassure himself that the potboy was out of danger. The smell in the attic was revolting but to his great relief it now looked as if Jack was over the worst. 'Open the window,' he told Lizzie, 'and take the slop bucket away. I doubt he'll need it again.' He came over and felt the boy's pulse. 'Certainly you still have much bile,' he told him, 'but you'll survive. I'll tell your mistress you must stay where you are for now. Lizzie must bring you only liquids and perhaps some broth towards the end of the day. You should be feeling much better by tomorrow.'

He then set off for his bedchamber only to discover as he tramped along a strange corridor, that once again he had mistaken where he was. He wondered if it was only he who had such difficulty, or whether other folk were constantly to be found wandering around unable to locate the right door or staircase. When he did finally arrive in his room he found John Bradedge there, busy packing their saddlebags. He had seen little of his man over the last two days, and from his appearance and attitude John made it obvious that he had not found his stay at the castle particularly enjoyable.

'These Dorset folk are friendly enough,' he began without any other greeting, 'but there's been precious little to do while you gentlemen have been sitting around chatting all day. God be praised we're going back to London tomorrow! Though from the state of the bed, I imagine you had company overnight,' he grinned. Then he gave his master a shrewd look. 'So, what about these folk who claim they've been poisoned?'

Simon shrugged. 'I don't believe it was the sea holly. Both could have eaten something tainted. I presume you also partook of the food left from the banquet? There was a great deal of it.'

John replied that he had and very good it was, but added that while it might well be the case that the cause of the sickness lay in the supper, the fact that they had experimented in such a way could well leave lingering doubts in folk's minds. 'It's to be hoped they don't spread it abroad,' he opined.

'Well, Sir Walter isn't alarmed,' said Simon, 'as at least half a dozen other people took the sea holly without ill effect, myself included.'

John looked puzzled. 'You say you also took it?'

'Certainly. Why?'

John went over to the small table by the bed on which stood a candle in its holder and a small dish or saucer designed to hold rings or other small pieces of jewellery. 'So what's this then?' He picked up the dish and thrust it in front of Simon. Sitting in the bottom were the two pieces of candied sea holly that he had taken out of the box the previous evening. He had quite forgotten to eat them. He went cold, looking at them with horror. God's Blood, he thought, trying to recollect the sequence of events. He remembered picking them out of the box then taking them upstairs and putting them in the dish beside the bed, but what with the wine he had drunk and his whirling thoughts, followed by his dozing off and then the visit from the countess, it was clear he'd never actually eaten them. 'Hell's Teeth,' he swore, and sat down heavily on the bed.

'If I were you, doctor,' commented John, 'I'd stow these away and say nothing. Otherwise there just might be trouble.' On the whole Simon was inclined to agree with him. Since no lasting harm appeared to have been done it would be better to keep quiet.

Once again the day passed in talk. Mary Herbert came late to it, yawning like a cat and smiling broadly. If anyone suspected that she too might have been tempted to experiment then nothing was said. Shortly before supper Carew also reappeared, still pale, but apparently little the worse for his sickness which mercifully had made him considerably quieter. The meal, possibly in view of what had occurred, was a simple one and afterwards Sir Walter asked his lutenist if he would play his setting of Marlow's famous lyric 'The Passionate Shepherd to His Love' as a tribute to their distinguished guest.

The man smiled, pulled a stool forward and raised his voice in song, listing the various romantic inducements offered to the shepherd's love: beds of roses, fine gowns, birds singing madrigals, shoes with gold buckles . . .

> 'A belt of straw and ivy buds,
> With coral clasps and amber studs,
> And if these pleasures may thee move,
> Come live with me and be my love.'

There was warm applause when the verses came to an end and Marlowe was obviously both flattered and delighted.

'And now,' said Sir Walter with a broad grin, 'you must hear my reply.' Once again the lutenist struck up the same melody, this time singing Sir Walter's mocking response to Marlowe in the poet's own style, ending:

> 'But could youth last, and love still breed:
> Had joys no date, nor age no need,
> Then those delights my mind *might* move,
> To live with thee and be thy love!'

The company rocked with laughter as they applauded again. Simon looked across at Marlowe since it was always impossible to know how that mercurial poet would react to mockery, however much he might enjoy provoking others, but Marlowe too was smiling broadly. Years later Simon was to be haunted by that scene, the brightly-dressed lively company at supper and Kit Marlowe, his dark and mobile face lit by the light of the candles, laughing across at his witty friend.

There was no further visit from the countess that night nor any sign of her when, after an early breakfast, Simon, Marlowe and John took to the road. Sir Walter had set a date some two weeks ahead for the School of the Night to meet in his Tower Room in

London, and before Simon left he again reassured him that he did not believe that the *eringo* had caused the two cases of sickness. Jack the potboy had made a complete recovery, as had Carew who was now riding west having been prevailed upon to visit his uncle at Antony House.

The three men rode as far as they could that day, as all were eager now to reach London, staying overnight in an inn near enough to ensure Simon and John would be back in the Bankside well before noon. They would be parting company with Marlowe before that as he was riding to Scadbury to the mansion of his patron, friend and sometime lover, Tom Walsingham, but as they settled into their beds in their shared room that night, Marlowe leant on his elbow and asked Simon if what he suspected was right, that he'd had a bedtime visit from the countess during their stay in Sherborne. 'Don't look so coy,' he said. 'It was obvious to me what was likely to happen.'

Simon admitted somewhat sheepishly that his friend was right.

'They say she's most hot in bed,' continued Marlowe, 'and knows many tricks that would surprise a whore.'

That she had so obvious a reputation somewhat disappointed Simon. He did not want to feel that he was only one of many. 'Is it not dangerous for such things to be put abroad about such great folk?' he asked.

Marlowe shrugged. 'The old Earl seems prepared to put up with it. Don't fret. Compared to some of the others she's alleged to have taken as her lovers, a physician must appear quite respectable. For at one end of the scale it's rumoured that after a good and exciting day's hunting she likes nothing better than to fling herself on the straw with her head groom, while at the other . . .'

'At the other – what?'

Marlowe became serious. 'I nearly told you when we were

riding over. It's said she also beds with Cecil.'

This Simon *did* find shocking, for Sir Robert Cecil, Acting Secretary to the Privy Council, the Queen's spymaster, had served him ill during the adventure to Scotland – indeed, had almost cost him his life. It also amazed him, for Cecil seemed the coldest of fish and was hunchbacked to boot, whereas the countess . . .

'Are you sure?' he queried. 'It seems very strange – especially for such a clever and beautiful woman who could take her pick wherever her fancy led her.'

Marlowe shrugged. 'Power's a strong drug, Simon, and not only for ambitious men. Mary Herbert wouldn't be the first woman to find it exciting and arousing in a man, even one deformed like Cecil. It might even add to the attraction.' He yawned. 'But I must bid you good-night. I trust I haven't spoiled your peaceful slumber but I can't keep awake any longer.'

They rode into London on a cold grey morning. John took their horses round to the back of the house while Simon let himself in through the front door. Usually Anna came out to greet him straight away but at first he thought she must be out shopping for he had to call her several times before she finally appeared. She greeted him with a worried frown.

'You have been much sought after, doctor,' she told him, 'and that most urgently.'

Simon looked startled. 'Why, I've been gone less than a week. Who has been seeking me?'

In answer she went over to the chest in the hall and picked up two letters which she handed to him. 'These need your attention, doctor. Also there were several callers: your friend, Mistress Allen, who was surprised not to find you at home, a messenger who came yesterday to discover why you had not replied to a letter that had been sent to you – a most pompous fellow acting as if he were servant to some great master – and also a very unpleasant stranger who refused to believe for some time that you were not in the house. He seemed to think I was concealing you, and he questioned me closely.' She had obviously been upset. 'I do not like to be called a liar to my face, doctor.'

'Of course not,' he said in his most soothing manner. 'This stranger must be an ill-bred fellow. Did he give his name?'

Anna replied that he had not.

'So,' Simon continued, 'what did he want of me? Was it to visit a patient? To seek my advice as to his health or to cast his horoscope?'

It transpired it was none of these things. 'I asked him all this first when he pushed his way into the hall,' said Anna, 'but he said not, that he was here on business for his brother, making enquiries of the most serious nature concerning his brother's wife. And when I told him again you were not here it was then he said I was a liar, a common Bankside trull who,' she became tearful, 'no doubt whored of an evening after my day's work. I told him then that if he said any more in that vein I would call the Constable and have him thrown out. At that he calmed down somewhat but repeated that he must have some knowledge of his brother's wife.' She paused. 'But I did wonder if it was his own wife he came about.'

Simon sighed resignedly. Here we go, he thought. Another jealous fellow trying to pretend he's come on behalf of someone else. Does he think his wife's playing him false with me or another man? Does he suspect any child she might be carrying isn't his? Such questions had been put to him at regular intervals over the years by jealous husbands and lovers wanting answers from the stars.

But it appeared that in spite of his raging concern, the enquirer had not been so explicit. 'He asked me continually if the woman in question had been here last week, before you went away. In appearance he said she is small and plump with hair almost as light as mine, and very curly. Her eyes are large and blue and she is very young and would have been richly dressed with much jewellery, possibly carrying a small dog with her. Also, she might have given a name not her own. But I told him the truth when I said I had no recollection of such a one visiting you either last week or at any other time.'

'Neither have I,' Simon rejoined. 'Well, no matter. It will either all blow over and they'll make up their quarrel, for surely it must be her husband. If it doesn't then no doubt he will come back again.'

She seemed uncertain. 'When he left he said again that the matter was deadly serious, indeed a matter of life and death, and that if you truly were not in London then he had to seek help elsewhere and that at once.'

In spite of being quite sure he had counselled no such young woman, Simon began to feel uneasy. Neither the visit of the mystery gentleman nor that of the pompous messenger did much for his peace of mind. He was suddenly assailed by a sense of foreboding, a feeling that he had experienced a few times before and which on occasion had presaged misfortune. He pulled himself together. He was reading too much into all this, there was no more to it than his having drunk too much wine the previous evening and the many and varied events of the last few days. He thanked Anna for her trouble, pressed a crown into her hand for the unpleasantness she had endured, asked after her child and took his two letters into his study.

He found the first one he opened very puzzling. It was from the apothecary in Colchester apologising profusely for still not having been able to supply the promised *eringo*. He had tried every avenue, Joseph Beck wrote, but so far without success.

However, Dr Forman could be assured that as soon as he found another supply, he would send it to London without delay.

Simon looked at the letter again in case he had misread it. No, it was quite clear. He wondered what on earth the man was prating on about. He could only assume that one of the suppliers the apothecary had approached had sent the sea holly direct to him and failed to inform his colleague that he had done so. He would pen him a note therefore, explaining that he had now received a box of sea holly, thanking him for his efforts on his behalf and trusting that he would pass the money on to the right person.

The crest on the seal of the second letter made his heart sink into his boots for he recognised it at once as that of the College of Physicians. Some years earlier he had clashed with that august body on various points of medical practice and they had forbidden him to practise within the City of London, indeed had only finally lifted their ban on the orders of Sir Robert Cecil who, it transpired afterwards, had his own twisted reason for making them do so.

The letter was curt and to the point. It demanded that Simon Forman (no 'doctor') present himself before them on 22 January, otherwise under the powers given to them by statute, they would have him arrested. The twenty-second? That was the following day. What in God's good name had he done that required not only such haste but such a threat? This at least went some way to explaining the attitude of the messenger who had been sent to ensure his compliance.

He shivered and felt cold, for the damp seemed to have seeped right through the house and although it was barely noon it was already growing dark. He went into the kitchen and asked Anna to light a fire in his study while he had some dinner.

'You look worried, doctor', she said, setting a bowl of stew down before him.

'I am somewhat,' he agreed. 'Both of the letters waiting for me are very strange. One was from the apothecary in Colchester apologising for not having sent the goods I ordered from him which, in fact, I received over a week ago, while the other is a summons from the College of Physicians. Sweet Jesu, *now* what am I supposed to have done to provoke them?' He began to eat his stew. 'Also I'm still at a loss to know who this mysterious young woman is, who is alleged to have sought my advice. But you're right, I'm sure she's never been here.'

Anna was adamant. Not only had no such woman called at the house, she had no recollection of ever seeing anyone fitting her description about the Bankside, though of course the woman need not be a native of Lambeth. Perhaps, she suggested, it was no more serious than that the girl had wanted to go to the Rose playhouse and her husband had forbidden her to do so. 'Perhaps he taxed her with where she'd been one afternoon and she told him she'd been to consult a physician or have her horoscope cast, but he suspected her of passing time with a lover.'

Simon had to agree that was a likely explanation. He then turned to the other matter exercising him. 'And Mistress Allen?'

'Sickly, poor soul, but the child has now quickened and I told her that very often once that happens, the sickness passes. She worries a good deal, but then I understand she and her husband have waited many years for this.' She gave him a bland look. She must know the nature of the relationship between himself and Avisa, thought Simon, might well have her suspicions as to the child's paternity, but if she had, discreet as ever, Anna said nothing more.

Before the end of the afternoon Avisa came herself. She was pale and had dark circles under her eyes. Her figure was fuller now than before but her kirtle hid the growing child. Simon made at once to embrace her but she moved away from him.

'What's the matter, my love? Aren't you pleased to see me?'

'I don't know,' she said wearily.

He was alarmed. 'Is the sickness persisting? If so, then I will give you some water of Lady's Mantle to take first thing of a morning.'

She waved him away. 'It is no longer so bad since the child quickened; your servant was right in what she told me. No, it's everything else, the situation I find myself in, the terrible deceit. What we have done is a mortal sin, Simon. Were it still possible for me to find a Mass priest, I would at least be able to confess to him, but you know that is now completely forbidden. So day in and day out I have to listen to William talking constantly of "his" child, or more often "his son", for he is convinced it will be a boy, his plans for his education and upbringing, the place there will be for him in the silk business and our various merchant ventures, the grand christening we are to have once I am safely delivered . . . and all the time I am as sure as I can be that the child is yours.'

He was at a loss to know how to help her. The situation was an impossible one. He made one final attempt to comfort her and for a short while she rested in his arms, but when he gently tried to take it further she stiffened and would have none of it. 'Not now, Simon, not ever again perhaps.' She gave him a bleak smile. 'Perhaps I will feel better in a while. If I do, then I'll send and let you know.'

With that she left him to his own thoughts. He had rarely felt so downhearted, yet until a few days before, things had seemed to be going so much better for him. He had plenty of patients, he was becoming much sought after, his invitation to join the School of the Night had given him friends in high places, and while the situation with Avisa was hardly ideal, she had seemed content to be his mistress and had been delighted at the prospect of bearing a child after so many years of waiting.

Yet now he found himself once more in trouble with the College of Physicians, he was still unnerved by the events in Sherborne and Avisa had as good as told him she wanted no more of him. All it would take now, he thought grimly, was for the jealous husband to bang on the door, accuse him of seducing his wife then threaten him with swordplay at dawn. No, he must rid himself of this mood and common sense told him that it was unlikely he would hear or see anything of the man again. No doubt by now he had cooled down and accepted whatever explanation of her conduct his wife had given him.

Not surprisingly, Simon presented himself the next morning at the Hall of the College of Physicians in Knightrider Street feeling unrefreshed after a restless and almost sleepless night. John Bradedge went with him in case it was necessary to send for papers or notes from home. Try as he might to conjecture what might have caused them to summon him, Simon remained at a loss. However, he was not kept waiting long before he found out. Within minutes he was called in from the waiting area where he left John Bradedge and once again was ushered into the large panelled room in which the physicians held their deliberations. He noted at once that among those seated at the long polished table were several aged doctors who had been particularly hostile to him when he had been called before them two years earlier.

The President, seated at the end of the table, eyed him in an unpleasant fashion. 'You took your time replying to our summons, Forman,' he said, with no other preamble.

'That was because I was out of town when your letter was delivered, and when your messenger came to see if I had received it, my housekeeper informed him of this fact. I have been in the country for a few days visiting Sir Walter Ralegh at his home in Dorset.'

This statement provoked a certain amount of muttering among the physicians.

'Do not think you can avoid what is to come by claiming friendship with the Queen's favourite, or rather *past* favourite,' the President informed him sternly. 'You are here on the most serious and gravest of charges.'

'Then tell me what I am supposed to have done,' cried Simon in exasperation. 'I can think of nothing.'

'You have killed a man by poison,' replied the President.

Chapter 4

The Counter Gaol

'Poisoned a man? God's Breath, what are you talking about?'
Sweet Jesu, thought Simon, has some message already reached
the College from a mischief-maker in Sherborne? If so, the
likeliest culprit would be young Carew since he'd seemed determined to make as much trouble as possible. Well, if that was the
case then at least he had a ready defence. Others had eaten the sea
holly and remained unscathed. His confidence was therefore quite
shaken by what came next.

'I have here,' said the President holding up a written document,
'a letter of a most serious nature received from a certain William
Tapworth, partner with his late brother – I stress the word "late" –
in a silversmiths' business in Cheapside.'

Tapworth? Oh no, the old fellow with the lusty wife! Simon
felt sick in the pit of his stomach at the broad hint of what was to
follow. 'He accuses you of prescribing for his brother a quack
aphrodisiac, *eringo*, possibly in collusion with his brother's wife,
and alleges that the *eringo*, which I understand was in small
candied pieces, was either poisoned by you or that you knew it to
be an inherently dangerous commodity.'

This was even worse than he had imagined. And such folly!

'A dangerous substance?' Simon managed at last. 'Poison in collusion with Tapworth's wife? But I've never even seen the lady, let alone conspired with her! I realise now who the rude visitor was who called at my house while I was in Dorset and upset and insulted my housekeeper, Anna Bradedge. This William Tapworth called Anna a Bankside trull and accused her of whoring when she told him truthfully that I was from home and that no such lady as he described had ever visited my house.'

'We have had you here before, Forman,' broke in another of the physicians, 'and listened to your ludicrous views on doctoring; indeed, the only reason that you're practising within the City now is because pressure was brought to bear by Sir Robert Cecil. I said at the time that we should never have given in to Sir Robert's demands. I thought you dangerous then and have been proved more than right now.'

At this, one of the most elderly of the physicians who had been dozing during the proceedings woke with a snort. 'Told you the man learned his medicine under a hedge,' he informed the rest. 'Told you before.'

Simon was in a quandary. If he informed the Council that others had taken the sea holly without ill effects, then they would want to know where and when, which would mean they would also find out that at least two other people had been taken sick. Even though he firmly believed it highly unlikely the sea holly was the cause, the members of the College Council would ignore such a possibility, bent as they were on proving their case. Nor, in confirmation of its harmlessness, could he stoutly swear that he too had eaten it without hazard since it now turned out that he had not.

'So what do you have to say about the death of this man?' barked the President.

'Little or nothing until I have spoken to the family and learned of the circumstances of his death.'

'Do you deny you treated this man and he died?'

'No – why should I deny that I treated him? And since you now tell me he is dead then I must believe you. But have none of the rest of you ever had a patient die on you? Do you all possess supernatural skills whereby the outcome is always positive? Have you never prescribed medicine or undertaken treatment in all good faith, and yet the patient has still died in spite of all your efforts and care?'

'But this man wasn't even sick,' objected the President.

'Not in the obvious sense,' returned Simon, 'but he came to me begging, nay *beseeching* me to give him something, anything, which would allow him to have sexual congress with his new young bride. As it so happened, I had just received from a most respected apothecary in Colchester a box of this *eringo*, that is candied sea holly root, and as I could think of no other cure for his complaint I offered him the chance to try it, pointing out most carefully that I did not know its effects and had not prescribed it before, but that I understood it to be widely used for this purpose in the Eastern counties. Indeed, those who grow and prepare it there make a good deal of money sending it abroad to France and the Low Countries, where it is much in demand. I cannot imagine they would continue to do so if word came from the Continent that the recipients were dying like flies!'

'And why had you sent for it in the first place?'

Simon hesitated briefly then decided to tell the truth. 'To see, by experiment, if its reputation was justified. It was to be tried by a circle of gentlemen who meet under the auspices of Sir Walter Ralegh.'

At this one of the physicians jumped to his feet. 'Here we have it,' he cried, addressing the whole room. 'I presume you talk of the School of the Night, a band of necromancers, alchemists, heretics and blasphemers that is a shame to our realm.'

'I doubt the Earl of Northumberland would sit quietly by while you described it in such a way,' retorted Simon, 'or the great mathematician Thomas Hariot.'

'It's time and more the proceedings of this so-called society were fully investigated by the Star Chamber,' continued the physician as if Simon had never spoken.

'You have made a good point,' responded the President, 'and if you are all agreeable I will suggest as much to the Privy Council, but we are not here to discuss the School of the Night. We must get back to the matter in hand.' He motioned the speaker to sit down. 'So, Dr Forman, are you saying that you did not prescribe this *eringo* at the express wish of Mistress Tapworth?'

'I repeat what I've already said. I've never met Mistress Tapworth and I prescribed the sea holly to Tapworth at his own request and with due caution. May I enquire how the man died? He was elderly and carried much flesh. It is not unknown for old men to have an apoplexy or for their hearts to fail during the act of love, as surely you must know from your own experience. Indeed, there have been most embarrassing instances where men in high places, men of religion even, have been found dead in the arms of a whore!'

The President glared at Simon. 'You are not helping your case with such cheap jibes. But, for your information, this was not the case. Tapworth was taken with severe spasms of pain, first in the stomach and then in the chest, shortly after eating the *eringo* and before going to bed with his wife. The spasms became worse, accompanied by breathing difficulties. A physician was brought to him but in spite of the latter's best efforts, Tapworth died.'

'I see,' said Simon, finally realising where all this was leading, 'leaving his child-bride an extremely wealthy widow, I presume.

Well, none of this has anything to do with me. If it was the sea holly then I prescribed it in good faith and with no ulterior motive whatsoever. What possible gain could I have by entering into such a plot? At the very least I would put myself in this girl's power as her accomplice and so live out the rest of my life fearful of being accused of the crime. Maybe she would even see to it that I did not continue to live at all if she is as scheming and ruthless as you imply,' he added.

But in spite of his brave words Simon was devastated. The description of Tapworth's illness did not really fit the symptoms suffered by Jack the potboy and young Carew, but if the College probed further into the subject and made enquiries the illnesses at Sherborne would certainly come to light. For the first time he began to have doubts about the safety of the sea holly. Was there something in it that affected certain persons but not others and in different ways? It was beginning to look like it.

The President pulled his papers together before him and stood up. 'Under the powers vested in this Council by the Statute of 1512 I have an officer standing by outside to take you to the Counter Gaol, there to be confined at our pleasure.'

Simon reacted in horror. 'Send me to prison? You can't do that! On what grounds?'

'Oh, I assure you we have every right and that you are by no means the first quack doctor we have sent to gaol. We could have done so the last time you appeared before us, when you refused to swear that you would no longer practise as a physician, but in the event you were fortunate; you were merely fined and forbidden to practise within the bounds of the City of London. But this time we are prepared to show no such leniency and I doubt very much that the Secretary to the Privy Council will intervene on your behalf again if what I've heard is true.' He motioned towards the door. 'Go, one of you, and call the officer.'

'But what about my patients, my household?' cried Simon. 'Surely you will at least allow me to go home and collect some clothing and money and tell my housekeeper what has transpired?'

'I understand you brought a servant with you,' said the President. 'Send him to do that for you.'

'That's right, throw him in gaol straight away,' advised the elderly doctor who had accused Simon of hedge medicine as a burly officer entered through the door.

The President agreed. 'Very well, Forman, go with the officer now and give your man his instructions without further delay.'

'Tell you something,' the elderly doctor broke in again, 'this hedge "doctor" reminds me of that quack Kelley. Fellow who coined money, practised Black Magic and dug up corpses for horrid purposes. Had his ears cropped and was branded at Tyburn. I'd have hanged him.'

How odd, thought Simon. I knew nothing of this Kelley until a few days ago and now his name has come up again. Is the old fool suggesting I also forge coins and dig up corpses?

The President motioned the officer to wait a moment then turned to Simon. 'Have you some past connection then with Kelley?'

'No. I'd never even heard of him until a few days ago when his name was mentioned in connection with Dr Dee.' There was an embarrassed silence. His colleagues had never come to terms with Kelley's inexplicable hold over so distinguished a member of their fraternity. 'All know of him is what I was told, that he was a fraudster who gulled half the nobility, fled the country and died abroad.'

'If no one else has anything to say then I will now close the proceedings,' said the President.

'For how long am I to remain in the Counter?' asked Simon desperately. 'Do you intend I should rot there indefinitely? God's

Blood, man, what's the purpose of all this?'

'The purpose is to put you where you can do no more mischief while we proceed with our enquiries. Take him away, officer,' said the President and turned his back on him.

The meeting over, the Council members prepared to go their separate ways. The President was about to leave when one of the physicians, who had remained silent throughout the proceedings, came over to him.

'I made no comment during the hearing but I would now like to say that I think you're making a mistake. From everything I hear, Forman is a most competent physician and is very well-liked. I cannot seriously believe he would stoop to poison.'

'Forman's a quack, not properly trained and insufficiently acquainted with even the basic tenets of the great Galen,' responded the President robustly. 'He's been a danger too long. I am proud of the fact that we have been able to prevent such impostors practising so-called medicine. I can't understand your concern. We have sent many like him to gaol over the years.'

'And not all the outcomes have been happy,' the man reminded him. 'Do you recall the case of Alice Leevers? How the great Sir Francis Walsingham intervened on her behalf after she had been confined to Newgate, saying that she had great skills and had saved the life of his daughter and that she must be released from prison forthwith? That case did us little good.'

The President looked distinctly uncomfortable. He himself had drafted the letter in response to Sir Francis Walsingham in which he stated that it was the duty of the College of Physicians to discipline all quacks and impostors who purported to practise medicine; this demented female Alice Leevers was manifestly one such, since she was 'merely a woman'. For several days he had waited for a further letter from Sir Francis begging the College's pardon for interfering in their affairs. Instead he had received one from the Queen herself. Having read the response to Sir Francis's reasonable request Her Majesty was now ordering them to release the 'mere woman' Alice Leevers forthwith, for she herself could vouch for her skills. The subsequent cringing and abject letter he had been forced to send to his monarch was not one the President wanted to recollect.

'The case is quite different,' he replied brusquely, waving the other doctor away. 'I am certain I have done the right thing. And now, unless you have anything else to discuss, I must be off. I have serious matters requiring my attention.'

When Simon told his servant what had transpired, John Bradedge was deeply shocked. 'You should never have come in the first place,' he said.

'How was I to guess this would be the outcome?' retorted Simon. 'Now go straight home and tell Anna what's afoot and say that I don't intend staying in gaol a minute longer than I can help. Then bring me a change of clothes and twenty pounds. Here's the key to my small chest in the study. I'm aware that I'll have to bribe everyone in sight, and when you come to the Counter, ask Anna to make me up a basket of food. But before doing any of this, tell Tom Pope and send word to the Careys of my plight. Surely these fools will listen to the Lord Chamberlain! One last thing: bring my small medicine bag as well – no doubt the place is riddled with sickness.'

'Are you coming or do I have to drag you out?' the officer snarled.

'That won't be necessary,' said Simon, then to John: 'Come to me in the Counter as soon as you can.'

The officer marched Simon out of Knightrider Street into Cheapside and from there along to Wood Street where the gaol was situated. The Head Gaoler at the Counter was somewhat surprised to see Simon, having only encountered him before in a professional capacity. He assumed at first that the doctor had either been arrested for debt at the suit of a creditor or for some misdemeanour committed when drunk as was the case with other gentlemen prisoners, but when the situation was explained he understood: it was not the first time he had been presented with a prisoner detained by order of the College of Physicians. In the circumstances and because he knew Simon could pay for the privilege, he readily agreed to provide him with a room, bed and bedding and allow extra food and drink to be sent in.

The room was a small and barren affair, the bed hard and the blankets less than clean, but it also contained a chair and table and was at least above ground level and had a small barred window in the outside wall. Compared to the conditions most prisoners had to put up with, Simon was fortunate. On the whole the Counter housed only debtors, those awaiting the hearing of civil actions, petty criminals, vagrants and sturdy beggars, the major felons being sent to Newgate or Bridewell. But it was still a grim place. Because Simon would be able to bribe or 'garnish' the Sergeant in charge and the warders, he was housed in what was known as the 'Master's Side'. Progressively downwards after that came the Knight's Ward, the Twopenny Ward and, finally, the notorious Hole, a dank underground cavern where prisoners slept on the floor in filthy straw. Since the 'garnish' usually increased as the weeks passed, it was all too easy for a prisoner to find himself on an ever-quickening slide down into the Hole.

Common sense told Simon that he had sufficient friends with influence to get him out before that happened, but the sound of the door being locked behind him spelled out only too clearly the position he was in. More than that it reminded him of his sojourn in Edinburgh where admittedly he had been imprisoned in a private house, but the feeling of helplessness was the same. This, in turn, brought back the memory of redheaded Kate who had given her life to save his.

The gloomy mood persisted all day even after John had returned, laden with bags containing clothes, a blanket, candles, money, food, medicines and, with great forethought, pen, ink and paper. 'I reckon you'll be needing to write to a few folk,' he said, laying them down on the table. He had sent word to the Careys of Simon's plight and had left a message to the same effect with Tom Pope's wife, Jenny, as Tom was on stage that afternoon.

The day dragged on followed by a sleepless night, and as the grey light of dawn filtered into the cold room through the grating above, Simon became impatient to see John Bradedge and find out if he had heard back from the Careys. His breakfast, a pint of small ale and a decent piece of bread and cheese, was brought to him by a fellow prisoner, one of a handful trusted by the gaolers to carry out such tasks. He was an unprepossessing-looking fellow of about thirty with what looked like a bad eye infection and was serving his time, he said, for the crime of crossbiting.

Simon knew all about crossbiting for it was rife among the stews of the Bankside. It was a plot in which a whore would dress and behave as a married or affianced woman on the look out for a little excitement. She would carefully choose her victim or gull, making sure beforehand that he was respectable and, preferably, married. She would then make an assignation with him in some inn or house of ill-repute, take him to bed and when matters had gone past the point of no return, her pimp would rush in posing as her enraged husband, threatening either to kill the lover there and then, broadcast his infidelity abroad or both. The outcome was usually a reasonable financial settlement of the affair unless, as had happened in this particular case, the wealthy merchant in question refused to give in to the pimp's demands and instead went straight to the nearest Constable with a detailed description of the pair involved – an action which had led to their arrest.

'My girl, Betty, is only now out of Bridewell,' he told Simon, 'and sends that she is feeling poorly but I trust now I'll be joining her outside within the month.'

Simon asked his name and was told it was Roger Warren. 'That's a nasty eye you have there,' he commented. 'I think I've something with me that might help, if you'll wait a minute.' He looked inside the small leather bag and brought out a phial.

'What's that?' queried Roger suspiciously.

'Distilled water of groundsel,' replied Simon. 'It's efficacious for all inflammations but most especially for the eyes.' Reluctantly Roger allowed him to dab some around his eye. 'I'll treat you with this every time you bring me my meals,' said Simon. 'You'll find it soothes almost at once.'

Roger was still doubtful but had to admit that at least it soothed the soreness. He had been prone to infections of the eye for as long as he could remember, he told Simon. Some years earlier he had been treated by a Bankside doctor who seemed to have cured it for good, but recently the old trouble had reappeared. No, he didn't know what the doctor had used, nor could he remember his name, for the man had disappeared shortly afterwards. However just before his arrest, Roger thought he had seen him again among the crowds in Cheapside and had tried to attract his attention, though without success.

After Roger left, Simon paced up and down his room awaiting the expected arrival of John Bradedge with increasing impatience. To his astonishment the day drew to an end without sight or sound of either him or any other visitor. What on earth could have happened to prevent his coming to the Counter as promised? Certainly not the Head Gaoler, who had agreed to Simon having free access to visitors.

First thing the following morning, when John was finally shown in and the door locked behind him, it was clear he was labouring under scarcely concealed emotion. Before Simon could ask him what was the matter he put his hand in his pocket and flung a ring of keys on to the bed. Simon looked from the keys to John in astonishment.

'Where've you been?' he demanded. 'I've grown mad with anxiety waiting for you. And why do you bring me my house keys? What good are they to me in this place?'

John snorted. 'Well, they'll be no good to us now, will they? And how could I come sooner when we've spent all our time packing to leave. In spite of the way you've treated us after all this time, I felt it unwise to leave them with your friend the fencing master as you asked.'

'Packing to leave? Fencing master?' Simon's head spun so much that he had to sit down on the bed. 'God's Blood, are your wits wandering? Why are you deserting me now when I'm in such need and when we've been through so much together? I thought I could trust you with my life.'

John looked back at him equally amazed. 'It's you that's lost your wits, doctor. It's not we who are deserting you, but you who's told us to go at once from your employment without a roof over our heads or work elsewhere.' He reached inside his doublet and produced a piece of paper. 'Are you trying to tell me you didn't write this letter?'

Simon read the missive with growing incredulity. It was headed from the Counter Prison, dated the previous day, and appeared to be in his own handwriting. It informed the Bradedges that whether or not he left prison in the near future he was proposing to give up his house and practice at once, leave London as soon as he was released and try his fortune elsewhere, possibly abroad. Therefore he wanted them to leave immediately so that he would not have the expense of their wages. They were to close the house securely behind them and give the house keys to the fencing master who lived beside the Green Dragon tavern. There was no need for him to see them again.

'I never wrote this,' Simon insisted. 'Surely you didn't really believe I would send you such a letter?'

'But it's in your very own handwriting, doctor,' replied John, though it was evident that doubt was now creeping in.

Simon went over to the grating in the wall and squinted at the letter. 'It's very like – indeed, I would say it is an excellent copy. But it's not my writing and I swear on anything you care to name that I never sent it. Who brought it to you?'

'It was pushed through the door when we got up this morning.'

'You should have come and seen me at once,' said Simon. 'How could you think I would treat you so?'

John looked uncomfortable. 'That's what Anna said: that she couldn't believe it. She wanted to come to you herself but I said no, if that's how you felt then the sooner we were off the better.' He managed a smile of relief. 'I'm sorry, doctor. She was right, I should have come here straight away. I'll go back and tell her. She'll be so relieved – I left her in floods of tears.'

'Go back at once but before you do, is there any word from the Careys?'

'Nothing as yet,' John replied, adding that now matters were resolved between them, he would go in person if no letter had come by the end of the day.

'You'd best take these back then,' said Simon, handing over the keys, 'and ignore any further messages which are supposed to come from me until you see me. Should any more such arrive, then bring them here without delay and try and lay hold of whoever delivers them.'

John nodded and put the keys back in his pocket but he looked serious. 'It's a strange business this, doctor, isn't it? Whoever sent the letter knows a great deal about your present circumstances. It's beginning to look as if someone's out to make really serious mischief for you.'

Simon agreed. 'Even before this hoax letter, I was full of misgivings. I know the reason for my being in here is this man Tapworth, who seems convinced I colluded with his late brother's wife to poison him, but he couldn't have forged my handwriting and sent such a letter without knowing far more about me than is possible and also having a sample of my writing to copy. Nor would I be surprised if that young coxcomb Spenser Carew had also tried to make trouble for me, but he's hundreds of miles away in Cornwall. No, the mystery seems to go back further than that, to the arrival of the box of sea holly sent to me by God alone knows who. Possibly this very mischief-maker.'

'Do you now think it was poisoned, doctor?' asked John.

Simon frowned. 'Not all of it, for had that been the case everyone who tried it at Sherborne would have been taken ill, possibly some might even have died. But it would not be beyond the bounds of possibility for individual pieces to have been tampered with in doses of varying amounts – though to what end? Such adulterated pieces could not be aimed at any particular person unless he were to eat the whole box, so the poisonings would be quite random. And now this letter . . .' He shook his head in frustration. 'Away with you now to set Anna's mind at rest and unpack your belongings. I beg you to see what you can do with the Careys on my behalf. I must be out of here before anything else untoward happens.'

Towards the end of the afternoon John returned again, this time bringing with him Tom Pope who was carrying a covered basket. 'This is all very strange,' said Tom, setting down the basket, 'and I'm sorry to see you in such circumstances. Jenny's most upset and has sent you some food for your supper and I a bottle of canary wine. The gaoler on the gate made me take all of it out and examined it so closely I was expecting him to rip the pastry off the pie to see if it concealed a master key but eventually I persuaded him to desist by giving him a sixpenny garnish.'

Simon thanked him heartily then turned to John. 'Any news from the Careys?'

'I called on them myself, doctor, as I promised, having had no message but I fear we're out of luck. The Lord Chamberlain is at Nonesuch Palace with the Queen and your friend, young Carey, away up on the Borders. His steward thought you must know that.'

Simon cursed. 'Of course, he would be. Time has gone so quickly these last months that I'd forgotten his post as Warden of the West March must have been confirmed by now. God's Breath, what am I to do? I have no other such powerful friends to persuade the College of Physicians to release me.'

'What about Sir Walter Ralegh?' suggested Tom. 'And you also told me the Earl of Northumberland is one of your School of the Night friends.'

Simon shook his head. 'Sir Walter is only now making his peace again with the Queen over his marriage and as to the Earl, well, the College members are hardly likely to take notice of a man known popularly as "the Wizard Earl", however highborn he might be. In fact, one of the charges levied against me was that I attended meetings of the School of the Night, which was more or less described in terms of a cabal that met secretly to practise necromancy and black magic.'

'Perhaps Kit Marlowe could ask Tom Walsingham if he might help,' suggested Tom, 'though he has not the standing of the Careys.'

Simon felt defeated. 'I wonder now if anyone can. Those imprisoned by the College who have been released at the request of people in high places have merely been accused of practising unlicensed medicine or for refusing to pay the fines levied on them by the College, but in my case I stand accused of having a patient die on me, indeed possibly of murdering him!'

'But I can't see how that can be proved, even if they think it to be so,' Tom averred, 'and surely they can't leave you here indefinitely? God's Blood, Simon, what situations you get yourself into! Perhaps we should find someone to write a play about you. Come to think of it, eating poisoned sea holly would make a good plot and one far more believable than those involving kissing poisoned pictures or wearing poisoned rings.'

'What about that countess woman?' broke in John Bradedge.

'What countess woman's that?' asked Tom.

'You know,' continued John, unabashed, 'the one you romped about the bed with in Sherborne.'

In spite of himself Simon flushed. 'The Countess of Pembroke? Mary Herbert? I scarcely know her.'

'You took her to bed on mere acquaintance then?' suggested Tom.

'It wasn't like that,' growled Simon. 'She presented herself to me in the middle of the night and before you get carried away,' he continued as Tom's face creased with laughter, 'Kit Marlowe informed me that I was in no way likely to be particular to her since she regularly did the same with her head groom! I can't possibly impose on her.'

They talked around the subject for some time after but made little progress and eventually Tom and John left, John promising to return again the next day. If anything, the visit left Simon even more uneasy and depressed. He simply could not see how he could persuade the College to let him go. He could be in prison for weeks, months, until his money ran out and he ended up in the Hole.

When Roger brought him his suppertime ale Simon again treated his eye infection which was definitely improving. The other man was full of gratitude. 'I can't see why they're so set on locking up a gentleman like you,' he said. 'I'm told you'd a man die on you after treatment, but then how many have these grand doctors put underground? Scores, I imagine. My mother would rather have called in the wise woman than any number of doctors or barber-surgeons, even if she'd had the money to pay for them – which she didn't.'

'How then did you meet up with the other doctor who treated you?' Simon asked curiously. Even talking to Roger was preferable to more hours locked up on his own.

'Can't recall properly now but he was something of a gambling man for he sometimes went to the gaming houses and taverns so I'd seen him about. Oh, it must be all of ten years or so ago. No chance of catching *him* with crossbiting – he was up to all the rigs. He knew as much as we did of "Fullam's dice" and coney-catching.'

'And he was a properly licensed physician?' Simon was becoming intrigued.

'So he said. He told me he was cleverer than all of them, that there was no doctor in London as clever as he was. He was most jealous of his reputation, quick to draw sword and fight any who didn't give him sufficient respect. No, there's been none on the town like him since that I know of, begging your pardon, doctor.'

'You still can't remember his name then?'

Roger's brow furrowed and he bit his lip. 'No, it's gone. I've never been good at names. Never forget a face, but names . . .'

'And he actually lived on the Bankside? I wonder why I've heard nothing of him.'

But it transpired that the Bankside was not the doctor's main place of residence or practice. 'He'd a libken – that's a place to stay in off and on – over the printmaker's shop in that alley near the Green Dragon which they call Grope . . .' He paused. Simon nodded. He knew the saucy popular name given by the locals to the alley frequented by whores. 'You might know the printer,' Roger continued. 'He's still there and they say he makes a good deal of money selling lewd pictures.'

Simon did not know the man himself but was aware that there was a brisk trade in such engravings in the most disreputable areas of the Bankside. The mysterious physician intrigued him and he decided he would ask John to call on the printmaker and see if he could discover the identity of the cleverest doctor in London. If he could be found, the fellow might even be persuaded to plead his case for him with his fellow members of the College of Physicians.

The actors had been getting out of their costumes after the afternoon's performance when the owner of the Rose Theatre, Philip Henslowe, bustled in in a state of great excitement.

'I want the very best from you tomorrow in *Tamburlaine the Great*,' he informed the company. 'The very best!'

'Who've you got coming then?' queried one of the actors. 'Good Queen Bess herself?'

'That's enough levity,' responded Henslow huffily. 'No, our distinguished visitor will be the great Countess of Pembroke with her train. A great and most civil lady.' He smirked. 'Indeed, she's asked me to sit beside her during the afternoon's performance and wishes you all to be presented to her on stage afterwards. See you're worthy of her patronage. Remember, the very best.'

'Here's our chance, lads,' the young actor guffawed as Henslowe disappeared. 'I've heard it said of her that . . .'

'. . . She's a great lady and sister to Sir Philip Sidney,' Tom finished for him.

There was more laughter, along with several scandalous remarks. Tom sat silent. If it was true that the countess knew Simon, then surely she might be persuaded to help bring about his release? Whatever the rest of the company might think, he determined that he would find some opportunity to speak to her privately, and beg for her help.

Chapter 5

Intervention of a Countess

When John Bradedge arrived at the Counter Gaol the next day, he brought with him a letter that quite wiped from Simon's mind his interest in the identity of the cleverest doctor in London. It was from Avisa, and it left him in no doubt that whoever had written the forged note to the Bradedges had struck once more. For in it, she informed him that she never wanted to see or hear from him again after receiving his own 'terrible letter', combined with which she had also heard 'on good authority' that he was confined to prison by the College of Physicians for luring young women into whoring.

At first I found this hard to believe, she wrote, *but I now have real doubts, for my informant tells me that you regularly used your women patients for your pleasure and that some of them have consequently been cast out by their families and have had no recourse but to go on the streets; indeed, this person offered to find such a one and bring her to meet with me. Then I recalled how you had laid siege to me from when I first came to you for advice, how I had caught you on your very daybed with the Lord Chamberlain's mistress and how I too had heard whispers from time to time that you were not averse to overtures from patients.*

But that is as nothing compared to your own letter to me. How dare you say I used all my wiles to seduce you, how I openly boasted of cuckolding my husband, how I begged you to give me a child that I could pass off as William's to ensure he did not put me from him as a barren wife. Then to claim that I had pestered and pursued you to that end in spite of your telling me to go elsewhere 'to stud'. Worst of all is your ending: that the child I am now carrying is neither yours nor William's but that of some obliging fellow from the Bankside. How could you write such monstrous things to me after all we've been to each other, when you've told me so often how much you love me and wish we were man and wife? I realise you took my mood hard at our last meeting but surely you of all men must know the humours of women when they are with child and I have been most sickly. But however hard you took it, I surely do not deserve such treatment at your hands. By the time you receive this I shall be on my way to my mother's home in Kent. I have no wish for a reply.

'I must get out of this place if I have to break down the door with my bare hands and kill the gaoler!' raged Simon. 'In the meantime, while you wait, I'll scribble a letter to Avisa and you must find a carrier to take it down to her in Kent. Perhaps you could also put in a note of your own explaining that this is not the only one of these false letters I'm supposed to have written, for you received one too.'

He sat down and dashed off his letter, first swearing he had not, nor ever would have written anything so cruel and unforgivable to her, then begging her at least to give him a chance to clear himself of all her charges. Also, that while it would take too long to explain to her why the College had put him in prison, it had nothing whatsoever to do with bedding women, whoring or any other similar charge.

'Look,' he said to John, beside himself, 'we must try anything to get me freed. It might be that we can persuade Tapworth's widow to intervene or persuade someone to do so on her behalf, young as she is. She can't want gossip about her having rid herself of an unwanted husband. The family have a house next to his business on the Cheapside as well as one in Chelsea. Call there, will you, and see where Mistress Tapworth is at present, then I can send a letter to her.'

Then he remembered his conversation with Roger. 'It's not really important, but if you have the time, could you look into a more minor matter? There's a printer of doubtful reputation who sells salacious pictures from his print shop in the alley near to the Green Dragon, the one they call . . .'

'I know the one,' John Bradedge chuckled. 'Surely after all this you don't want me buying saucy pictures for you?'

'Of course not,' snapped Simon. 'All I want you to do is to ask the printer if he recalls renting a room to a doctor some years ago and if he does, can he tell you that doctor's name, his present direction and where he practises now.' He paused. 'I admit to being intrigued for he bragged of being "the cleverest doctor in London" yet I've never even heard of such a one so close to home, though admittedly that was before I came to London. But before doing that or anything else, find a means of forwarding my letter to Mistress Allen. I have written her mother's direction on the outside and will trust you to seal it with my ring when you've returned home and added your own note.'

Tom Pope, meanwhile, had found himself the subject of much gossip and speculation. When the cast of *Tamburlaine* had been lined up to meet the Countess of Pembroke – with Edward Alleyn, of course, well to the fore – he had attempted to ask her, when it came to his turn to be presented and in as quiet a voice as possible, if he might have a word in private with her afterwards. All he had succeeded in doing, alas, was to draw the attention of Philip Henslowe to his efforts. The owner of the playhouse was already annoyed since his greatest actor and now son-in-law Ned Alleyn had been highly offended that the lady had spent so little time with him after such a tremendous performance. The more cynical members of the company considered that the reason for this was likely to be Alleyn's new wife, Joan, who was standing protectively close beside him at the time, for the lady's eyes had swept most admiringly over Alleyn, who looked truly magnificent dressed as Tamburlaine.

'What are you muttering there, Pope?' enquired Henslowe irritably.

'Master Pope was asking if he might have a word with me in private,' returned the Countess, her eyes sparkling.

'What?' bellowed Henslowe. 'What possible matter need you discuss with the Countess that cannot be said in front of all of us?'

Aware of the broad grins, nudges and scarcely concealed leers of his fellow actors, Tom stood his ground. 'The matter concerns someone else,' he said, 'who has asked me to act as messenger on his behalf. It is a private matter.'

'Then we will go apart and you can tell me of it,' declared the countess. She looked along the line of actors. 'Is Kit Marlowe not here?' she asked. 'I had hoped to tell him how much I enjoyed his play.' But it seemed the poet had not been in the theatre for some days. 'Come then, Master Pope,' said the countess, 'and tell me what concerns you.'

The rest of the Lord Admiral's Men looked on in no little astonishment as the Countess swept Tom away with her. The boldest of players with a string of conquests behind him, including court ladies, would have thought twice before making such a suggestion to so great a lady in a public place, but that it should be Tom Pope! In a craft where all too many actors never married and made do with a string of mistresses or, if they did, kept a long-suffering wife at home seeing to house and children while they lived much of their lives elsewhere, Tom Pope was legendary for his devotion to his pretty wife and two sons.

'You have a room in which we can talk privately?' the Countess demanded of Henslowe. Through clenched teeth the famed entrepreneur suggested that she might make use of his own business office if she wished, humble and bare of furniture as it was.

'I do not imagine Master Pope and I will wish to recline at our leisure on daybeds nor eat and drink the night away,' she replied, brushing this aside. 'Once he has given me his friend's message then I shall be on my way. I must call on my dressmaker to see if my new gown is ready for I dine with the Queen tomorrow.'

Left to himself with so splendid a lady, for the Countess was beautifully attired and decked out with jewels, Tom himself marvelled at his own impertinence. Also, a frightful thought struck him. Suppose she thought he had taken her aside to make some kind of advance to her? But as soon as the door closed behind them she turned to him briskly and came straight to the point. 'Well? I assume this must be a serious matter that requires my attention so urgently.'

As well as he could Tom explained Simon's predicament to her – how he had been blamed for the death of a man for whom he had prescribed the sea holly and thus been imprisoned by the College of Physicians, although they had no proof that he had done any wrong. Worse, that some unknown person seemed out to make particular mischief for him, including the writing of forged letters. Simon desperately needed to be released from the Counter so that he could clear his name and try to discover who was behind such black business. Mary Herbert heard him out in silence.

'I will certainly see what I can do to press the College Council to have him released,' she said at once. 'I know how ready they are to blame anyone who is not part of their small circle and to refuse licences to many who are highly skilled. As to the other matter, I find that very interesting indeed.' She paused for a moment. 'You would seem to be a man of discretion, Tom Pope, so I will tell you in confidence that other members of the School of the Night have also suffered strange and embarrassing happenings, which mostly they have kept to themselves.' She gave him a reassuring smile. 'Leave the matter with me now. I will do all I can. If, as I understand, Dr Forman is skilled at solving mysteries then it would help us all if he were able to solve this one.'

The next morning the President of the College of Physicians was informed that Mary Herbert, Countess of Pembroke, had arrived and wished to speak to him. He found this somewhat surprising as he was not acquainted with the lady although he had seen her from a distance at great state occasions, usually accompanying her brother, Sir Philip. Rumours had reached him that she dabbled in scientific experiments; indeed that on some occasions she was aided by Dr Adrian Gilbert himself. He hoped she was not planning to discuss such matters with him or ask his advice on some aspect of chemistry, for he would feel impelled to inform her, albeit most civilly, that it really was not possible for the minds of women to grasp such things however highborn they might be. In spite of what the Queen might say, he added to himself.

But if he was expecting a little light chat possibly accompanied by some kindly admonishment on his part as to the place of ladies in the scheme of things, he was to be briskly disillusioned. The lady swept into his fine panelled room accompanied by her maid and after the briefest of greetings declared: 'I understand you have confined Dr Forman to the Counter Gaol?'

The President was taken aback. Yes, he agreed, he had ordered that the man, Forman, be imprisoned in the Counter while enquiries of a serious nature were being undertaken.

'And how far on are you with these "enquiries"?'

The President had to admit that so far nothing had been done. He was sure the Countess understood; the members of the Council were occupied with many great affairs and had little time to spare at present to look into the activities of an obscure fellow from the Bankside who purported to be a physician. But, if it interested her, then he hoped they might turn their attention to Forman in a month or so. He trusted that answered her question to her satisfaction.

No, she told him loudly, it most definitely did not. To his great astonishment it appeared the Countess was *au fait* with the situation. 'I understand you've locked him away on the word of some silversmith who alleges that Dr Forman poisoned his brother at the request of the man's wife. No doubt he has his reasons, an obvious one being that the woman in question now presumably inherits his wealth. How sad that under church law a man may not marry his brother's wife, for if *that* had been the case I doubt you'd have heard any more of it – supposing, that is, that the brother is unwed.'

The President grappled with his temper. 'I am at a loss to see why this should interest your ladyship,' he said as coolly as he could, 'but there is more to it than that. Forman prescribed for this man a supposed aphrodisiac, *eringo* – candied sea holly, without any knowledge of its effects. Even if he did not collude with the woman to commit a heinous crime, then at the very least he is guilty of gross carelessness in so prescribing.'

'I understand the man was old and fat and could not satisfy his wife,' continued the Countess, unabashed. 'No doubt his dismal exertions hastened his end. However, you should know that Dr Forman's *eringo* was used experimentally by willing participants at Sherborne Castle the other week.' She hesitated for a moment then decided to be bold. 'At least half a dozen men ate it without any ill-effect whatsoever.' That, she told herself, was quite true. There was no proof that it had made either the servant or young Carew ill.

God's Blood, cursed the President under his breath, how do I get rid of this dreadful woman? He attempted a respectful smile. 'I will give some thought to what you have told me,' he intoned, making it clear that so far as he was concerned the meeting was now at an end. 'When I have done so I will, as I have already told you, discuss the matter further with my Council and we will then decide how best to proceed. If it would please your ladyship, I'll send word to you in, say, a month from now and let you know the outcome of our deliberations.'

But the Countess made no attempt to leave. 'It does not please me in the least,' she told him. 'I want Dr Forman out of prison. *Right now.* I want to see it done before I leave for Nonesuch to dine with the Queen tonight, otherwise his continuing in gaol will offer an interesting topic of conversation at the supper table.'

Sweet Jesu, not the Queen again, groaned the President. Did this termagant know of the unfortunate affair of the Leevers woman? Grudgingly, he realised he had little alternative but to comply with her commands – or at least appear to do so. 'Very well,' he said with a sigh, 'I will send for my secretary as soon as you have left and despatch a letter to the Governor of the Counter asking him to release Forman.'

'I am not so short of time that I can't wait a little longer,' the Countess advised him. 'Send for your secretary now, and as for taking the letter over to the Counter, my carriage is outside. One f my grooms will deliver it personally and then there can be no ossibility of its going astray.'

After four days in prison Simon was at his wits' end to know what o do with himself, racking his brains as to who might be making o much trouble for him. His old enemy, Giles Escourt, was now ead and, as he had told John, the Tapworths could only be esponsible for the complaint to the College of Physicians. It was aost unfortunate that James Tapworth had died so soon after eing given the *eringo*, but Tom was surely right: there was no roof whatsoever that it had been the cause of his death. However made Simon think of other patients he had been called on to 'eat and who had later died – the victims of scrofula, blood loss r fever – and to consider whether his unknown enemy might be rawn from the ranks of their families. If that was the case, surely e would have learned of their suspicions before now! Indeed, as ne of the very few doctors who had remained in London during ist year's plague epidemic in order to treat its victims, their urviving relatives – always supposing there were any – had been nly too grateful for the fact that he had tried to save their lives at ll.

The most eerie thing was that whoever was doing all this ppeared to be so familiar with his way of life, his household, ven his mistress, not to mention his handwriting, and if the sea olly really had been poisoned then his enemy knew he had sent way for that too. He paced up and down his small room. He had, e just had, to get out.

The sound of his door being unlocked made him swiftly turn ound. The Sergeant stood there, accompanied by Roger Warren, le prisoner with the infected eye. 'The Head Gaoler says you're come and look at a prisoner in the Hole,' the Sergeant said, 'for :ar it's the plague.'

'I know him, you see,' Roger piped up. 'I don't think it's the plague but he's very sick, mortal sick. Would you come and help him like you helped me, doctor?'

The Sergeant led Simon down endless stone corridors, through the Knight's Ward with its dingy rooms and the Twopenny Ward where dirty white faces were pressed against cage-like rooms, often with a dozen or more people in each. The stench from the Hole hit Simon at the top of the steps leading down to it – a grim miasma of damp, dirty humanity, urine and sickness. 'Wait a moment,' grunted the Sergeant, 'I'll fetch a candle.' It was like a scene from the Judgement Day. Dim figures stood or lay on filthy straw, the only light coming from one small barred window. The sound of sobbing, coughing, streams of oaths and pitiful cries filled the choking air.

As his eyes became accustomed to the gloom Simon saw half-starved women struggling to give babies the breast, men who had spent their last pennies on strong spirits and were hardly able to stand, falling over those lying apparently senseless, or dead, on the ground unaware of what was going on around them.

'Lord have mercy on us!' he breathed. 'What a fearful place! Where is your friend?' Roger led them over to a corner while the rest of the prisoners clustered round them, frantically begging for money for food and drink. Overwhelmed, Simon was almost glad he had none on him and clung firmly on to his bag. He found Roger's friend almost insensible. 'Hold the light nearer,' he ordered the gaoler. 'How am I supposed to examine him in the dark?'

He gently turned the man over and held the candle to his face. There were no blotches. 'Help me get his coat off,' he said to Roger. 'Let me see if there are any buboes under his arms.' Between them they did so but there was no sign nor, when reluctantly Simon drew down his breeches, were there any swellings in his groin. They dressed the man again who was now muttering to himself.

'Well,' said Simon, 'it's not plague, so you're in luck. But God knows what other foul diseases you breed down here. Whatever these benighted folk have done, surely they should be put where there is light and fresh air?' The man on the floor moaned and opened his eyes.

'See, now, Luke. I've brought you a real physician,' Roger told him.

The sick man blinked at the candle. 'Fetch me some water – some *clean* water,' Simon instructed the Sergeant, 'if there is such a thing in this place. We should at least try and get his fever down and I have a remedy here that might help. Though if it is, as I suspect, gaol fever then you might lose almost as many of them as if it had been the plague.'

The Sergeant shuffled off and returned a few minutes later with a tin cup of reasonably clean water. Simon put in some herbs and stirred them as best he could. 'The water should be boiling but I'm unlikely to get that here.' He put his arm round the man's shoulder and raised him up, trying not to breathe in the smell, and made him drink.

'Thank you, doctor,' the sick man said, then, alarmed, he looked at Roger. 'But I've no money. Doctors don't treat you if you've no money.'

Simon reassured him that there was no question of payment and the man clung to his hand. As he laid him back again on the filthy straw, his patient looked intently at his hand. 'There's no mark,' he said, 'no mark.' Then, 'So I don't know you, do I? Who are you?'

'My name's Simon Forman,' said Simon. 'But what is this about a mark? What mark do you mean?'

'On your hand ... no mark,' and he lapsed back into unconsciousness.

'What on earth did he mean by that?' wondered Simon. Roger shrugged and shook his head while the Sergeant said the fool was out of his wits and no heed should be taken of it. Simon stood up. 'Well, if you've an ounce of sense you'll tell the Head Gaoler or, better still, the Governor that he should get this man out of here immediately and put him in isolation unless he wants gaol fever to run rife through the Counter. I hardly need to tell you it carries off the gaolers as well as the prisoners.'

They retraced their steps towards Simon's room to find the door standing wide and no lesser person waiting for him than the Governor of the Counter, who greeted him with a smile. 'I have good news for you, Dr Forman,' he said. 'You are to be released forthwith.'

'Released? Are you sure? On whose authority?'

'Quite sure, and it is on the authority of the President of the College of Physicians. I thought it surprising they put you here in the first place and presumably they have now thought better of it, particularly as you appear to have noble friends. There is also this letter for you with a great crest on it. You may take up your things and go. I bid you good-day, sir.'

Simon thanked him, still bemused, then told him of the sick man in the Hole. 'I'm almost sure it's gaol fever,' he said. 'If that's the case he should be put somewhere away from the others.' He went to his bag. 'Here's a guinea, sir. Use it to put the man elsewhere at least until he recovers and I'll leave him my blanket. As for this leftover food, Roger here may have it. He's been good to me while I've been in here.'

The Governor went on his way and Simon began ramming his belongings along with the letter into the bag John had left him. Whatever had persuaded the President to change his mind? Had

William Tapworth withdrawn his complaint? Still, that could all be gone into later. As Simon carried on gathering up his few belongings, he became aware that Roger was still standing looking at him. The inflammation around his eye was now almost gone.

'I must go back to the Twopenny Ward,' he said, 'but I'm glad for you that you're getting out. I'll be free soon too, by the end of the week they say.' He pulled up his ragged shirt and showed Simon the marks of old weals on his back. 'They said I could either have a whipping and be out in three months, or no whipping and be here for twelve or more. I chose the whipping. My Betty's got us lodgings in the alleyway down by Henslowe's warehouse so we'll be neighbours, so's to speak.'

'And how will you make shift to live?' Simon wanted to know.

'Well, there'd be no more crossbiting again, that's for sure. But there's plenty of other means for a sharp lad on the Bankside without going in for nip and foist or charming locks, ways of keeping just this side of the law,' replied Roger with a broad grin. 'But thank you most kindly for seeing to my eyes as you have. If there's ever any way I can repay what you've done, you've only to call on me. Ask at the lodging house, third door on the left down the alley going towards the river. You never know, I might be useful. I was brought up by the Thames among the watermen; I doubt there's any place either side of it that I couldn't find if I wanted to. In fact, if I can find the bung I might buy a boat myself.' He extended a grubby hand and Simon shook it then handed over the remnants of his food which Roger seized eagerly and took away.

Outside in Wood Street, Simon took in great gulps of air, though the stink of the Hole still hung about him. But he was free, free to walk the streets and go to his home and, above all, free to try and discover who was behind his troubles. He crossed the busy Cheapside, wondering if John had managed to discover the whereabouts of the widow Tapworth, and from there made his way to London Bridge. He was halfway across it when he saw John coming the other way, obviously *en route* for the Counter.

'Well, doctor,' John hailed him from some yards away. 'So they've let you out. I reckon you've Tom Pope to thank for that.'

'Tom? What's he got to do with it?'

'Only talked to your countess, that's what.'

'The Countess of Pembroke? She's hardly *my* countess and I scarcely think she'd thank you for saying so. But how did Tom come to meet her?'

As they walked back to his house, John told Simon what he had learned from Tom, how the Countess of Pembroke had visited the Rose Playhouse the previous day and how he had drummed up the courage to approach her on the subject. 'I think he has some doubts about it now,' declared John, 'for not only has his forward behaviour offended Master Henslowe but he's now the butt of many jests and lewd comments among his fellow players. You see, he was closeted with the lady in a private place for above half an hour.'

It was with the most tremendous relief that Simon entered his own house once again. After throwing his bag down on the floor, he went out to the pump in the yard with a towel and sluiced his hands and face under it. He then went into the kitchen and, after asking Anna to boil up as much water as possible so he could wash the stink of the gaol off himself, he poured out a cup of wine and went into his study to read the letter the prison Governor had given to him. He had almost forgotten it in the excitement of getting out.

It was, as he suspected, from the Countess. She had been sorry to learn, she wrote, that he had suffered such an indignity and trusted that her intervention had proved successful. If it was convenient she would be grateful if he would come to her London house in two days' time to attend a meeting to which she had invited several other members of the School of the Night, including Ralegh.

While you seem to have suffered most, she continued, *you may be surprised to know that you are not alone in having been the victim of what at best is an unpleasant hoax and at worst something a great deal more dangerous. It would seem sensible therefore for us to share our experiences and see what might be learned and what can be done before something even more untoward occurs.* She signed herself *Yours affectionately, Mary Herbert.*

Sometime later, having scrubbed himself free of lice in a tub of hot water and rolled his clothing up in a bundle for Anna to do what she could with, Simon dressed in clean clothes and made his way to the kitchen to enquire if there had been many patients calling on him while he had been in the Counter. No, he was told, it had been strangely quiet, uncannily so. As to the other matters, they were no longer so pressing, but had John managed to discover the whereabouts of Mistress Tapworth? The widow, he learned, was not after all in the country seeking solace for her loss in the Chelsea house, but back in the City. The servant to whom John had spoken had told him 'the mistress was very busy with *her own affairs*' and had rolled her eyes to make her point. 'I see,' said Simon thoughtfully. 'Perhaps after all she did find some way of disposing of Tapworth. I think I'll pay her a visit, seeing how I was alleged to have assisted her. And what of the printer? Did you also manage to find him?'

Not surprisingly, given the way he made most of his money, the printer had not taken kindly to enquiries of any kind about anything at all. He had greeted John with patent distrust, opening the door only a crack and that on a chain, and had seemed reluctant to believe that he wasn't there on behalf of a Justice or Sheriff's

Officer. Pressed on the matter and still deeply suspicious, the printer grudgingly agreed that some years earlier a doctor had rented a room above the shop. No, he couldn't remember the man's name, why should he? It was all a long time ago and it had only ever been a temporary arrangement. A man must live and he must have had a score of casual lodgers since then; he'd be hard put to remember any of them.

Asked if he knew the doctor's permanent direction or where he practised, the man snapped that he'd never said, 'And I never asked. People don't ask many questions around here. So long as his money was good and he paid for the room, that was all I cared about.'

'I suppose that's possible,' Simon agreed when John had finished his account. 'Perhaps he just came to the Bankside for entertainment of a somewhat doubtful kind and kept his professional life altogether separate from his jaunts south of the river. It does happen. I take it you learned nothing more?'

John had not, for at that point the printer had slammed the door in his face. But he'd looked both shifty and uneasy and John felt that the man was worried about something altogether different, a matter of more immediate concern. 'I might be wrong but I had the feeling he wasn't alone, that there was someone else there, either in the back of the shop or up above.'

'Well, if he does sell the kind of pictures he's reputed to, it's more than possible that some of his customers don't want to be seen buying them,' asserted Simon, 'and he won't want to embarrass them and so lose business.' John agreed but added that the man had given him the impression that he was expecting trouble of some kind. 'He must be used to that,' Simon said dismissively. 'I wonder how many times he's been hauled up before the Justices. Anyway, it doesn't really matter. It's the least of my problems.'

The unnatural quiet continued throughout that day and the next. Not a single patient knocked on the door asking for Dr Forman's services, no young blade or wily banker desirous to have their horoscope cast, no young woman keen to discover whether or no she was with child.

'I simply can't understand it,' Simon said to John and Anna. 'It's never been as quiet as this since I set up practice on the Bankside. What in the name of all that's holy can have driven everyone away from my door? Surely not my being in the Counter, if news has got out? Few folk can have known I was in the gaol, and surely it would not stop any who did from seeking my advice. Half the population of the Bankside have spent time in there, if for nothing more than nonpayment of debts or someone taking a suit out against them for an imagined slight. Not to mention the actors. The last time I saw Henslowe at the Rose he was grumbling about how it had cost him two pounds to bail out two actors and a playwright after they'd had a night out on the town and knocked down a member of the Watch. He told me he intended taking it out of the money he owed to them. No, there has to be some other reason for it and I intend finding out what it is. There's been too much mystery by half.'

Chapter 6

The Widow's Story

It could be, Simon thought, that the Tapworths had been making more trouble for him, warning all and sundry that he thought nothing of the odd poisoning. Therefore he would visit the young widow and see how matters stood. So young a girl, even if precocious in bed, would be naive in the ways of the world. Even if she were not unhappy at the death of her elderly spouse then she was likely to have been overwhelmed by the funeral, the arguments over the will and not to mention being accused of making away with Tapworth. He walked briskly across the Bridge and made his way over to Cheapside. The Tapworths' silversmith's shop was easy to find, not least because of the fine house standing back a little way from it. He plied the elaborate knocker and asked the maid who answered it if Mistress Tapworth was at home.

'I'll go and ask her if she'll see you,' she replied doubtfully, but with a glimmer of a smile. 'She's most occupied at present and has asked not to be disturbed.' Occupied with what, thought Simon in some amusement. Perhaps she's already found consolation. A vision arose in his mind of a pretty, plump young woman dallying on a daybed with a handsome youth. 'Who shall I say it is, sir?' enquired the maid.

'Er . . . John Bradedge,' responded Simon quickly. After all, he could hardly tell them his real name; for all he knew, the other Tapworth was lurking about somewhere and would have him dragged straight back to the Counter on his own suit. The maid reappeared a few minutes later. The mistress did not know the name but said he might come in so long as he did not take up too much of her time. As she led him through the hall, Simon wondered what to expect. A tearful nymph? A wily elf of a girl already calculating what kind of a husband she could buy for her wealth? A lost child in a harsh world? All he knew of her was that she was sixteen years old and pretty. He was unprepared for what he found.

Lavinia Tapworth was seated at a large table almost hidden from sight by ledgers. She was indeed pretty and very young but the rest was quite unexpected. Small curls of fair hair escaped from the widow's cap she was forced to wear although Simon noted it was of the finest lawn and trimmed with lace. Her gown, naturally black, was of expensive velvet and very neat but had a tracery of silver embroidery on it. Her fingers, he noticed, were stained with ink from the pen with which she was busy writing. She looked up at him as he entered and motioned him to sit down.

'You have come to buy from us, Master Bradedge?' she asked.

'Is your brother-in-law not here then?' he returned in some surprise.

She gave him a level look. 'I have no idea. I am in charge of the business now, you may deal with me.' She caught his expression. 'Do you find it strange? I was used to looking after my father's books for him and organising his affairs almost from when I learned to read, write and number. My late husband would not, however, allow it.'

'I was sorry to hear of your loss,' he told her, wondering whatever she would come out with next.

'Thank you. But James was, after all, an old man,' she replied serenely. 'Now, what is it you want? The books have been sadly neglected and I am doing my best to get them in order.'

'Then I will put my cards on the table since you seem an astute young woman,' said Simon. 'I misled your maid. John Bradedge is the name of my servant. I am Dr Simon Forman.'

This did produce a result. She looked at him open-mouthed. 'I'd been told you were in the Counter Gaol.'

'Was it you who sought to put me there?' he continued. 'God's Teeth, woman, I've just spent the best part of a week in that stinking hole having been accused of colluding with you in the poisoning of your husband.'

'It was none of my doing,' she assured him. 'It was down to William, my brother-in-law. In fact, I thought I might well find myself in the Bridewell accused of being a murderess. I think he would have been quite content to see me hanged at Tyburn.' She shivered. 'Though at least that is preferable to the punishment of years back when a husband-murderer was burned at the stake.'

But she had not been so accused – at least, not publicly. Simon began to feel somewhat annoyed. 'You obviously managed to convince him otherwise. Might one enquire how? Was it by throwing suspicion on me?'

'Most certainly not,' she assured him. 'It was not my idea that James went to a physician to try and cure his problem. He blamed his first wife, poor woman, for all his troubles. No doubt she would tell a different tale. Anyway,' she added mischievously, 'I know it was not the sea holly, for I took two pieces and ate it myself. So far as I could tell it made no difference, though matters might have been otherwise if there had been another kind of man in my bed.' She really was a most unusual girl, thought Simon.

She stood up and came round the table to him, putting her hand on his arm. 'I'm so sorry, Dr Forman. William did not even inform me at first that he had written to the College of Physicians. I told him that if it came to court then I would insist on appearing and telling all who cared to hear that James died of an apoplexy, that I too had tried the sea holly without ill effect and that the whole business was to do with the fact that James had left the largest share in the business to me. If he had any more to say about it, I swore that I would have him arrested on my suit for slander. I realise now I should have done more about it, but first there was the burial and the will and then these affairs to be dealt with.'

'Apoplexy? I was told your husband had spasms of pain in the gut which could be poisoning.'

She agreed that had been the case, but that they had been quite mild. 'However, when he also complained of a pain in his heart, we sent at once for a physician who came almost immediately. There was nothing he could do.' Her voice was matter-of-fact. 'My husband died some half an hour later, struck down in exactly the same way that my uncle was years ago, which is why I feel sure the real cause was apoplexy.'

'What did your physician say?'

'First, following James's complaints of stomach pains he asked him if he had eaten anything that might have disagreed with him and James pointed to the pieces of sea holly and muttered "poison". That was not long before he died.' It was clear she was quite unmoved by the event. 'I told the physician then that I did not think that could be the cause and that the symptoms seemed to me to be those of apoplexy, but he dismissed this. He obviously did not care for the advice of a woman, informing me that he was a member of the College of Physicians. He then shook his head, looked grave and asked my husband where he had obtained the stuff. James told him that he had consulted you and that you had given it to him. The man claimed to know you and declared that this was a serious matter and he would look into it further.'

So, thought Simon, that was why the College had taken the issue up so quickly. One of their own had also complained about him as well as the man's brother. He wondered which member of that august body it was: it might actually have been one of the Censors present at his own hearing – possibly the old man who had ranted on about hedge doctors. It was important he found out.

'I presume he is your usual physician?'

She shook her head. 'As it happened he wasn't, for our own man lives here in Thames Street. It came about by a fortunate chance. A few days earlier, discussing business with a colleague in an inn in the City, James had found himself in conversation with this doctor. You must have realised James was fearful of the slightest thing where his health was concerned and no doubt he was delighted to hold the man captive, describing his symptoms! It turned out that he, too, was bound for Chelsea the next day to visit an acquaintance on his way south and so they arranged to ride together. James had pressed him to join us for supper but he said he had a previous engagement and so he left him at a nearby inn. When James was taken ill therefore I sent a servant to the inn straight away and the doctor came at once.'

'Of what like was he? Old? Of middle years?'

'Not old, more of middle age, but he was very serious, pompous and old-fashioned-looking, and that made him seem older than he was.'

That could be any one of the Censors, thought Simon. 'And his name?'

'Dr North.'

Well, if it was one of their own who'd attended her husband, no wonder the College had been so harsh on him, Simon thought. Perhaps this doctor had given Tapworth some remedy or other or tried a treatment of his own and then, when the man died, was frightened he would be blamed. When, on top of that they received William Tapworth's letter, it gave them the perfect excuse to blame him.

'He seemed competent enough, did he?'

She nodded. 'Oh yes, he did all the right things. Made James pass water and examined it, ascertained which humour governed him.'

'Did he give him any elixir?'

She told him no, for her husband had died before he could do so. 'He really did have the grandest manner. I think he must be doctor to some great households. When I asked him if there hadn't been anything more he could do for James, he turned to me and said if he couldn't save him, then no physician could for he had often been called the cleverest doctor in the world. What arrogance!'

'The cleverest doctor in the world.' Where had he heard that before?

There seemed nothing more to learn and Simon thanked the brisk young widow for giving him her time.

She smiled. 'You can come again if you think I can help you. Do you cast horoscopes?' He replied that he did. 'Very well then, I will visit you shortly to see if you can tell me what my future holds. That would be most interesting.'

'You want to know if you will marry again soon and what kind of man he will be?'

She laughed. 'I am in no hurry to marry again. I am enjoying being independent of father and husband and have a great deal to occupy me. If or when I change my mind then I can promise you he will not be in the least like James Tapworth.' He believed her and wondered if he should envy or pity the next man she accompanied to the altar.

Once outside the house he decided, being so near to Thames

Street, to see if there was any word there from Avisa. No letter had come to him from Kent. The door was opened by a maid he disliked who gave him a knowing look when he informed her that he had called round to enquire after her mistress's health. Mistress Avisa, she told him, was still in Kent but was expected home within the week. The master, who had visited her a few days earlier, had found her better in health but low in spirits. He could come in and wait for the master if he liked, she added with a disagreeable smile, he would be back from Billingsgate harbour directly.

He turned down the offer and began making his way home. Then he stopped rooted to the spot. *The cleverest doctor in the world* – that was what Roger Warren the prisoner had said of the physician who had treated his eye trouble – the one who had lived over the print shop by the Green Dragon! It might, of course, be just a coincidence but it was worth looking into. It sounded more like the kind of boast a quack doctor might make, but if the man was properly licensed then possibly even the College of Physicians would be uncomfortable at one of their members making such an extravagant claim.

He was halfway across London Bridge when he saw the first handbill. It was affixed to the post of the drop-down counter of a haberdasher's stall which served as a counter in the day and secured the building at night. It informed all and sundry that Dr Simon Forman had given up his practice on the Bankside as of now. He thanked the people of Southwark and elsewhere for their support during the last two years but he had decided to leave at once for the country. The lease of his house was for sale and anyone interested could apply to his housekeeper who was staying on in a caretaker capacity. The hoaxer had struck again! No wonder no one had been to consult him for days.

He roared into the back of the shop and hauled out the

unfortunate haberdasher who disowned all knowledge of it. He had noticed it there during the morning and had not bothered to take it down, proposing to do so when he closed his shop for the night. No, he had no idea who had put it up. Hundreds of people crossed the Bridge both ways all day; anyone could have done it when his back was turned. 'Anyway,' he said, 'it's not the only one. You'll see plenty of others.'

He did. Between the haberdasher's shop and the entry to the Bridge on the south side, Simon discovered another six, all of which, he was assured, had been placed there without the owners' knowledge. He tore them down and instead of going straight back home, went along the lanes and alleys of the Bankside in search of others. He had no problem finding them. They had sprouted on every post and piece of blank wall like strange fungus. But there was worse. Side by side with some of them, printed in exactly the same way and on similar paper, were others complaining that the Bankside, like the rest of London, was overrun with foreigners who were responsible for the last epidemic of plague and were now living off the backs of hardworking citizens.

This was distinctly frightening – and not just because of the unpleasant nature of the material. Of late the government had brought in a law prohibiting the pasting up of bills in public places without authorisation, following a spate of nasty and slanderous handbills which had appeared inciting violence towards the recent influx of persecuted refugees from the continent. Therefore those wanting to put up any kind of bill were supposed to ask permission of the relevant authorities, while anyone caught posting those aimed at the refugees faced the severest of penalties. Indeed, so concerned was the Privy Council, that its edict authorised law officers to enter and search the premises of anyone suspected of so doing and, if such material was found, to take them away and question them.

It ended in a chilling fashion with words Simon recalled all too well: '. . . and after you have examined this person and, if you should find them to be suspected and they shall refuse to confess the truth, you shall, by the authority hereof, put them to the torture in Bridewell and by the extremity therefore draw them to discover the knowledge they have. We pray you use your utmost travail and endeavour.'

It was clear that whoever had arranged for the bills to be printed and posted up had not only sought to ruin his medical practice but, by putting the two side by side, had deliberately given the impression that he was responsible for both – thus putting him at risk of being arrested, dragged off to Bridewell and racked. He shuddered. He had seen enough when abroad of what torture did to the bravest to know that he would be likely to confess to anything rather than it should continue. It was a wonder no one had knocked on his door already.

He ran frantically around wrenching the handbills down wherever he could find them, then returned home to fetch John to help him in the task of seeking out any he might have missed. There were even a couple in an inconspicuous place on the wall of the Rose Theatre.

'What scum from the sewers has done this?' John asked when they had finally, so far as they could tell, completed the task and were back home again.

Simon ran a frantic hand through his hair. 'How am I to counter it? God's Blood, no wonder I've had no patients but that's not the worst. With every knock on the door I'll expect to be dragged off to Bridewell.'

'You could go into the country for a while,' suggested John.

'And give this person the satisfaction of driving me away? No, I'll have to find this vermin before he destroys me. But I must admit the idea of getting out of the Bankside's a tempting one.'

'Are you going to alert the authorities?' asked John.

Simon began to pace up and down as he always did when disturbed. 'How can I risk it? They'd make enquiries, discover I'd just come out of the Counter Gaol and decide I was trying to cover my tracks. No, we must do two things. We must put it around as widely as possible that the handbills were a slanderous hoax and that there is no question but that I am staying on the Bankside while at the same time trying to find out who is the author of this outrage.'

He stopped his pacing and went over to the window. 'As to the first there is nothing to stop me going to the printer near Henslowe's warehouse and having him print some small notices saying only that Dr Forman has *not* given up his practice on the Bankside. We can place these in the shops of apothecaries, the fencing school, the tavern and even the Rose. It might be strictly against the law but I doubt much notice will be taken of it.' He picked up one of the offending handbills and tore it into shreds. 'Then we must next discover who printed this stuff and see if he can lead us to the perpetrator.'

He remained thoughtful as Anna ladled out his noontime soup. It would be like looking for a needle in a haystack, for London now had dozens of printers on both sides of the river. In fact, it was worse than that for they could as well have been printed outside London in some other town or city. Indeed, it would make sense: a country printer, ignorant of the edict prohibiting the printing and publishing of dangerous libels against foreigners, would be unaware of the risk he ran. Simon wondered where on earth to begin but he had to start somewhere.

Some time earlier he had had a small volume of his own work published by a printer near to St Paul's; this fellow might be able to suggest a possible culprit, as might the man whose shop was close by Henslowe's warehouse. He tried the latter first but the man was unable to help. He could, of course, have been lying but Simon did not think so, for he was a respectable craftsman of good reputation and most fearful of the consequences of posting up any illegal handbills.

'But why would I do such a thing, Dr Forman,' he asked, 'unless you had requested it yourself? Nor would any other round here, I dare swear.' Simon left him and briskly crossed the Bridge and made his way to his own printer in St Paul's who was equally adamant that no printer worth his salt – or indeed his reputation – would print such slanderous material.

'But presumably there are those who are not so nice about what they do, as there are in all trades,' Simon persisted.

The printer looked thoughtful. 'It's only a suggestion, but you might try that fellow who has a print shop close to the Green Dragon on your side of the river.'

'The man who sells lewd pictures?'

The printer laughed. 'You know of him then? Well, I believe he's none too fussy about what he undertakes.'

Simon thanked him and made his way quickly back home, cursing himself for being such a fool for not thinking of it himself. This was the same fellow he had sent John Bradedge to see, to enquire after Roger's 'cleverest doctor in the world' – the self same words used by the Tapworth widow that morning to describe the physician who had attended her dying husband.

He called for John as soon as he reached home. 'That printer I sent you to in the alleyway by the Green Dragon, you say he seemed most shifty and that he didn't even let you into his shop?'

'No, doctor. He kept the door on the chain which, looking back on it, seems strange being as it was during the day. For all he knew, I could have been a customer. But when I told you, if you remember, we both thought it was because of the stuff he peddles.'

Simon nodded. 'It's a reasonable assumption, but might it not be that he was already worried before you came to his door? That he had some dirty business on hand such as the printing of illegal handbills and that he was fearful you might be a law officer sent to search the premises?' He went into his study and returned with his sword and swordbelt. 'Let us pay a call on him and find out, shall we?'

Chapter 7

The Printer's Tale

It took only ten minutes to reach the printer's workshop which was under the living accommodation of his house. The lane, in which it was part of a terrace, certainly lived up to its bawdy nickname, for not only were there a good many whores plying for trade along its length, it was obvious that many of the establishments on either side were brothels. Indeed, one young lady, dressed only in what appeared to be a piece of thin green material slung over one shoulder, leaned out of an upstairs window and offered both gentlemen a good time.

'No wonder he does a roaring trade in his prints,' noted Simon as they reached the door. 'I'll speak to him first, John, since he might remember you and be suspicious, then you follow me in.' They tried the door but it was locked. 'A strange artisan this,' commented Simon, 'who has no open shop into which his customers can walk.' They had to knock for some time before they heard the sound of feet approaching from somewhere at the back of the building; the door opened a crack and the printer squinted through it at Simon.

'Well?' he demanded suspiciously.

Simon assumed a bashful and hesitant manner. 'I – er – hope

I've come to the right place. I've been told you have . . . that you sell . . . in short, I would like to see some of the rare engravings I understand you keep here for sale.'

The printer relaxed slightly and opened the door an inch or two wider. 'I might have such matter,' he agreed.

'Will it be possible then for me to see it?' enquired Simon, motioning to John to follow close behind.

At this the printer opened the door. 'Very well then, come in.' Immediately Simon pushed past him, followed by John who locked and bolted the door behind them. 'Here, you, what's the meaning of this?' cried the printer, then recognising John, 'Haven't you been here before with some cock and bull story about seeking a doctor? Thought then you was up to no good.'

The front part of the shop was laid out with shelves containing boxes of type, large jars of printer's ink and reams of paper of different varieties, and sizes. In front of the shelves was a trestle table scattered with examples of the man's work and rough pulls of handbills and pages of print. At present the window on to the street was shuttered and Simon decided to leave it that way. What light there was came from a room built on to the back of the building which housed the printing press and was reached through an open doorway.

Simon turned to the man. 'Ah yes,' he said, 'the doctor. Before we discuss other matters, have you as yet recollected his name? If so, I'd like to hear it.' The printer shook his head. 'It wouldn't be North, by any chance?'

'I don't believe so, but as I told your man then and I'll tell you again now, I don't recall it. It was years since. Now will you get out. You've no business in here.'

'Oh, but I have,' Simon assured him, 'pressing business,' and half drew his rapier out of its hangar.

The printer looked at it warily. 'I'll call the Constable,' he threatened.

'How?' enquired Simon pleasantly. 'Now, Master . . .? What's your name?'

'Holt. William Holt.'

'. . . Master Holt, if you'll just answer a couple of civil questions there will be no need for that.' He pulled one of the handbills out of his pocket and shoved it in the man's face. 'Did you print this?' he demanded.

'Don't know anything about it. Never seen it before,' the man asserted, avoiding Simon's eye.

Simon nodded to John who picked him up by his jerkin and pushed him up against the wall. 'Think again, you foul undigested lump or I'll ram it down your throat to jog your memory.'

Holt swallowed. 'Put me down,' he croaked, 'and I'll have a look. It could be I *might* have . . .'

'I'm looking for certainty,' Simon informed him, fingering his rapier again, at which the printer scurried to the table and delved among the heaps of paper.

There was a brief pause and then Holt cleared his throat. 'Yes, well, it looks as if I did print them. Some days ago. I forgot,' he explained. 'I've been very busy of late.'

'If your memory is this bad, I wonder you keep in business,' returned Simon. 'Who ordered them? And don't tell me you can't recall who it was or I'll ask John here to take you into that back room where you can't be heard and see that you do.'

'Maybe he didn't give a name,' replied the man sullenly. 'Some people don't.'

'This is like drawing teeth!' Simon exploded. 'Surely you must have taken a note of the man's name, how many bills he wanted printing, what he wanted on them and how much it would cost so that he could pay you when he returned? Have you no record of this transaction?' There was no response. 'Then let me show you the other bill. I take it you printed this one too since the paper, ink and typeface are exactly the same.' The printer did not reply. John twisted his arm behind his back and yanked it upwards.

'Aaah,' he shrieked, 'stop! You'll break it.'

'If you don't tell me the truth,' Simon told him quietly, 'I will leave my man here while I go and find a law officer and tell him that you are printing seditious libels as set out in the recent Order of the Privy Council. Then, when John has finished with you, the law officers can take the remains to Bridewell and put them on the rack. Keep him there, John, while I see if I can find copies of the second bill too.'

He searched through the papers on the trestle table while the printer moaned in John's grip. There were piles of examples of pamphlets, small handbills advertising everything from quack medicines to entertainments in the Paris Gardens, a few odd printers' blocks and even one or two of the notorious engravings seemingly featuring men and women of athletic, indeed acrobatic, tastes. Finally Simon discovered two or three copies of the second handbill. 'Now,' he said, 'I want to know who ordered both this and the other one and where I can find him. Let him go for now, John. And be quick,' he told Holt. 'Any delay and I call in the law officers.'

The printer went back to the table, rubbing his shoulder and upper arm, opened a box and took out a grubby piece of paper. 'See here then. He wanted forty copies of one and twenty of the other. They was ordered four days ago and picked up yesterday morning.'

'By the man who ordered them?'

'No. They was collected by the same tall young fellow who'd first brought in the order for his friend. Well-dressed. Spoke all smooth.' He paused for a moment. 'Looked well-heeled, he did, and I told him about my gentlemen's prints but he said he'd no time to look at them then. There's nothing wrong with those pictures,' he said, looking at their expressions. 'They're classical, most of them.'

'We're not here to talk about your other trade,' said Simon, 'and personally I don't care if you do sell bedroom pictures to those prepared to pay you foolish amounts of money for them. Now, one last chance. Will you tell me who ordered the handbills! Surely the man who brought in the order told you who they were for?'

By this time Holt realised there was no point in prevaricating any further. 'Very well,' he replied, obviously wanting to get it over, 'it was a doctor who ordered and paid for both of them.' He flourished a piece of paper. 'Here, see for yourself. They were for a Dr Forman, Dr Simon Forman.'

'I don't believe you,' declared Simon.

The printer gave him a surly look. 'It's the truth. His friend said he'd to leave London quick and on the quiet because he was in trouble, bad trouble. Something to do with a poisoning and he was off to Deptford to pick up a ship. As to the one about the foreigners . . .' he went over to the box again and came back with a piece of paper on which were a few scrawled lines . . . 'he said he didn't think anyone would come looking here but if they did, I'd to give them this piece of paper admitting he was responsible for having them printed so that I wouldn't get no blame for it. Look, it says so here and it's signed "Simon Forman".' He looked from one to the other but the revelation did not seem to have had the desired effect.

'*Now* what's the matter?' he grumbled. 'Do you know this doctor then?'

'Indeed I do,' said Simon through gritted teeth, 'for *I* am Dr Simon Forman. The Devil knows who this other man was and I'll warn you now, you haven't heard the last of me. And for your information, whoever it was who ordered this rubbish was wrong. If the law officers came here looking for proof that you printed those seditious handbills, that letter wouldn't help you even if it really had been me that signed it. Under the law, the printer's life's as forfeit as he who orders such bills. The Bridewell rack and the Tyburn gallows await both. As regards the other bill, if I find you publishing any more slanders alleging I'm leaving London, I'll personally drag you off to Newgate and stand and watch when they brand you a felon!'

The mood of those members of the School of the Night who met at the house of the Countess of Pembroke the next day was a sombre one. They included most, but not all, of those who had gathered at Sherborne Castle as well as some who had not and, as the Countess had informed Tom Pope when they spoke together, nearly everyone had a tale of some kind to tell of an unpleasant communication or black joke. Even the widely-respected Thomas Hariot had been the recipient of an anonymous letter accusing him of practising magic, raising the Devil by use of calculations and black spells and threatening him with an indictment for witchcraft.

'As for myself,' Mary Herbert informed them without the slightest loss of composure, 'my husband received an anonymous letter about my supposed activities, the content of which was later printed as a small pamphlet and circulated around the court. According to its unknown author, I have a small hole in the floor of the loft above my stables so that I may peer down when the stallion is brought to a mare in order to inflame my lust which I then slake with the nearest fellow to hand.'

This, understandably, produced no little embarrassment among her hearers and caused Marlowe, who was once again looking strained and heavy-eyed and until this time had taken little interest in the proceedings, to raise an eyebrow and nod slightly at Simon.

'Have I made you blush, gentlemen?' enquired the countess. 'I can assure you there's no need. I dealt with it by offering any who were interested a chance to visit our estate at Wilton and see for themselves if there is such an arrangement for a peepshow, while my husband let it be known that if he ever laid hands on the fellow who had put out such scurrilous stuff he would dispense with bringing him to justice and hang him himself from the nearest post, after whipping anyone he discovered dining out on the tale.'

There was some laughter at this then Ralegh turned to Simon. 'I hear you have been a particular target of this dangerous prankster, Dr Forman. Will you tell us about it?'

So Simon told of the chain of misfortune which had begun with the mysterious arrival of the *eringo* and the two cases of illness at Sherborne following the experiment, and continued with the death of Tapworth and his subsequent week's imprisonment on a charge of poisoning. 'And, by the by,' he added, 'the man was attended by a Dr North whom I very much wish to meet. If any of you know of him and his direction then I'd be grateful if you could tell me later, but next, while I was in prison,' he continued, 'my servants received a letter in a cleverly forged hand, supposedly from me, dismissing them from my service and at the same time a friend received a similar missive which caused them deep offence. Last but not least I too, like the countess, have been the victim of printed slander, for yesterday I discovered these two bills posted on London Bridge and around the Bankside.'

He produced a copy of each. 'Both are slanderous, as you can see, but the second could have had me dragged off to Bridewell since in some places they were posted up side by side, thus implying they were the work of one and the same person.'

'Good God preserve us!' exclaimed Ralegh. 'This could have

hanged you. I hope there are no more of these publicly displayed.'

'I trust not,' Simon told him. 'My servant and I searched for several hours removing all we found and when I finally discovered the whereabouts of the printer who had printed them he told me there were but twenty of the worst and forty of the other, and of the twenty I found I had them all. There were two or three more in his shop and I burned those along with the rest, keeping only a couple of each back for my own use.'

'Did the printer tell you who had supposedly ordered them on your behalf?' asked the countess.

'He replied – after much persuasion – that he had done so on the orders of a Dr Simon Forman who was fleeing the country. He even produced a letter allegedly scrawled by me taking responsibility for the handbills. The printer was fool enough to believe this would prevent his being put to the rack if copies were found in his shop.'

'How did you discover the printer?' Ralegh asked curiously.

'With a certain amount of luck,' answered Simon. 'I tried one or two near to home then went to my own printer close to St Paul's, who suggested a fellow with a dubious reputation. It so happened that my man had called at this very print shop a few days earlier on another matter altogether and was treated in a surly and suspicious fashion. Therefore, before trying another dozen or so print shops, I decided to pay the man, whose name is Holt, a visit and so it was we found the culprit.'

There was a flurry of conversation, the leaflets were passed round and examined again and then Ralegh called for quiet. 'It seems you have been most particularly singled out, Dr Forman. Have you an enemy who might have chosen to destroy you in this way?'

Marlowe, who still appeared strained, lounged back in his chair. 'What about our mighty Acting Secretary of State to the Privy

Council, Simon? You made yourself quite an enemy there.'

'Sir Robert Cecil?' exclaimed Ralegh, startled. 'How was that?'

Simon gave Marlowe a speaking look. 'That's in the past, Kit, as you well know. Sir Robert sent me to Scotland on . . . on a mission,' he explained, 'which turned out to be very different from what I had thought it to be. I will say no more about it except that Lord Hunsdon took my part when I returned and I remain under his protection. But in any event I can't imagine Sir Robert Cecil being behind this. If he really wanted to do away with me then he could find the means without pasting up handbills to bring it about – nor would it explain the tricks played on everyone else.'

Mary Herbert looked across at Simon thoughtfully. 'So you went on a mission for Robert? Dear me, what an intriguing man you are, Dr Forman. You must tell me all about it some time. I am quite fascinated.' Only then did Simon recall Marlowe's gossip on the way back from Sherborne, that it was said that the Countess shared her bed not only with her head groom but also with Robert Cecil. Suppose it were true, at least where Cecil was concerned? What on earth had possessed Marlowe deliberately to bring the matter up?

'And what about you, Kit?' Ralegh demanded. 'Do you too have enemies? Or have you so far avoided the notice of this mischief-maker?'

For once Marlowe had no witty or clever response at hand. 'Enemies?' he replied bleakly. 'Too many to count. I fear they are all around me but not, I think, this fellow – whoever he is. I am quarry of a different sort.' He shivered slightly. 'In this case, I can't help you.'

'How about Thomas Nashe?' enquired Marlowe's friend Matthew Roydon. 'He's always publishing something and he's a gadfly if ever there was one with his pamphlets and such. You've been thick as thieves with him since the death of Robin Greene. If he is our man then that would explain why you haven't drawn his fire.'

Marlowe gave him an unpleasant smile. 'If I were you, Roydon, I wouldn't let Nashe hear you say that, or you might find yourself the subject of one of his publications. He can be biting, even dangerous, in his writings and I know he views all of us with extreme disapproval and suspicion, but not even he would risk breaking the Privy Council Order just to anger us.'

There was an uneasy pause and then Ralegh spoke. 'Very well, we take your point. Now let us put our heads together to see if we can come up with anyone who might feel a sufficient grudge or grievance against our association in general, and Dr Forman in particular, to go to these lengths.'

They talked for an hour or more without reaching any conclusion, having considered a host of possible reasons for what was happening. No, they had never asked any members of the loose association of seekers after truth to leave the School against their wishes or because of a quarrel with another member. Only those who were felt to be sympathetic and of a questing turn of mind were invited to attend meetings in the first place, and only then after careful consideration and discussion both as to their suitability and the field of knowledge they had to offer.

A chilling suggestion from Hues, the geographer, that one or other of them present might not be all they seemed and had been set there for some unknown reason by unknown persons in order to destroy the School was greeted first with appalled silence then, by Ralegh quietly intervening to say that he would stake his own honour on the integrity of every one of those present; but the thought hung in the air and the uneasiness was palpable.

Ralegh continued, 'But while I do not believe there really is a spy among us, I have received some other ill news it is perhaps best you know now, though I do not think it is connected with the matter in hand. That is that sufficient stir has been made among enough worthies to have them petition the Star Chamber to mount an inquisition into the activities of what they describe as "the devilish society of necromancers, warlocks and blasphemers known as the School of the Night".'

The others looked at him in horror. 'Are you so sure that this is not part of the same business?' Hues asked.

Ralegh paused for a moment. 'At present my instinct is that it is something altogether different, although of course I may be wrong.'

'I don't think you are, Sir Walter,' Simon told him, 'for I heard such a suggestion made when I appeared before the College of Physicians.'

'Therefore,' Ralegh went on, 'it is best for the present that we do not meet on a regular basis and busy ourselves instead with our own affairs, for the last thing we need is to draw any further attention to our activities from the Star Chamber. But it becomes even more essential that we discover the identity of this dangerous hoaxer.' He turned to Simon. 'I think all of us present know that you have acquired no small reputation as a solver of mysteries and in this case you have a pressing need of your own to do so.

'Mary, gentlemen, I propose we should ask Dr Forman to use all his expert skill to try and unravel this mystery and to that end give him every help and pledge our support. Are you willing to undertake this task on our behalf as well as your own, Dr Forman?'

'I will do my best,' Simon replied, 'though you will appreciate I can't promise success. I may also need to question some of you to see if there is anything at all you might know, however unimportant it might seem, that can help throw some light on the situation before worse befalls. Whoever is doing this is either thoroughly evil, deranged, or both and therefore most dangerous.'

The meeting began to break up and as it did so one of those attending came over to Simon. 'You spoke of a Dr North, Dr Forman. I am almost certain that was the name of the doctor who had his practice close by Canon Row and was much respected but if so, then he removed to the country some years since.'

Simon thanked him and was about to leave when Ralegh came over to him. 'Should you need any funds to enable you to carry out this task, then you must apply to me. I realise the burden we are putting on you.'

'What of this Star Chamber inquisition?' queried Simon. He shuddered slightly. 'I would take an oath that Sir Robert Cecil's behind it, however many "worthies" have allegedly petitioned him, apart from the College of Physicians.'

'So I think also,' nodded Ralegh, 'but I agree with you that it's unlikely he has anything to do with this other business. At least, I hope we are right,' he added cautiously, 'for the alternative is deeply unpleasant. Cecil is still consolidating his own power base and I am not part of it.' He paused, then said very quietly, 'Rumour has it that Cecil and Mary Herbert are close; which is yet another twist. How true it is, I don't know. It could be no more than friendship.'

'I'd heard as much from Kit Marlowe,' Simon told him. He looked across at the countess who was still chatting with Hariot. As if she felt his gaze she turned and smiled at him and he went over to bid her farewell. She offered him a shapely hand to kiss.

'I note you wish to question us all separately. I am at leisure during the mornings over the next few days.' She gave him an arch look. 'We can also discuss other matters such as . . .'

'Chemistry?' suggested Simon quickly. 'I am told you have conducted experiments with Adrian Gilbert himself.'

The countess laughed. 'Most certainly chemistry. I am a great believer in experiment.'

He returned home with mixed feelings. Certainly it was flattering to have so many great men willing to give him such responsibility, but what if he failed? So far he had not the faintest idea where to start looking for the culprit and there was always the possibility that whoever was stalking him had nothing to do with the mischief suffered by everyone else. As he was close to the water steps at that end of the Strand, he ran down to hail a wherry to take him across the river to the Bankside rather than walk down to London Bridge. He was met by the usual shouts and cries of those touting for custom. It must have been a quiet day for there were half a dozen empty boats all jostling for position.

'Here,' a voice yelled. 'Dr Forman! It's me, Roger.' It was his fellow prisoner from the Counter. 'Let me take you across. I'll do it for free for your curing my eyes and seeing to poor old Luke.'

This caused an immediate reaction and Simon feared his fellow boatmen were about to turn on Roger and smash his boat to pieces. There was a chorus of the insults for which the boatmen were famous, among the more respectable of which were 'whoreson slave', 'gallows rat', 'louse of a lazar house', and 'cankered scum'.

'Be still,' he called out, 'let him alone. I know him and need to have words with him.'

One of the boatmen looked up. 'It's Dr Forman, isn't it? You'll take your life in your hands, good sir, if you let him take you over in that old heap of rotten planks. You'd be safer in my mother's washtub.' The other boatmen laughed jeeringly.

'You may well be right,' Simon agreed, critically regarding Roger's craft. It was smaller than the others, its paint was peeling and there was a good three or four inches of water in the bottom. 'But if I go across with him it will save me seeking him out later. So on this occasion, if you'll let me pass, I'll take a chance. You know I make use of all of you from time to time.'

There was a good deal of grumbling and the wherryman who had spoken first informed Simon that Roger was a convicted felon, an outsider and no member of the Company of Watermen, for the wherrymen had their own rules, regulations and livery company and guarded their rights jealously. However, Simon was finally allowed through; he clambered out to Roger over two other boats and they set off for the Bankside.

'You'll have trouble if you really cross those wherrymen,' he advised Roger as the latter strained against the current, for the tide was racing in. 'They've been known to take violent action against freebooters.'

Roger shrugged. 'I'll take my chance. I bought this old craft for next to nothing but as soon as I've earned some money I'll find something better. As I told you, I know a good many wherrymen myself though most of them are downriver from here. I'll ask for their help in setting up for I intend turning over a new leaf.' He panted slightly then pulled hard until they were almost over to the other side. 'So, what was it you wanted to talk to me about, or were you just fending off the other boatmen?'

'The sight of you reminded me of the doctor of whom we spoke, he who cured your eyes some years back but you couldn't remember his name. "The cleverest doctor in the world" you said he called himself. The one that lodged with a printer?'

'Aye, and I still can't, if that's what you want to ask me. It's been annoying me too. Are you looking for him then?'

'Let's just say I'm interested. Could his name have been North?'

Roger thought hard then shook his head. 'No, that rings no bell. Is it important?'

'Most likely not. It was just an idea I had, for it was partly through a complaint from a Dr North that I landed in the Counter accused of poisoning a patient, and this man too boasted of how clever he was. However, I've more pressing matters on hand at present for now someone is making a deal of mischief for me and having handbills printed in my name saying I'm giving up my practice and leaving the country. The connection is that it just so chances that the printer, a William Holt, who carried out the order is the very man with whom your doctor lodged, but he says that he can't recall the doctor's name either – and when I demanded to know who'd ordered the bills, he'd the nerve to reply that it was a Dr Simon Forman!

'In spite of my servant using his best efforts at persuasion, we could make him tell us little else. He claims that whoever was behind it all did not come in person, sending another man in his stead. But I still think he knows more than he told us.' He sighed. 'We'll have to pay this Holt another visit.'

They had reached the water steps by Simon's house by this time. Luckily, there were no other boatmen there to cause trouble for Roger. He secured the boat for Simon to disembark. As he did so, Simon remembered the sick man from the Hole and asked how he'd fared. Roger said that Luke was still alive when Roger had left the Counter, and that if he survived a further week then he would have served his time and would be released.

Roger screwed up his face in thought. 'I'll remember the name of that doctor if it's the last thing I do. Serious-looking cove when he was up in his room playing the grand physician but you'd expect that from one of you piss-prophets – er, that's what some call those of you that's always needing to look at a man's piss to tell him what's wrong with him!' He frowned. 'He dressed the part too in a long gown and an old-fashioned hat, the kind that fits close over the ears to the neck like you see in pictures of grave old fellows in our fathers' or grandfathers' day even though when I went to him the weather was hot. Reckon he thought it made him look more learned.'

Simon thanked him and insisted on paying him the ferry fare.

Roger bit the coin, threw it in the air and pocketed it. 'I might well bring my Betty to see you soon anyway, Dr Forman,' he grinned. 'It seems I got her with child before we was both locked up and we'd like you to cast to see when it might be born and if she will carry safely.'

Back at the house Simon found a man with a carbuncle on his chin patiently waiting for him in his hall and quickly gave him a salve of his own making to put on it morning and night, telling him to return if it had not improved after three days. Then he went into his study quite overwhelmed at the thought of the task he had taken on. Perhaps the stars could help. He sat down and made a series of complicated calculations based around a figure and then looked at the result. The way ahead looked dark. There were no certainties, just a series of paths leading off in unknown directions. He sighed. The most sinister possibility of all was that in spite of Ralegh's stout defence of his colleagues the unpleasant hoaxer was, after all, one of them.

He heard a nearby clock strike one and came to a decision. Yes, he would take John and go back again to the printer. In spite of Holt's insistence that the man who had ordered the bills had not come in person he might well be lying, possibly out of fear. Somehow he must be persuaded or forced to tell the truth and, at the very least, his memory jogged with descriptions of some of those whose names had come up that morning. As for the younger accomplice, the brief description would fit both Thomas Nashe, who must know many printers since he was always having work published, and the malicious and unpleasant Spenser Carew – but when his name had cropped up during the morning, Ralegh had confirmed that the young man was safely back home in the West Country.

On arriving at his house, Simon informed John that they would set off as soon as he had eaten but as he was finishing his dinner a woman arrived with a sick baby and hard on her heels a seaman, desperate for him to cast to see if he was likely to return from his imminent voyage without shipwreck. It was therefore nearly three o'clock in the afternoon before he and John set out once again for the printer's shop. As before the door was firmly closed and again John knocked hard on it. There was no response. The shutters were back however from the small front window, which was glazed with bottle glass. Simon peered through it with some difficulty but could see no sign of life.

John drew his dagger and applied the hilt to the door as a hammer. 'I'll bring him down if he's in there. The rat's probably lurking upstairs peering out to see who it is.' They both stepped back and looked up above but if the printer was there he was keeping well out of sight. John hammered on the door again then rattled the latch. 'That's strange, doctor. It seems to be open.'

'Well, let's go in then,' said Simon. 'We might as well have a good look round while we have the chance and if he is upstairs then he'll soon come down when he hears us moving about.'

The print shop was much as they had seen it the previous day. A neat pile of new handbills advertising a coming bear baiting was evidence of the day's work. Simon stood at the bottom of the stairs leading up to the top floor and shouted up to see if the printer was indeed concealed above but there was still no response.

'I don't care for this,' said John. 'You'd think if he'd gone out he'd have locked his front door. You don't think we've walked into some kind of trap, do you?'

They shouted again but there was silence, except that they became suddenly aware of a strange creaking noise coming from the back room. The two men looked at each other then went over to the inner door and peered into the gloom beyond.

'Jesus wept!' exclaimed Simon.

The printer was, after all, at home. He was hanging from a

noose, the rope thrown over a beam which creaked as he swung to and fro.

Chapter 8

The Hanged Man

For a moment the two men stood transfixed. 'Has he taken his own life, doctor?' whispered John.

'Let's see if we can find out.' Simon went over to the body then looked round the room. 'Hardly. See – there's no chair or stool on which he could have stood and then kicked away, and he must be all of two feet off the floor. He could hardly have thrown the rope over the beam then hauled himself up! We'd best cut him down. Fetch something to stand on from the shop, a stool or box will do.' John was about to do as he was told when they heard the sound of firm footsteps crossing the shop from outside and a minute later an authoritative voice called from behind for them to, 'Stop where you are at once!' followed by, 'God's Mercy, what have we here?'

They turned to find that they had been joined by the Parish Constable, a man with whom the doctor had dealt several times in the past. The Constable looked equally surprised to see them. 'Dr Forman? I didn't realise it was you.' He looked from one to the other then up at the swinging body. 'Is he dead?'

'I'm afraid so.' Simon lifted up the printer's hand as he swung to and fro. 'And has been for some time, I'd say, since he's cold.

We were about to cut him down when you came in. I'd just asked my man to get me something to stand on.'

'Then you'd best do that,' the Constable agreed. He looked up at the hanging man. 'If it was anyone else I'd be tempted to think you'd put him up there. I take it this is the owner of the premises?'

Simon agreed that it was and told the Constable that his name was William Holt. When John returned with a wooden chair, he climbed on to it, the other two men supporting the corpse as he sawed through the rope with his dagger. Then they laid the unfortunate printer down on the floor and Simon bent down beside him. The corpse was not a pretty sight for the face was purple and congested with blood, the eyes and tongue protruding.

'Is it possible that it's self-slaughter?' the Constable wondered aloud.

'That's what I thought at first,' replied John, 'until the doctor showed me it was impossible.'

The Constable looked at Simon enquiringly. 'It can't be,' Simon explained, 'for, as I pointed out to John, there was nothing in the room on which he could have stood to do the deed. You saw for yourself that we had to fetch a chair from the other room.' He bent over the body again. 'I don't think he's been up there all that long. I'd say it must have been some time during the morning, for as yet there's no death stiffening.' He pulled the noose away from the neck where it had left a deeply embedded bluish line. 'The rope's common enough. It was probably lying to hand. Ugh, let's try and make him more seemly.' He felt in his pocket for two coins and, after closing the man's eyes, placed the coins on his eyelids before forcing the tongue back into his mouth and tying up the jaw with his own handkerchief.

The Constable looked grave. 'If you're saying this is murder then the Coroner and the relevant authorities will need to know.'

'What brought you here then, Constable?' Simon asked, rising to his feet.

'It's all very strange,' the man replied. 'Some twenty minutes or so ago there was a knock on my door and when I opened it a fellow was standing there muffled up in a cloak. When I asked him his business he said I must come at once to the print shop as there was trouble. I tried to ask him more but he was off and I assumed he must be returning here, having been sent by the printer to fetch me. I came as quickly as I could, only to find you here.' He paused. 'And now perhaps you should tell me why you *were* here.'

'I'm here because of this.' Simon felt inside his doublet for a copy of the offending handbill which he then handed to the officer.

The Constable went over to the back window so that he could read it in the light. 'Well,' he commented when he had perused it, 'I'm sorry to hear you're leaving us, Dr Forman, but it doesn't explain why I should find you both here with the dead man.'

Simon decided to give him a guarded version of the truth which, among other things, left the printing of the second handbill unmentioned. 'Because I'm not leaving the Bankside nor do I have any intention of doing so, and I was wondering why I had no patients and everyone was staying away. These bills were plastered around the place by some unknown mischief-maker or prankster; indeed, I'm surprised no one's drawn your attention to them since such unauthorised billposting is in direct contravention of the recent Order in Council.

'So naturally I've been searching both for the culprit and the printer of the bills, making enquiries everywhere including asking the wherrymen since they always seem to know what's going on. When one of them told me that I should try this man since he'd a reputation for doubtful practices, he proved to be right for we found copies of this very bill out there in the print shop.'

'You're sure there was no one about when you arrived?' the Constable asked.

Simon shook his head. 'At first we knocked and there was no reply, then John rattled the latch and found the door unlocked. We thought it odd since there was no sign of Master Holt in the shop, but we came in and I called up the stairs to say he had custom in case he was above. When there was still no reply we looked around and found the copies of the handbills. Soon after that we ventured in here and found our man exactly as you saw him, for you were here yourself immediately afterwards.'

'Well, he certainly must have made himself an enemy or enemies,' the Constable noted grimly, 'and I imagine the cause to be something more than the printing of slanderous handbills – there's recourse to the law for that.' He grimaced. 'I must start making some enquiries, I suppose, though this is not an area where the local folk are famed for assisting law officers.' He looked around the print shop. 'I'd heard it said he traded in lewd pictures. Maybe that was at the root of it. Possibly he was in thrall to one who made him pay money for their silence or, I suppose it could even be that he fell foul of one of the extreme Puritan tendency believing he was carrying out God's will by ridding the world of such wickedness. Such things have been known.'

'Oh, he sold the pictures all right,' John assured him. 'There's some out there in the shop.' They followed him through to the front and he went over to the table and spread out a handful of prints. They were certainly graphic, though given an air of respectability by titles based on classical themes such as *The Rape of the Sabine Women*, *Venus and Adonis* and *The Judgement of Paris*, the latter bringing a smile to Simon's face in spite of himself as he remembered having seen it enacted at a private party in Edinburgh. The author of the fourth print had turned to the Old Testament for his inspiration, and had entitled it *A Wild Night in King Solomon's Harem*.

The Constable shook his head. 'There's always a market for this kind of thing, especially among youngbloods and old lechers.' He took another look around the print shop. 'Ah, here's the door key,' he said, picking it up from a shelf. 'I suggest we go now and I'll lock up behind us.' He looked across at John. 'You'd best put everything back as you found it.'

John was standing behind the table tidying away the prints when the shop door was flung open and a young man stood in the doorway.

'So I've found you in at last then, printer,' he called out, peering into the gloom from the light outside. 'I came earlier but found no one at home so I paid for some entertainment next door. It's hardly the best establishment of its kind – half the whores are as old as my grandmother and the rest as rough as rats as they say in Cornwall. I've come to buy some of those unusual engravings you sell which are suitable for a gentleman's chamber.' He came into the shop and stopped in his tracks, peering into the gloom at John. 'Don't I know you? Haven't I seen you somewhere before?'

It was Spenser Carew. He turned to the other two and took a step back. 'I don't know who you are, my good man,' he said to the Constable, 'but God's Life, if that isn't the doctor who tried to kill me in Sherborne by feeding me poisoned sea holly!'

The Constable looked at Simon in some surprise. 'I assume the young man speaks in jest, Dr Forman?'

'I was present when Master Carew here was taken sick during a gathering at Sir Walter Ralegh's estate in Dorset,' Simon told him. 'So, also, was one of the house grooms. The candied sea holly root had been taken by those who wanted to participate in . . . to investigate its medicinal properties. It is by no means certain that either of the illnesses were caused by it since it was also eaten by at least half a dozen others with no ill effects whatsoever.'

'Thought no one would know of it, did you, so that you'd get away with it?' Carew sneered.

'It makes no difference who "knows" of it, since it isn't true,' countered Simon steadily. 'But I had understood from Sir Walter that you were in Cornwall?'

'I changed my mind. My mistress had a whim to come to London and see the sights, the lions in the Tower, St Paul's, the playhouses. Today she went to a sempstress for a fitting for a new gown and so I've been pleasing myself. I was – er – told the man here sold interesting pictures and so came to see for myself.'

He paused. 'Where is the fellow then? I don't want to risk the pox in another Bankside brothel.'

'He has met with an accident,' returned the Constable. 'He is through there.'

Before he could say any more Carew pushed past them into the back room. There was a short silence and then he reappeared. 'Accident!' he exclaimed. 'The man's been strangled or hanged, the mark on his neck's clear to see and the very rope's there beside him.' He looked up at Simon. 'Is this more of your work then, *doctor*?'

'You foolish, loud-mouthed bragging Jack,' exclaimed John. 'How do we know you're telling us the truth about your tumbling with the whores? What really happened? Did you fall out with the man over the cost of the prints or some other matter and string him up yourself?'

Carew made to draw his sword, at which point the Constable tried to intervene only to be roughly thrust aside. 'Out of the way, fellow, unless you want to get hurt. I'll settle this myself and then go and find a Constable. I presume they have such things even in these stinking back alleys.'

The Constable thumped on the table. 'I *am* the Constable and that will do, young man, unless you want me to take you in charge for a breach of Her Majesty's peace!' He gave him a stern look. 'We will all leave now and I will lock the door so that all stays as it is. I will then inform the Coroner what has happened and make arrangements for Master Holt's body to be taken elsewhere. He seems to have lived alone and I must also make enquiries as to whether or not he had any family. I suggest you all go home too,' he concluded adding, 'I know where to find you Dr Forman. No doubt you will be called again as a witness – you must be used to that by now.'

'Regularly involved with murder, are you, Dr Forman?' asked Carew.

'And you, if you please, will give me your direction,' the Constable said, raising his voice. 'For you may also be wanted at the Inquest.' For the first time Carew looked uneasy. 'Well?' the officer persisted. 'Where do you lodge?'

'Oh, find out for yourself,' Carew told him. 'This is nothing to do with me,' and he ran out through the doorway. They followed after but he had already disappeared in the maze of alleyways. John looked up and down the narrow lanes but there was no sign of him.

'We'll keep our eyes open for him,' said Simon, 'but it's a waste of time looking for him here. I'll ask Sir Walter Ralegh, though. He may know and if he does, I'll send word to you.' The Constable thanked him and set off to alert the authorities.

The two men watched him go. 'Well, doctor, surely you've no further to look for your villain,' commented John. 'He was down with us in Sherborne, blames you for supposedly poisoning him, and is not as we supposed safe in the West Country but here in London actually visiting this very printer's shop. What's more, he fits the description of the fellow who came and collected the handbills.'

'Maybe,' Simon agreed, 'though if he is the mischief-maker, it doesn't explain how I came to be sent the sea holly in the first place or how he could have tampered with it if, indeed, some of it really was poisoned.'

'He could have done so at the castle,' suggested John. 'There were any number of ways to get around the place.'

'I suppose so,' said Simon doubtfully, 'although it would mean his risking poisoning himself as must have happened if it was him. He was genuinely ill. No, it might well be that the arrival of the sea holly was mere coincidence and has nothing to do with anything else. But certainly Carew could have had the handbills printed in an effort to get his own back at me and paid an accomplice to order them in my name. He might even have been able to copy my handwriting and so have written the letters too, for I left a number of notes lying around at Sherborne. He also knew you were my manservant and I suppose it's not impossible that he should know of my . . . my friendship with Mistress Allen.'

He thought for a moment. 'Say he followed us straight to London, bent on revenge, or even arrived before us and heard shortly afterwards that I was safe out of the way in the Counter Gaol. It would be easy for him to put your letter through the door and as to Mistress Allen, if he'd heard gossip then there's a maid who works for her who knows too much and dislikes me . . . he could have set out to make her acquaintance. Yes, it all fits; and of course, he knows most of the School of the Night circle and so could have been responsible for the other matters as well.'

John nodded. 'So he came back to the printer to see if anything had happened as a result of posting up the bills and to make sure he kept his mouth shut, found out that we had visited him, was frightened he'd be recognised, and so killed him in a fit of panic.'

John stopped. 'It would have been mighty difficult for him to string the fellow up alone. Do you think he'd an accomplice?'

Simon thumped his thigh. 'God's Blood, what a fool I am! Of course he could never have got him up there alone, or even at all unless the man had been stunned or drugged first. Where were my wits? I never thought to look and see if he'd suffered a blow of any kind and now I can't get back in to have a look.'

'There was no bleeding from the head that I noticed, doctor, nor blood on the floor anywhere.'

'No, there wasn't, was there?' Simon looked thoughtful. 'But it's possible to stun a man or even kill him without leaving a mark if you hit him in the right spot. His face was so suffused and his neck so swollen around the rope that it would not be noticeable unless one were looking for it. Possibly Carew trusted it would be considered suicide. He might well carry it out quite expertly but then not have the wit to realise there would have to have been a chair or stool present. Although young Carew is quite sharp in many ways I wouldn't say he was clever.' He looked up and down the lane again. 'Before we go back home, we might make a start on our own enquiries by asking the ladies next door if they really did entertain him this afternoon.'

The ladies next door proved difficult to convince that two hearty men were visiting their establishment only to ask questions. The madam, a dreadful old hag with a painted face and a red wig (no doubt covering up her loss of hair due to the pox), dressed in a garish purple gown decorated with tarnished copper lace insisted on producing a selection of the goods on offer to tempt the 'gents'. Carew was at least right in this respect for the choice was grisly. Some were indeed old and wrinkled while the younger women were, with only a couple of exceptions, unattractive. All were far from clean.

'A real twopenny whorehouse,' whispered John to Simon.

'I imagine disease comes as part of the service,' Simon murmured back.

Finally, however, and after some coins had changed hands, the ladies resigned themselves to mere talk. Yes, a young man fitting Carew's description had visited them that day and pleasured himself with Doll. Doll was one of the two better-looking young women and she agreed that she had taken him upstairs to the pallet that served as a bed and done as he'd asked. She had not thought much of his performance. He'd bragged about his virility, how women begged him on their knees to take them to bed once they'd experienced his expertise but when it came to it he'd proved a sad disappointment. Indeed, finally he'd asked Doll if she would whip him lightly with his riding crop to stimulate him.

''E blamed is doxy,' Doll told them. 'Said she'd'ad'im at it day an' night this last week. Dunno if it were that or not but 'e was in a funny state, sort of excited yet worried, as if 'e was thinkin' of somethin' else.'

'About what time did he visit you?' Simon asked. 'Can you remember?'

'Oh, I can remember all right,' Doll asserted. 'It's been quiet as a churchyard in 'ere today. It were just on eleven. I'eard the clock strike at St Mary's just as he got his breeches off.'

'Just on eleven,' repeated Simon as he and John made their way home, 'and he'd led us to believe he'd come straight from the brothel to the shop. There's nearly four hours missing and I'm sure he didn't spend all that time being whipped by Doll.'

'Funny what tricks your well-off folks get up to,' commented John. 'I've had whores in my time and been to brothels – though not since I married Anna,' he added hastily, 'but I've never had to ask a girl to whip me. What else do they want, I wonder – putting in the stocks or standing in a pillory?'

Simon laughed then became serious again. 'Well, as you rightly say, we now have at least one person in our sights who could well be our man. I'll go straight to Sir Walter's house on the Strand and see if he knows that Carew is here and, if so, his direction. I was to see him again tomorrow but this won't wait.'

But, having taken a wherry from the Bankside to the Strand and almost run to Ralegh's house, he found he was out of luck. Sir Walter's steward, who opened the door to him, informed him that the master was out visiting Master Thomas Hariot and if the night was clear, they were to look at the stars through Master Hariot's great telescope and so Sir Walter was not expected home before midnight.

Simon slept badly that night, for as well as the pressing matters on his mind he was deeply uneasy that he had heard nothing more from Avisa. Had she received his letter of explanation and, if so, did she believe him? He rose early and, going into his study, cast a figure to try and see if there would ever be a future for them. Once again it was not encouraging. They would come together again soon, he ascertained, but their way was strewn with difficulties; there was no obvious solution. He broke his fast and while he was considering what time he might decently call again on Ralegh, Anna showed in a young man suffering from scrofula, the disease simple folks still called the King's or Queen's Evil, believing that their sickness could be cured by the laying-on of hands of a royal personage.

An unpleasant weeping abscess on the man's neck showed how far the disease had advanced. Simon knew a number of remedies for alleviating the symptoms of the disease but nothing that would certainly cure it, although he had come across cases where the patient seemed to shake it off without any other intervention. This patient had tried to put himself in the way of Her Majesty on her progresses through the City but had never been able to get near enough to her to be able to beg her to touch him. 'You look doubtful, doctor,' he said, glancing at Simon. 'Don't you believe that being touched by those with royal blood cures my ailment? We've been told for hundreds of years that it does.'

'I don't know' Simon told him truthfully. 'Perhaps in some cases God allows such an outcome, but I myself have never seen one. In the meantime let's see what we can do to ease you. First I'll clean the wound and then I'll give you a special mixture for a poultice.' He cleaned the wound with water and vinegar then went to a jar and measured out a paste which he put into a small pot.

'What's that?' asked the young man suspiciously.

'A mixture of mallow, hollyhocks, rose leaves and sheep's suet. Take it home and boil it up in half a pint of ale, thicken it with crumbs of bread and get someone to apply it as hot as you can bear. It should help dry it up. If that doesn't work then come back and we'll try something else, but I think you'll find that at least it rids the swelling of all venomous matter.' The man thanked him, paid him two shillings, and went on his way. Simon watched him go, relieved to be back in the world he knew even if he recognised his impotence in the face of so much disease. But scrofula had always interested him and he made a note to spend more time on the subject.

Half an hour later a messenger arrived from Ralegh, apologising for not being at home when Simon called the previous day and suggesting he came to visit him as soon as possible since, presumably, there was some urgency. Within the hour Simon was seated in Ralegh's attractive Tower Room, a glass of canary wine in his hand, watching the busy shipping going up and down the river and the wherrymen plying their trade across the water.

Ralegh heard him out in silence as Simon described his second visit to the printer, how he had found him dead and the quite unexpected arrival on the scene of Spenser Carew. Ralegh expressed astonishment that Carew was in London, not least because usually when the young man visited the capital he stayed with him in the Strand house, and on the rare occasions when he did not, was a frequent caller. 'I take it you suspect him of at least some of this mischief?'

Simon had to agree that he did. 'It seems a most remarkable coincidence that he too should have business with that very same printer who not only published the slanderous handbills but is then found dead.' He paused. 'But I fear there's more to my suspicions than that. His description fits that of the person who ordered the bills on behalf of another and then returned to collect and pay for them; he had the opportunity of tampering with the sea holly when it was still in my chamber – though if he did, then also he suffered the consequences; he knew the name of my manservant and of course he knows virtually all the inner circle of the School of the Night and is no doubt privy to any gossip there might be about any of them.'

Ralegh looked grave. 'I see your point,' he said heavily, 'but you must admit it is only conjecture until we know more.' The news had obviously upset him. 'Carew's family are of the best, with a fine reputation throughout both Devon and Cornwall. One of his uncles is the Earl of Totnes, another the recusant scholar and poet who I thought he was visiting at Antony, and our respective families have known each other for ever. Up until now I'd have sworn his worst faults to be no more than hot-headedness and arrogance, as is the case with many young men of his age.

'He's not much of a scholar but when he wants to he can show a real interest in the New Sciences, which is why I've let him join in some of our meetings. I agree he must be found without delay and his conduct and activities must be investigated. I'll do my best to discover where he lodges and also send word to his home to see if his family know – though I fear it will take at least a week before I can expect a reply.'

He looked at Simon. 'I feel you've almost made up your mind.'

Simon agreed but felt sorry for Ralegh who had obviously a fondness for the young man even if it was largely based on his friendship with the Carews.

'I did not of course give any consideration to Spenser as a culprit,' continued Ralegh, 'and concentrated my thoughts elsewhere. So, if you're agreeable, let us look at the list I have drawn up of those associated with the School of the Night, along with others whose names were brought up the other day, for we cannot know for certain if you are right. And while I meant what I said about staking my honour on the probity of our own circle, we must consider every eventuality.'

Neither believed either Hariot or Hues needed to be considered though Ralegh suggested it might be useful to talk to Hariot who was famed for his attention to detail. 'He might have noticed something that we have missed.' Likewise the Earl of Northumberland. 'It could be that Percy's made an enemy who is now set on making trouble for all of us. He is such a pleasant and charming man that he might well be unaware of it, but he is still heir to one of the oldest and most powerful families in the realm and such men can unwittingly provoke jealousy and spite.'

They continued down the list until they reached Marlowe's name. Ralegh leaned back in his chair. 'Some of the cleverer aspects of this malice might be attributed to Kit in one of his black and evil moods, but not the rest. I simply can't see him wasting his time in such a way. Yes, he can offend even his best friends when the mood takes him; he can be adder-tongued, reckless even, but he's far more likely to challenge you to a duel when in drink or burst into your house and tell you what he thinks of you than fester in so underhand a manner.'

Simon agreed. 'He would never stoop to slanderous bills nor secret murder, and of all men I can't believe he would serve me such a turn. If it hadn't been for him I might well have never returned from my fateful visit to Edinburgh. We've had our arguments and I consider some of his ideas to be dangerously wild but no, not this.' He paused. 'Also, I fear he is in some deep trouble of his own.'

Ralegh looked pensive. 'He has certainly something on his mind. Have you any idea what it might be?'

It was in Scotland that Simon had first learned of Marlowe's longstanding involvement in the world of the intelligencers and he had kept it to himself ever since. Possibly Ralegh also knew, but in any event Simon thought it best to continue to say nothing and so replied that he did not, adding, 'Perhaps he and Tom Walsingham have fallen out. I had a young lady visit me recently who expects to marry him and came to have her horoscope cast. It might well be that Kit is facing the fact that he will most certainly lose a lover and maybe a patron as well.'

Ralegh ran his finger down the list. 'Matthew Roydon the poet hangs about with some strange people – you might talk to him. Then there's Emery Molyneux the globemaker.'

Simon shook his head. 'As unlikely a possibility as Hariot, and I would have real difficulty there for he's something of a patron of mine. As is George Carey.' He was becoming more and more frustrated. Surely the most urgent matter was to go after Carew; none of those mentioned were anything like as suspect. But he could hardly press Ralegh further and he resigned himself to hearing him out.

'I think you should most definitely seek out Thomas Nashe,' Ralegh was saying. 'He thrives on trouble and I hear he's about to publish a pamphlet on those he calls quack doctors and bogus astrologers, and so it seems he bears ill-will to all your profession. He makes no secret of his dislike of the School of the Night. There is another remote possibility,' he added finally, 'and that is that the mischief stems from the Earl of Pembroke. He would not dirty his hands personally, of course. While not all the gossip about Mary Herbert is true, she does take lovers and the fact is widely known. It's usually thought that the old Earl is complaisant about it so long as she does not create an overt scandal and she has already given him an heir. But suppose he only pretends complacency. It would be a clever way of getting back at all her associates though, if that were indeed the case, I cannot see how you would figure in his scheme of things.'

Simon said nothing but coloured slightly. Ralegh laughed. 'I see. Presumably she set her cap at you at Sherborne? I had, of course, assumed that the candied sea holly was only of interest to the men in our party!'

Ten minutes later Simon prepared to depart. They had added no more names to their list of suspects. It stood at Carew, Roydon, Nashe and (a bow at a venture) the Earl of Pembroke, though how Simon was to set out to investigate the latter was far from clear. 'The countess has suggested I visit her again to see if she can offer any help,' he told Ralegh to the latter's obvious amusement.

'Mary Herbert's a clever woman and a shrewd one,' Ralegh responded, 'and you might even feel you could confide our suspicions to her regarding her husband. She won't be shocked. And it *is* a possibility, though we would be in deep water if we tried to prove it.'

'Regarding the countess,' said Simon tentatively, 'if it's true that she's involved with Cecil in some way, even if only in friendship, do you think she tells him what is discussed among us at the School of the Night? I don't for a moment imagine she has had anything to do with this business, indeed she seems determined to get to the bottom of it, but if, as we suspect, Cecil is behind the proposed setting up of this inquisition into our activities, is she not a risk? At the very least she must be pulled both ways.'

'I have thought of that,' Sir Walter conceded, 'but as I've already implied she is a most unusual person and I think if she wishes, she is capable of keeping the different facets of her life in separate boxes as it were. Why she should find Cecil attractive, in whatever capacity, is a mystery but it is inconceivable that she would betray us.' So saying he closed the subject and with that Simon had to be content.

They parted shortly afterwards on the understanding that Simon would seek out Roydon and Nashe while Ralegh would make every effort to discover the whereabouts of Carew and ensure he was brought to his house for questioning. Once outside in the street Simon decided to walk to Canon Row to see if he could gather any information on Dr North. Here he was almost immediately in luck, for the merchant who was issuing from his front door as he passed was able to inform him that a Dr North had leased the house next to his some years earlier.

'A most respected gentleman,' he told Simon, 'and of a pleasant disposition. We were sorry to lose him as a neighbour.' On being asked as to his possible whereabouts the man shook his head. 'All I know is that he was a Lincoln man and returned to Lincoln. He did call on us once not long after he removed from London but I've seen nothing of him since.'

So that was that. Dr North was genuine and, presumably, had once again been visiting the capital when he had the luck, or misfortune, to find himself in the company of James Tapworth.

Simon walked back across London Bridge with a heavy heart and fearful, in spite of Holt's death, that he would find another crop of handbills had appeared overnight; thankfully there were none. He was becoming ever more convinced, in spite of everything Ralegh might say, that the most likely culprit was Carew.

From his vantage point on the Bridge he looked across to Avisa's house on Thames Street, wondering if she were now back home and if so, whether they would ever again be able to pick up the threads of their relationship; and all the time she was carrying his unborn child.

He opened the door to find two letters waiting for him on the carved chest in the hall. He took them up eagerly, hoping that one was from Avisa, but a closer inspection of the handwriting on both missives showed that neither were. The first, bearing the now familiar coat of arms, invited Simon to visit the Countess of Pembroke the following morning; at least it would give him the opportunity of trying, if he found the courage, to raise the issue of her husband's possible attitude to her activities.

The second was in the form of a thin packet of stout paper sealed with a ring bearing a device he had never seen before. He wondered if it was foreign. He opened it up and at first thought it was another hoax, for there seemed to be nothing inside it, yet when he shook it there was a faint rattling sound. He tipped the packet up and a playing card fell on to the floor. Simon reclaimed it with a feeling of foreboding. The back of the card was ordinary enough, dark blue with a small red design. He turned it over, to discover its face was not that of an ordinary court card from a regular suit of cards but came from a pack he had seen several times on the Continent though never before in England.

It was from the Tarot and the card was the Hanged Man.

Chapter 9

A Verdict of Murder

Simon took the card through to the kitchen and found John sitting with Anna, young Simon on his knee. He laid the card down on the table and both looked at it in horror.

'Funny man,' said little Simon, grasping it firmly. 'Why's he upside down?'

'The Lord protect us!' exclaimed Anna, taking it from him. 'Where would one find such a terrible thing?'

'Peace, wife,' said John. 'I've seen such a card before. Isn't it part of some strange pack from foreign parts?'

Simon agreed that it was. 'It's called the Tarot. There are suits, like ordinary playing cards, and court cards, but also what is called "the Greater Trumps" – cards with magic images. There are over twenty of them as I recall, including the Hanged Man.'

'Is this a threat of some kind then?' asked John.

Simon sat down at the table and regarded the card again. 'I don't know. These cards can be used to foresee the future, though I've never used them to do so myself.' He shook his head. 'The Tarot was never part of my studies though I recall a seer in Italy telling me of their powers years ago. I wish now I'd taken more interest in what he had to say. I do remember that there are several ways of setting them out and that all the cards, but particularly the Greater Trumps, can mean different things depending on where they are in the pattern and which way up they are placed.' He picked the card up. 'In France they call him *Le Pendu*. As to whether this is a warning to me, a black joke from the printer's murderer or a clue to the mystery, I'm as much at a loss as you are.'

Before leaving for the countess's house the next morning he sat down and wrote a letter to Avisa addressed to her London home. In it he poured out his heart as to his feelings about her, his desolation at receiving no reply to the letter he had sent to Kent (which he trusted she had received) and pleading with her to see him as soon as she was able. He then gave it to John to deliver to Thames Street. He also wrote again to the Colchester apothecary asking him if he would lose no time in discovering where the box of sea holly had come from.

Since you were the only person I approached for it, he wrote, *if it did not come directly from you then it* must *be from someone you know. This is as urgent for you as it is for me since at least two people were taken ill after eating it and an elderly man, to whom I prescribed it, died. I have subsequently been taken before the College of Physicians as his family accused me of poisoning him. This appears now to have been resolved, for the man carried too much flesh and it seems likely the cause of death was apoplexy; also there was a disputed will and a young widow in the case. Since I cannot leave London in the immediate future I beg you use every diligence to trace who sent me the* eringo.

He set off to the countess's house more or less convinced he was on a fool's errand. What could she possibly tell him that he and Ralegh had not already discussed? As to the Earl of Pembroke's possible involvement, it appeared less and less likely with every step he took. He rang the doorbell and a very grand servant, having ascertained who he was, showed him in at once informing him in a deferential tone that her ladyship was expecting him and that he would find her in her study. He found Mary Herbert poring over a number of books spread out before her on a table.

'I'm obviously disturbing you,' he said. 'I can come back at some better time.'

She looked up and smiled. 'There's nothing here that cannot wait. Hariot has been showing me his papers on calculating the declination of the sun at any time of year and on the movement of stars in the heavens. He is a very clever man.' She stood up. 'Let us go into my sitting room and I'll send for wine to mellow our talk.' She led the way into a chamber with a view of the river. 'Pleasant, as you can see, but not so fine as that from Ralegh's Tower.' They passed the time in general talk until a servant had brought in wine and shut the door behind him whereupon the countess leaned forward. 'Now,' she said, 'is your investigation progressing at all?'

'Well, your . . .' he began, then stopped, unsure as to how to address her.

'I think you might call me Mary, Simon, at least when we are being informal, given our coming together in Sherborne,' she prompted, quite unabashed.

He cleared his throat and enlightened her as to his second visit to the printer, what he had found there and his increasingly strong suspicions of Spenser Carew.

Like Ralegh, she expressed some surprise. 'Carew? The boy who bragged of his prowess in bed and boasted of sending for his mistress? I know him only slightly, but I wouldn't think he had the wit to make so much mischief.'

'But he arrived at the printer's shop just after we'd found the man hanging and he follows the description of the person who collected the offensive handbills. It would fit,' Simon continued, trying to convince her. 'He had the means, he is linked into the School of the Night, albeit he isn't one of the inner circle, and he was convinced I'd poisoned him.'

'I can see how it looks,' she agreed, 'but I think you would be unwise to put all your eggs in one basket. Discover where he is and question him closely, certainly, and if you are convinced he is to blame then send to the nearest Justice. But keep your eyes and ears open for other possibilities as well. Have there been any other happenings?'

He drew the Tarot card out of his doublet and laid it down before her. 'This was awaiting my return after my discovery of the hanged man.'

'How very disagreeable,' she said, picking it up and examining it closely. 'The design is different from that in my own pack. Mine is French but I would say this comes from the East of Europe. I wonder if that has any significance? Wait, let me show you my own pack.' She went over to a drawer and drew out a handsome wooden box from which she took a pack of fine cards, riffling through them until she found the Hanged Man. 'See – in my design he looks quite unconcerned at his fate; indeed, he is smiling.'

She put the card down on the table beside the other and spread out the rest of the Greater Trumps. 'How much do you know of the symbols?' she asked.

'Not a great deal,' Simon admitted.

'I'm sure you know that the Greater Trumps can be used to prophesy, to which end they can be laid out in a number of ways so that the images also have different meanings. Like the rest, the Hanged Man has several. It can mean violent death encountered by tragic accident, but it doesn't sound as if that applied to your printer. Punishment – does someone wish that you should be punished? If so, for what? Great change – well, that can come to any of us. Redemption, even . . . we must all hope for that at the end, whatever our beliefs.'

She regarded the card thoughtfully. 'I am no teller of fortunes like you, Simon, but sometimes I have an instinct for these things and in this case I think you should take heart, for while I believe you're right in surmising that it was sent you in mischief by one with a dark purpose, I was told once by Dr Dee that this figure has yet another significance: it can also mean a better knowledge of the future and a new understanding of the past.' She gave him an odd look. 'I feel quite inspired. I think it is telling us that while you are presently in no small hazard, you will survive if you face it bravely even though that was not its sender's intention.' She gathered the pack together to put them away but before doing so showed him another of the Greater Trumps – *Les Amoureux*, the Lovers. 'Now, imagine how intrigued you would be if you had received *that*.' With a smile she returned the cards to their box.

'I must find a set for myself,' said Simon. 'There's a shop near to St Paul's that sells such things. It might be useful.' He picked up his own card. 'From Eastern Europe, you say? Do you know anyone who's travelled there?'

'Dr Dee visited those parts years ago with Edward Kelley. I will send word and ask him if he has any knowledge of such a pack or of anyone who has one, but I hope you don't imagine that he is our villain and that the card comes from him. He would never have done such a thing even when he was most under the influence of that appalling fellow.' She shook her head. 'It's a blessing Kelley died.'

'Kelley? Oh yes, the quack doctor, necromancer and supposed scrier who so influenced Dr Dee. I remember being told of him at Sherborne. How exactly did he die? Is it known?'

'I was told he offended some minor princeling on their travels, was first clapped into gaol then put to death. It caused a great deal of trouble for Dr Dee who had to flee home for fear of his life. That's all I know. Now to business, for I am again summoned to Court. Tell me who else you and Ralegh suspect might be the author of all this trouble even if, as I can see from your face, you think it most unlikely.'

'Ralegh says the poet Matthew Roydon mixes in strange company and has some doubtful friends, though he has always found him honest, as does the pamphleteer, Thomas Nashe, he who calls himself "Pierce Penniless" and publishes scurrilous and sometimes slanderous material. If you recall, he was mentioned at our last meeting. But I can't imagine he would be so senseless as to post up handbills against the law, let alone one that might take him speedily to Bridewell. We even discussed Kit himself but not in any serious way. With all his faults he's proved a good friend to me and if he wants the world to know he is aggrieved then he roars it across the taproom after two bottles of wine. However, I will seek out Nashe who I'm told has a low opinion of doctors and see what he has to say to my face.

'Then there was . . .' Simon stopped, quite unable to go on now it had come to the point.

'Then there was who?' prompted the countess with a laugh. 'You look as if the words stick in your throat.'

'There was . . . We thought . . .' He gulped. 'God's Breath, there's no good way of putting this, er – Mary. It crossed our minds that your husband might have taken against your involvement with . . . with the School of the Night and had set someone on to destroy it.'

He wondered how she would take such a suggestion. With a torrent of abuse? Cold indignation? In the event she did neither, merely looking thoughtful. 'I can see why you might consider such a possibility but I do not honestly think so. Ours is not a conventional marriage. I am, after all, Harry's third wife and was a very young girl when we wed fifteen years ago. His father was still alive then and shook his head and warned Harry against the match, not only because of my poor dowry but because he thought me both fair and clever, a dangerous combination, telling him that if he insisted on going against his advice then he must keep me securely in the country for fear I would cuckold him.'

She smiled. 'But Harry liked the idea of a witty wife rather than yet another respectable pudding. I have given him children, prove a good hostess to all his friends, and he accepts my . . . foibles so long as I am passably discreet for he knows that in my own way I both love and respect him. As he does me. We are also very straight with each other and I am almost certain that if Harry had wanted to stop my association with the School of the Night or saw its members as his enemies, he would have told me so in no uncertain terms and then sought out Ralegh and said the same to him.'

It certainly was not a marriage of the common sort but what she said had the ring of truth. As to her relationship with Cecil, Simon simply did not feel brave enough to embark on asking for an explanation of that as well, though the very thought of the Acting Secretary to the Privy Council made him shudder, let alone the notion of him and the countess disporting themselves in bed together.

They discussed the matter a little further but without coming to any conclusions and the Countess rose to make her preparations to go again to Nonesuch. 'But I promise we will meet again soon. I might even come and visit you at your home. I would be fascinated to see where you work and talk with you of remedies and elixirs.' He bent to kiss her hand but she took hold of it then kissed him on the cheek.

'I must admit that a finger points to Carew but perhaps that also is intentional. Have you thought of that? It's as if we're all walking blindfold in the dark.' She paused. 'I can't help but think that there is someone out there playing a game with all of us, someone we would recognise if only we could bring him to mind. If so then he is older, more experienced and far subtler than Spenser Carew and thus infinitely more dangerous.' She called for a servant to show Simon out. 'Expect to see me at your home in the not too distant future,' she said with a smile, 'and however sure you are, give some thought to what I've said and have a care. Call it women's instinct.'

He arrived home to find a formal summons for both him and John to appear as witnesses at the Inquisition before the Coroner into the death of one William Holt, master printer of Southwark. It was to be held in the upper room at the Green Dragon at ten o'clock prompt the following morning.

'What do we say to the Crowner when he starts asking questions?' John demanded when Simon had given him the news. 'Do we have to say it wasn't our first visit?'

'We tell him the truth,' Simon told him, 'or at least as much of it as we think he needs to know. If you're asked, tell him no more and no less than we told the Constable: why we were there – referring only to the slanderous handbill – that we found the door open and that when we investigated we found the fellow swinging from a beam. To that I will add, if the opportunity arises, that shortly afterwards a young man of the name of Spenser Carew appeared.' He stopped, looking thoughtful. 'If possible, I'd like to take another look at our corpse before the hearing, this time to see if I can find any trace that he was stunned first.'

In spite of what the Countess had said, he was almost completely convinced that Carew was his man but agreed with her that it was sensible not to rule out any other possibility. As to her last remark about a shadowy gamesman lurking in the darkness, it made his flesh creep.

The upper room of the Green Dragon was fairly full by the time John and Simon entered next day. Violent death always attracted those who enjoyed hearing the ghoulish details, along with others who simply had time on their hands and felt like being entertained. A couple of elderly women had brought their knitting with them and sat chatting as if by their own firesides. Noticeable on one of the long benches was the madam of the brothel, marginally more soberly dressed than when they had seen her before, along with a couple of her employees whose profession was unmistakable. There was no sign of Carew but then it was unlikely the Constable had been able to trace him.

Simon had appeared as a witness several times before the usual local Coroner but on this occasion it was a different man, a weary-looking person of the name of Sir Matthew Long who gave off an air of irritation at having been called to preside over such a trivial matter. He looked on indifferently as the clerk swore in the jury of local good men and true, suppressed a yawn from time to time and seemed scarcely more interested when the clerk explained the circumstances of the case: that the said William Holt, master printer, had been discovered hanging from a beam in the back of his print shop by the Constable of the parish and others. That the jury had viewed him lying in his coffin in the stable outside and that he had been formally identified by the – er – owner of the house next door since he seemed to have no known next-of-kin.

The first person called as witness was the Constable who explained how he had been summoned to the print shop by a stranger and had arrived to find Dr Forman and his servant there before him.

'You did not recognise your informant then?' enquired Long.

'No, sir.'

'Did you know the dead man or anything of him?'

'I've seen him about,' replied the Constable, 'but I didn't know him personally. He had something of a reputation, however.' He paused.

'For what?' yawned the Coroner. 'Come on, man, don't be all day about it.'

'He had a reputation for selling salacious pictures, sir, of naked women disporting themselves. That kind of thing.'

The Coroner raised an eyebrow then continued, 'I understand you do not consider the man hanged himself.'

'I did at first, sir. But then Dr Forman pointed out why that wasn't possible and I agreed with him. There was nothing in the room on which he could have stood to do so.'

'I see. Is it known then if he had any enemies?'

The Constable shrugged. 'Anyone who trades in obscene pictures might well have but none are known, though it seems he was a man who kept himself to himself. I made enquiries locally to see if anyone had heard the sound of a quarrel or seen strangers hanging about but no one has been able to help. Or is willing to do so,' he added. 'It's a very rough neighbourhood.'

Long considered this. 'Very well. You may go, Constable.' He looked round. 'Now, is Dr Forman here?'

Simon duly made himself known and stepped down to face the Coroner while the Clerk whispered in the Coroner's ear.

'Dr *Simon* Forman, is it? The necromancer who attempts to raise spirits and casts horoscopes?' For the first time in the proceedings Long showed more interest.

'No, Sir Matthew. I am no necromancer but a physician recognised by the University of Cambridge and I cast horoscopes as part of my trade. As does the President of the College of Physicians himself.'

Long gave him a calculating look then continued, 'First tell us, doctor, why you were present when the Constable arrived. Had you also been sent for by an unknown emissary?'

Simon replied that he had not. He told his story yet again and produced a copy of the first handbill which he passed to the clerk who then handed it on to the Coroner who briefly cast his eye over it. He hoped the Constable would not raise the matter of the second and decided it was unlikely. Admitting knowledge of such a dreadful document was like touching pitch; dirt stuck.

'How did you know this man Holt printed it? It does not say so.'

'Obviously I made enquiries as to who might have done such a thing,' Simon informed him, 'and his name was given to me as a possibility. That is why we went in search of him first before starting out to visit every other printer between here and St Paul's. Fortunately it turned out that he *was* the culprit, for when we went into his print shop we found there some further copies of it.'

'Do you have any idea who was behind this slander?'

'No, sir. That's what I had hoped to discover from the printer.'

'You did not know the man before?'

'I did not,' replied Simon steadily.

'And he was hanging as the Constable has described and was already dead when you entered?'

'He was. My servant and I were about to cut him down when the Constable arrived. Had he not come when he did, I would have sent for him.'

'And you are certain that Holt could not have hanged himself?'

'Not unless there was someone else present to connive at his suicide and who took away the bench or chair on which he stood to do it. However, before coming in here this morning I took another look at the body and I am now certain he was murdered, possibly in the hope that it might appear to be self-slaughter.'

There was a murmur from the public benches at that, causing the Clerk to frown at them and shake his head.

The Coroner ignored it. 'I see. Pray enlighten us then.'

'After I left the print shop it struck me that the man would have to have been drugged or stunned to allow himself to be strung up in such a way, even if there was more than one assailant, but there was no obvious head wound or blood which would have been the case had he been struck down.

'On examining the corpse again this morning, this time with some idea of what I was looking for, I found behind his ear a narrow mark which had later spread into a bruise which was almost completely concealed by the larger mark made by the knot of the rope.' This piece of news prompted a further rumble of interest among the onlookers, causing the Coroner to announce that if there were any further disturbance he would ask the Clerk to clear the room. He then motioned to Simon to continue, enquiring how he thought the blow had been administered.

'My personal opinion is that the printer had no suspicion that his killer meant him any harm, either because whoever did the deed had no such intention until something happened which prompted it, or because he was clever enough to conceal from Holt that he had come with murder in mind. As to how he was able to deliver the blow, then what could be easier than for him to ask the printer to show him a sample of his other wares, possibly even one of those notorious prints. Holt would have spread it out on his table and both would have bent over to look at it, which would give his assailant the opportunity he needed to strike him with the edge of his hand so.' He made a chopping motion. 'That would stun him sufficiently. Indeed, when I was in Italy I recall being told that so subtle a blow could kill a man. It would not be all that easy to hoist the body up, it being a dead weight, but then Holt was a small, thin fellow. If you wish, sir, I can point out the mark I've described to the members of the jury.'

'I think we'll take your word for it, Dr Forman, though it's hard to understand why this villain went to so much trouble.' He looked round. 'I understand there was another man with you.'

'My servant, John Bradedge, who is here if you wish to speak to him. Also, while we were discussing the printer's death with the Constable, a young man arrived to buy some prints. Coincidentally, we had met before.'

The Coroner sighed. 'There must have been quite a crowd. And *his* name?'

'Spenser Carew. He is of a West Country family and I made his acquaintance some weeks ago at the home of Sir Walter Ralegh in Sherborne. Carew told us that he had called earlier and receiving no reply, assumed the printer was from home, and so passed the time until the man returned in the bawdy house next door.'

'That he did,' the madam bawled out on hearing this. 'And don't you go thinking we had anything to do with it. I'm only here 'cos I was summonsed.'

The Coroner raised his eyes heavenward. 'God's Breath, this is interminable! Very well, you'd best come down here and say what you have to say. You may go back to your seat, Dr Forman, though I'll tell you now I think there's more to this than you're prepared to say.'

An unpleasant but shrewd fellow behind that lazy manner, thought Simon as he sat down again beside John Bradedge.

The madam had obviously had a great deal of experience of courtrooms, addressing the Coroner variously as 'your worship', 'your lordship' and 'your honour' and even 'your grace', prompting Sir Matthew to inform her acidly that he was not the Archbishop of Canterbury, after which she agreed that the smart young gent she now knew to be Master Carew had passed a pleasant hour in her establishment being entertained by one of her young ladies. 'We wasn't doing nothing wrong,' she told him firmly. 'I'm fussy about who comes to my house. We don't hide no villains or murderers if that's what you think. What we does is a service and I look after my girls. They don't have to have no pimps nor nothing.'

The Coroner looked over at the Constable. 'Have you had any complaints about this . . . establishment? Is there need to close it down?'

The Constable shrugged. 'It's no worse than many others hereabouts, sir. They take all the money they can off their customers but so far as I know they don't actually steal from them, and if it was closed down they'd only go and set up elsewhere a week later.'

The Coroner agreed then looked again at Simon. 'Carew, you said? Would that be the Carews of Antony in Cornwall? Are they not recusants, Dr Forman?' Simon, thinking at once of the problems Avisa had suffered by holding on to the old Faith, replied that he did not know. There was enough of mystery as it was without adding Catholics to the brew.

'This man Carew was not summoned to attend then?' the Coroner asked the Clerk, who in turn motioned to the Constable.

'I did not know where he lodged, sir, and have had no luck in finding him,' the man replied.

'And you didn't think to ask Dr Forman, who claims to know him?'

The Constable shook his head unhappily at Simon who at once responded that he had no idea of the whereabouts of Carew either, grateful that the officer of the law had not brought up the matter of Carew's obvious antipathy to him, adding, 'I myself went to Sir Walter Ralegh to ask if he knew where this young man was. He did not, but said he would do his best to seek him out.'

The Coroner gave a thin smile. 'Well, since there seems to be no further light to be shed on the matter, I will call an end to our proceedings.' He turned to the man elected foreman of the jury. 'Consider your verdict then, gentlemen. I can't think it will take you long.'

The jury filed out, returning some ten minutes later to inform the Coroner that their verdict was one of wilful murder by a person or persons unknown. The Coroner thanked them, dismissed them and walked swiftly towards the door but paused as he reached Simon. 'You interest me, Dr Forman. As did what you said and left unsaid.'

'You are not convinced then that the man died in the manner I described?' countered Simon.

'Oh, I will take your word for it since you seem to know a great deal about such things. What interests me is that I now realise I've heard your name before in connection with violent death. Since as a physician your calling would seem to be to cure the sick and heal the wounded, one wonders why such matters hold such a fascination for you. I intend making further enquiries as to your previous activities.' And with that, he swept out.

Simon returned home pondering over the Coroner's words and wondering whether they boded yet more trouble, only to find it already waiting for him. Avisa was now once again in Thames Street and she had finally responded to his letter. She wrote that she believed him when he swore that the offending letter she had received had not come from him, and she thanked him for the other two. But unless she suffered a change of heart, she thought it best they did not meet. *Please accept what I say,* she wrote. *I know it is for the best*. She finished by assuring him of all her love and would pray that God and the Holy Virgin would protect him.

Chapter 10

The Terrors of the Night

Spenser Carew sat morosely over his tankard of ale in a cheap tavern in Deptford. In a chamber above there was a large wooden chest and a several bags containing many of his personal possessions, stoutly bound for a long journey. The young poet, Matthew Roydon, had just left him, having tried unavailingly to cheer him up.

'Think how many people would envy your chance to visit the New World,' he had said in bracing tones, 'and the opportunities you will have to make your name and fortune.'

But Carew had never had the slightest desire to visit Her Majesty's colony in Virginia or any other such far-flung foreign parts. The fact that he had brought himself to this pass only made matters worse. His thoughts drifted back to the start of it all, to the foolish act that had triggered off a train of events which had begun badly and ended worse. The brief interlude in Sherborne had been a welcome diversion, in spite of his illness which he was still convinced had been caused by poisoned sea holly. He grimaced. At least he had got his own back on Forman first, although the repercussions of that made his need to leave the country even more urgent.

But now there was a delay, for he had just learned that the ship in which he was to sail required unexpected and urgent repairs, and therefore according to the captain, it would be at least another three or four days before they could leave port.

He took another swig from his tankard and was about to call for more when a voice said quietly in his ear, 'Don't you think you've already had enough?' The speaker, a distinguished-looking man wearing the long gown much favoured by academics, then settled himself beside him at the table. Carew greeted him with a sinking heart before enquiring what he was doing in Deptford. His new companion smiled unpleasantly. 'I might ask you the same, Carew. However, I am here because from what you told me I'd assumed you would have been gone these three days so I was somewhat surprised when I learned that you were still in Deptford.'

Carew's mouth went dry. 'Further repairs were needed to the ship,' he managed after some effort.

This was greeted with a marked lack of enthusiasm. 'I see.' The newcomer called over to the tapster for a cup of wine, waited until it had been brought, then continued: 'Tell me, will you, what possessed you to return to the print shop?'

Carew went cold. How on earth had he learned that? 'I had time to spare', he said at last, 'and wanted to buy some of the fellow's prints. There'll be little enough entertainment of that kind where I'm bound,' he added, gaining confidence. 'Anyway, I didn't think . . .'

'You never do. That is why you find yourself in this pass.'

'How *did* you know I was still here?' Carew asked curiously.

The man shrugged. 'Word came to me. It always does.' He looked across to the window through which could be seen the masts and rigging of several large vessels. 'So there is to be yet more delay. I must tell you that I'm not the only one who will be seeking you out if you linger here much longer. Ralegh is asking far and wide as to your whereabouts and then there is also the busy Dr Forman you have been so eager to damage. Your foolish visit to the printer will only spur him on. Oh, by the way, the Inquest verdict was one of murder and your name was mentioned several times. Oh yes, you are much in demand.'

'What then am I supposed to do?' demanded Carew, now becoming angry. 'I can't repair the ship with my own hands then arrange an outgoing tide with a following wind!'

The man beside him looked thoughtful. 'I have learned that there is another vessel that leaves in the early hours of tomorrow morning. I think you should be on it before Ralegh, Forman or the law catch up with you. You seem to have caused your family enough disgrace without compounding it by your being hanged at Tyburn.'

Carew looked at him in horror. 'But I haven't . . . it wasn't me who . . .'

'Try telling that to the Judge.' The man stood up, put his hands on the table and leant over Carew. 'Stay close here while I make enquiries of the master of this other ship to see if he is willing to take you now. I will send you word later as to when and where we can meet up to make the final arrangements.'

'But I told you! All has been settled with the master of the *Spirit of Venture*.'

'And I am telling *you* that if you value your skin, not to mention your neck, you'll take ship tonight!'

As silently and quickly as he had appeared, the man left. Now what do I do, thought Carew desperately. Was he telling the truth? *Am* I sought far and wide for murder? If that is the case then he's right when he says I should leave without further delay. He made his decision. If the captain of the other vessel was agreeable he would board that ship tonight. There was nothing to be gained in hanging around Deptford for the next few days. Indeed, all might well be lost.

There was certainly no time to be lost, thought Simon. Speed was of the essence. As well as looking for Carew he must also search out Matthew Roydon and Thomas Nashe and see what they had to say for themselves so that he could be certain they'd played no part in the mystery. The first problem was finding them.

The two most popular taverns with the poets and dramatists were the Anchor on the Bankside and the Mermaid over the river by Puddle Dock, and so it seemed sensible to start with them. He began near home with the Anchor, in the hope that Kit Marlowe might be there and would be able to tell him where he was most likely to find the other two men. He was at a particular disadvantage where Nashe was concerned for, so far as he was aware, he had never seen him and so did not even know what he looked like. But there was no sign of Marlowe in the Anchor although there were a number of actors from the Lord Admiral's Men enjoying a drink after the morning's rehearsal, among them Tom Pope.

'You want Kit, you say? He's not been into the Rose for several days nor have I seen him about. Have you?' he asked the other actors. They shook their heads. 'He's drinking ever more heavily,' Tom confided, 'looks dreadful and seems worried to death. If you ask him what's afoot all you get for your trouble is curses and dark mutters of betrayal and being surrounded by enemies. He does admit to finding it difficult to work at present and I suppose it could be that's the problem. It seems he still hasn't nearly finished *Hero and Leander*, by which he sets so much store.' There was a general move towards the door by the actors who were to play that afternoon and Tom made ready to join them. 'Have you tried the Mermaid?' he suggested. 'I've heard he drinks more often on that side of the river than this these days.'

But when Simon arrived on the north side of the river after walking over London Bridge, he found the Mermaid tavern almost empty of custom although, when he enquired of the landlord if he had seen Marlowe recently, the man replied that of late Master Kit had taken to coming in most afternoons. With no clear idea of what to do next, Simon went out again into the street and stared almost unseeingly over towards the great bulk of St Paul's Church. The sight jolted him out of his trance and reminded him of the shop close by to it that sold Tarot cards, crystal balls, amulets and other such paraphernalia. Well, he decided, having come this far he might just as well see if he could buy a pack of the cards before returning again to the Mermaid.

The shop, with its shabby front, was in a lane so narrow it could be spanned by a man standing in the middle and extending his arms. A sign swinging over the doorway showed a seated alchemist or wizard surrounded by the signs of the Zodiac and cabalistic figures. The owner was a small crabbed fellow who, when asked if he had any Tarot cards for sale, made a great performance of opening a drawer and looking into it as if he expected demons to be lurking there. He then brought out a pack of the cards in a small box and placed them on the counter with a flourish, informing Simon that he was fortunate as he had no others in stock at the present time.

The design of the pack was different again from both that of the countess and the card of the Hanged Man put through his door, and the shopkeeper informed him that it was Italian, demanding a guinea for it. It seemed a very high price but the pack was a fine one and eventually, after much haggling, Simon bought it for sixteen shillings along with a small booklet explaining the various patterns in which the cards could be spread out. Pleased that at least this one small goal had been achieved, he was walking back towards the Mermaid when his eye was caught by a notice pinned to the door of a stationer's shop.

NEW IN! BUY NOW! it proclaimed in large red letters. Then, underneath: '*The Terrors of the Night or a Discourse of Apparitions!* by Thos. Nashe. *Post Tenebris Dies.* Printed by John Danter for William Jones and to be sold here and at the sign of the Gunne near Holbourne Conduit.' Simon stopped in his tracks. Was this the pamphlet Marlowe had mentioned? Well, there was only one way to find out. He entered the shop to find it crowded with customers, most of whom were eagerly buying the new publication. Simon duly paid his shilling, took it outside, and looked at it in the dying light of the afternoon. He was amused at its over-flowery, indeed sycophantic dedication to: *That clear Lamp of Virginity and the excellent adored high Wonder of Sharpe Wit and sweet Beautie, Mistress Elizabeth Carey, sole daughter to the renowned Sir George Carey, Knight, etc.* Elizabeth Carey was cousin to his own friend, Robert Carey, and niece to the Lord Chamberlain. Well, so far so good. He turned the page to find the work began with a discourse on dreams, a subject which interested him greatly. Suddenly aware that he had eaten nothing since breakfast, he quickened his pace towards the Mermaid where he ordered some food, then sat back to read Nashe's discourse, deciding he would give Marlowe half an hour and if he hadn't come by then, would return home.

Simon realised how hungry he was when the bowl of soup, platter of bread and cheese arrived and he made short work of it, reading as he did so. The stuff on dreams and nightmares was interesting enough, though its author took a somewhat cynical approach to the subject, but it was the next section which made him cry out, causing the handful of drinkers in the taproom to turn and stare at him.

It was a diatribe aimed at those Nashe described as quack physicians, astrologers and 'famous conjurers'. Such so-called charlatans, he wrote, armed only with a little sprinkling of grammar in youth and having spent their all on halfpenny ale and riotous living with harlots, would of a sudden decide to take up doctoring. They would then 'rake some dunghill for a few dirty plasters and candle ends, tempered up with ointments and syrups' and set up as physicians, at first in the remote countryside among the ignorant since their learning was based at best only on three or four old rusty manuscript books (Nashe was a university scholar and liked to remind people of it). But soon these 'doctors' would venture to London and there commence practising, 'hanging out their rat banners like aqua vitae sellers or stocking menders'.

'God's Blood!' muttered Simon, seething inside. 'Is this meant for me? Since I never studied at university here, practised first in the country and am now set up in London, it must be! Perhaps I've been wrong after all and chasing after Carew has been nothing but a wild goose chase.' He turned over the page only to find it got worse. After touting his wares in taverns and ordinaries and bragging of his ability to cast fortunes by astrological means, the supposed doctor would prescribe his own remedies, often poisonous, 'killing twenty for every one he restored to perfect health'. By such means his reputation would grow apace as he went from strength to strength, acquiring wealthy clients by the day, called to attend the nobility at Court, and all the time pretending to an expertise he had never learned, and to foreign travel and study never undertaken, having only been as far as Ireland or the Low Countries, 'enforced to fly either for getting a maid with child or marrying two wives'.

Simon thumped the table in rage making the tankards and trenchers rattle. 'Hell's Teeth,' he swore under his breath, 'he *must* mean me. How on earth did he find out about my child in Salisbury?' Suddenly he recalled his conversation with Marlowe on the way to Sherborne. That was it then. Marlowe must have told him, for who else could it be? There was nothing for it but to have it out with him.

He did not have long to wait, for a few minutes later Marlowe entered the taproom, saw Simon sitting in his corner and came over after calling for the tapster to bring them some wine and two cups.

'Do you know anything about this?' demanded Simon, throwing the pamphlet down in front of Marlowe without any preamble.

Marlowe picked it up. 'It's out then? I had thought it wasn't published until next week.'

'I take it you know what's in it?'

Marlowe laughed. 'Nashe told me something of it. Am I to gather it's mightily offended you? Oh yes, I remember. Doesn't he have his say about quack doctors and astrologers?' He opened it up and ran his eye over the pages. 'Ah yes, I see, here it is.' The tapster arrived with a bottle and two cups, leaving Marlowe to pour out the wine. 'You'll join me, I presume, Simon?' Simon said nothing. Marlowe poured out a cup of wine and put it down in front of him. 'God's Blood, man, what have I done to warrant so ferocious a scowl? *I* haven't written it. It's nothing to do with me.' He carried on reading for a little while then threw it aside. 'Why take it personally? It applies only to quacks and charlatans and since you are neither, why should you worry?'

'He writes of country doctors who have no training at Oxford or Cambridge,' replied Simon in a fury, 'idlers who waste their substance and then turn to medicine to make a fortune. I spent only two years at Oxford and so was unable then to take a degree. He speaks of quacks who return from the Continent pretending to be qualified and poison their patients. I learned my trade in Italy and have just spent the best part of a week in the Counter accused of poisoning a patient. Nashe even writes of this supposed doctor having fled abroad for getting a wench with child. I told you of my bastard son, thinking you would keep my confidence. Presumably it was too good a story and you repeated it to Nashe.'

Marlowe raised his eyes to the ceiling. 'For heaven's sake, calm down, will you! For your information I haven't even seen Nashe since we returned from Sherborne. I have been either with Tom Walsingham at Scadbury or at the Rose with the Lord Admiral's Men. I have my own reasons for keeping close at the moment, reasons which I do not intend to divulge.'

Simon had to smile at this. Possibly he had overreacted; he did not want to look foolish. 'I must believe you then, but do you know where he lives?'

Marlowe shrugged. 'Who knows? He flits here and there like a butterfly, or rather a flea, for he is annoying, lives off his host when possible and then bites the hand that feeds him. Having said that, he's an amusing fellow and good company and you'd probably get on well with him. You'll have to ask around the taverns and lodging houses.' He smiled broadly. 'What do you intend to do? Call him out? Will it be swords at dawn in Finsbury Fields?'

'I doubt it but I'd still like to know if this stuff really is aimed at me personally, for if that is the case then he might be involved in the other matters too. Ralegh thought I should see what he had to say.'

'Then seek him out by all means.' Kit looked thoughtful. '*If* Nashe did have anyone particular in mind, then I would put my guineas on his using Dee's man Kelley as his model.'

'The countess brought his name up only yesterday, saying it was as well he died. It's odd how many people remember the fellow after so long. Did Nashe know him?'

'I shouldn't think so, it was before his time. But, as I recall, Edward Kelley remained notorious for a good while after he left the country. He still is to some extent; the name Kelley has become synonymous with quackery.' Marlowe hailed the tapster and ordered some more wine.

Simon picked up his cup and drank gratefully. 'Truth to tell, Kit, this coil is becoming ever darker,' and he told Marlowe of his discovery of the hanged printer and his very real suspicion of Spenser Carew.

Marlowe listened in silence, becoming increasingly serious as the tale unfolded. 'It seems you find yourself yet again in deep water and I agree that it's urgent you track down Carew. But I'm sure you and Ralegh are wrong in suspecting Nashe might have a hand in any of it.

'As to murder . . . never! He has no stomach for violence and would be hard pressed to defend himself in a fight, let alone cold-bloodedly string a man up on a beam even if he had the strength, which I doubt. Oh, he's brave enough with his tongue and full of sharp thrusts with his pen but no more. I know too that he intensely dislikes the School of the Night and all its works, but that's as far as it goes and he, like many of us, puts his own self-interest first. That's another reason for thinking he was aiming at Kelley. He knows he's quite safe since the man's dead! Poor Nashe, he's always looking for patrons among the nobility and is likely to step carefully seeing that we have an earl and a countess among our number, neither of whom he would want to offend. Think, man! Why in God's name should he set out to ruin you? He aims his arrows at all and sundry and this time it happens to be physicians. I don't believe there's any more to it than that.'

Simon agreed Marlowe had made out a convincing case but added, 'Whatever you say, though, I will tackle him about his wretched pamphlet and warn him that if it is aimed at me, then I shall have him arrested at my suit for slander!'

The afternoon was nearly over and he was on the point of leaving when Matthew Roydon walked in. He came over to them, picked up Marlowe's cup, drained it and flung himself down beside them.

'I've fought men for less,' remarked Marlowe. 'It's as well I'm in one of my increasingly rare good humours today.'

'You can afford it', countered Roydon. 'I have no money and you are always in funds, thanks to your patron.' He turned and squinted at Simon. He had obviously been drinking elsewhere. 'What are you doing here – Dr Forman, isn't it?'

'Seeking Tom Nashe's blood!' mocked Marlowe, picking up the pamphlet.

'This is the new one, is it?' said Roydon, taking it off him. 'What's your quarrel with Nashe then, Forman?'

'I want to know if the quack doctor of whom he writes is supposed to be me,' Simon told him. 'Also what he knows, if anything, of the spate of mischief that has befallen so many of us.'

'You think Nashe is to blame?' Roydon shook his head vigorously. 'No, no, no. You're quite wrong.'

'I told him so,' said Marlowe, 'not least because this "mischief" now includes the murder of a man by hanging,' and he told Roydon of Simon's discovery.

'Well, someone's responsible for all this evil business,' declared Simon, 'and since you're here, Roydon, I tell you now that I've also heard your name mentioned in connection with our present troubles.'

Roydon looked incredulous. 'Me? That's even more stupid. I presume you've been in here drinking all day and are out of your wits or that you've been seized with a fit of madness.' His face reddened. 'If you mean it, Forman, then come outside and we'll settle it here and now.'

'Stop this nonsense, will you,' growled Marlowe, 'or I'll take on both of you which would be a pity as I'm by far the best swordsman of the three of us. Come now, Simon, you said yourself that the most likely suspect was Spencer Carew.'

Roydon looked startled. 'Carew? What do you mean?'

So Simon explained his suspicions yet again, adding that he and Ralegh, along with the Parish Constable, were searching London for him so far with a signal lack of success.

'You need look no further,' advised Roydon. 'He is even now lodged in the Red Bull tavern in Deptford waiting to take ship to the New World. I ran into him a day or two ago in the City and he told me of his departure and invited me to meet him for a farewell drink. I've just come from there,' he explained. He paused. 'He's most definitely in dire trouble of some kind which is why he's fleeing the country.'

'Didn't he tell you why he was making off in such haste?' asked Marlowe.

'Not exactly,' Roydon replied thoughtfully, 'but he spoke darkly of an offence or offences he'd committed which makes it essential he leaves the country.'

'Then I must go downriver to Deptford without delay,' said Simon, getting to his feet, 'and see if I can catch him before he sails.'

By the end of the afternoon Spenser Carew's nerves were on edge. He had enquired of the hostess of the tavern, who seemed to know everything, which vessel was expected to sail to the New World on the dawn tide but she expressed her surprise at his question, telling him that so far as she was aware, the first one bound for the New World was the *Spirit of Venture*. The others were sailing for nearer ports, for the Low Countries, Bordeaux and Lisbon.

He tried not to feel alarm at this; after all his informant had seemed so definite and hitherto he had always been right. The afternoon dragged on towards its end with no sign of any message.

Finally, unable to contain himself any longer, he went out and looked up and down the street outside. It was nearly dark and a fine rain was falling. Behind him the clock of St Nicholas Church struck five. He was turning back into the tavern when a lad appeared making purposefully towards the door. He stared up at Carew.

'I'm looking for a cove that's expecting to go to sea tonight,' he said, 'a Master Carew. Do you know him?'

'That's me,' Carew told him. 'What do you want?'

'Then I'm to give you this,' said the lad handing him a letter then making off at a run.

Carew took it back into the taproom and over to his corner, calling for a candle to read by as he did so. The letter was unsigned but he recognised the writing as that of his companion of the afternoon. The captain of the new vessel, he was informed, would take him to Virginia subject to agreement on the terms on both sides. He should make his way to the river steps at the Watergate at eight o'clock bringing nothing with him. Arrangements would then be made for his box and other baggage to be collected.

'I fear the hounds are getting ever closer on your trail,' he read, *'so do not tell the hostess that you leave tonight. I will settle your account with her.'* Carew gave a sigh of relief. Eight o'clock then. In three hours he would be safe.

Chapter 11

Deptford Strand

Simon raced out of the Mermaid and was about to hail a wherry to cross to the Bankside when it occurred to him that he had better inform Sir Walter Ralegh that Carew was in Deptford, about to take ship for the New World, that he was hastening down to see if he could prevent it and, hopefully, persuade (or force) Carew to return to Sir Walter's house with him. He hailed the wherry, cursing inwardly at its slow progress as the boatman made his way upstream against the downward pull of the river and the fast-slackening tide. It was almost on dead water.

Once again Sir Walter was from home, though expected back within the hour, but Simon felt the matter was too urgent for him to wait; Carew might even now be boarding his ship. After calling for pen and paper he left Ralegh a hastily written note explaining what had happened. *If it proves impossible for me to persuade Carew to return to London with me to resolve this matter once and for all, then I will send to you at once to see if you can prevent his leaving the country. It might be that even his family do not know of his plans. Certainly there is something amiss for he admitted to Matthew Roydon, who visited him in a Deptford tavern, that he had committed a wrong that made flight inevitable.*

He had asked the boatman to wait for him, assuming that it would not take long to tell Ralegh his news, but when he went back to where he had left him, boat and man had disappeared. The tide was just on the turn and the water along the bank almost completely still apart from the small waves kicked up by a freshening wind. It was growing dark and beginning to rain. He looked at the empty expanse of water and wondered what to do for the best. It would take forever to walk back to the Bridge. He cursed again. It was always the way. When time was of no importance, dozens of boatmen jostled for your custom; when speed was of the essence there were none. He was about to retrace his steps and walk down to the next place where he might reasonably hail a wherry, when a boat shot into view.

At this glad sight he raced down to the water's edge, calling out and waving his arms, and of a sudden it changed course and the boatman began pulling strongly in towards the shore. When it got to within a few feet of him, Simon realised it was Roger once again but this time in a different boat, a much finer craft complete with a small post in its stern from which dangled a lantern. Simon climbed in, wetting his feet in the rising water as he did so.

'Surely you can't have been this successful so soon?' he asked as he settled himself down opposite the boatman.

Roger grinned. 'Told you I'd friends downriver. Well, I went to see some of them yesterday and there was old Ned Snout laid up with aches in the joints – this weather always gives him the screws – and he said I could use his boat so long as I paid him a reasonable sum from my fares. I was on my way to Westminster but then thought I saw someone on the waterfront waving for a boat. You were in luck. So, where do you want to go, doctor?'

'First to the Bankside to fetch my man then, if you're willing, down to Deptford.'

Roger gave this some thought then said, 'Fair enough. But it'll cost you. It's a long way in the dark and can be hazardous. There's always lots of rubbish floating in the water.'

'That I expected, but there's little time to lose and it's quicker than having to walk out to where I keep my horse, then hire one for John and go down by a road which winds all over the place.'

Roger looked at the water. 'I can only go so fast as my arms will let me and the boat allows with two of you in, but we'll soon have the tide running strongly down with us and that will help a good deal. What's the hurry?'

Simon leant forward. 'I told you someone had been making mischief for me. Well it seems the person I think it is might have killed a man and I've just learned he's at Deptford, at the Red Bull tavern, about to take ship for the New World. I must stop him going at all costs.'

'I can't see me being able to haul three of you back here if you do find him,' commented Roger, 'and that in the dark against the tide, especially if this fellow doesn't want to come.'

'I realise that,' Simon told him. 'We'll just have to try and hold him there while I get word to Sir Walter Ralegh that we've found him. Perhaps Sir Walter will come to Deptford to collect him in his own carriage. The important thing is to prevent this man leaving the country.'

The boat was now making steady progress along the Middlesex bank towards Blackfriars. 'I'll cross there,' Roger told Simon, 'it's as good a place as any. Faugh!' he snorted a little later. 'What a stench!'

'The Fleet?' enquired Simon. The Fleet River had been little more than an open sewer emptying its contents into the Thames for a hundred years or more.

Roger nodded. 'Mind you, there's even worse. Yesterday I'd a fare who wanted taking from Bread Street to Holbourne; that meant rowing him up the Fleet, then the Old Bourne. I swear I'll never do it again. I could hardly get my oars into the water. The Fleet was scummed inches deep with grease from the cookshops and ordinaries that the cooks had thrown out, along with offal, fish heads and bits and pieces of dead meat. After you'd got through all that lot and up towards the Old Bourne then it was the night soil from the night tubs of the poor and what comes down from the privies and jakes of the better houses. Not to mention dead cats and dogs, while on every ledge and walkway the eyes of the rats glint at you.'

Before he could expound further, he turned the boat sharply and made his way across the river, cleverly using the tide and current to help him. 'You're certainly skilled enough,' Simon told him, 'so why didn't you turn to this in the first place instead of a life of crime?'

Roger shrugged. 'Thought there were easier ways of making a living. But not after twice being in the Counter and the last time I came up before the beak he told me if he saw me again he'd have me hanged and I believed him. Reckon now I'll settle down and marry Betty before the child's born, make an honest woman of her. Plenty of whores have turned honest and made good wives.'

He tied up at the steps below Simon's house and Simon leapt out of the boat to fetch John Bradedge. It would have taken much less time to go on alone, but he had no idea what awaited him at Deptford. He found it hard to imagine Carew would calmly give up his planned voyage and come tamely back with him to Ralegh, but even in the unlikely event that he agreed to do so, Deptford was a rough place where many a seaman fresh home from a voyage had found himself knocked on the head or stabbed in a back alley and his purse taken. Sightseers visiting Drake's ship *The Golden Hind*, preserved there in memory of his great voyage round the world, usually went in parties. No, on all counts it was better there were two of them and John was always dependable however desperate the situation. They would go together and well armed.

As he reached the top of the steps he heard the clock strike the hour on St Mary Overy. God's Breath, it was seven o'clock! He must have spent longer in the Mermaid than he'd realised.

Just before eight o'clock Spenser Carew reached for his thick cloak and throwing it over his arm, left the taproom of the Red Bull and went out into the damp night to make his way along Deptford Strand to the Watergate. For a few minutes he gazed out across the river to the anchored ships, their masts silhouetted by a watery moon. He wondered which of them it was that was shortly to set sail for the Americas, finding it odd that there were no lights on any of them, no sign of the noise and bustle of a vessel making ready for sea.

He sighed and thought of London, well hidden now by the bend in the river and for the thousandth time cursed himself for a fool. His life on his parents' Devonshire estate that had seemed so dull and boring only a few months before, now seemed like paradise. As to what those same parents would make of it when they found out that he had left the country rather than face up to the consequences of what he had done, he could scarcely imagine.

Surely it must now be eight o'clock? He muffled himself in his cloak and walked to the Watergate, and as he did so the clock struck the hour. He reached the stop of the steps and looked down but there was no sign of anyone there nor any boat tied up below to show a recent arrival. He peered out into the river and although there were now several boats plying their trade, their lanterns bobbing over the water, they were wherries ferrying passengers over to the Isle of Dogs or from the Isle to Deptford; none was making its way towards him. He looked round to see if anyone was coming on foot. There were several houses on the street leading down from St Nicholas's Church to the water, one particularly fine one on the corner. Hearing a noise from it he turned and thought he saw a crack of light from an open door, but he must have been wrong. Perhaps a curtain had been twitched aside. Where, oh where was the wretched ship's captain? He hunched himself in his cloak. Should he stay where he was? Go back to the tavern? The letter had told him not to do so once he had left, that his goods and chattels would be collected, his reckoning paid. More minutes passed.

He was hardly aware of the footsteps behind him, they were so soft, but at the last moment he turned, felt a slight sting under his shoulder-blade and saw a dark figure running fast away from him back up towards St Nicholas's Church. He put his hand under his cloak to the place where he had been stung and brought it back sticky with blood. He dropped his cloak and tried to run after his assailant but after only a few paces the dark buildings and the wet sky whirled and eddied around him as he fell to the ground.

The tide was running strongly downstream helped by the rain that had fallen steadily into the upper reaches of the Thames during the last few days, and although the wherry was burdened with three people, it made good progress. Lights glimmered here and there on the river banks though mostly on the north side, for there were fields and orchards between Southwark and Deptford on the Kent bank. From time to time they saw the nodding lantern of a boat though all were crossing the river from one side to the other rather than making their way up or downstream.

They passed Wapping on their left then the river bent dramatic- ally south-east and its lights disappeared. They were now in unknown territory so far as Simon was concerned. He had been to Deptford only once before and that with Avisa when her husband was away on business and they had visited *The Golden Hind* together and had even sat inside the ship and had food and wine. A further cluster of lights appeared on their left which Roger informed him was the Isle of Dogs, home to the boat's owner. 'After I've dropped you off and had something to wet my throat I'll go over and beg a bed for the night then go back upriver on the morning tide.'

Ten minutes later he was pulling into Deptford Strand. 'There's two sets of steps,' he told them, 'one at the Watergate and the other further along. There's a couple of taverns there.'

He manoeuvred his boat adroitly in among others tied up there and Simon and John disembarked. 'Will you come with us and have a drink?' asked Simon.

'You go and find your man,' said Roger. 'I'll have a look round and stretch my legs. I might see you later in the Red Bull.'

The two nearest taverns proved to be the Ship and the Wharf and Yard; it took them some time to find the Red Bull. The taproom was full of men, mostly seamen, but with a scattering of those who worked on wharves and in the chandlers' shops and repair yards. The crowd was clearly rough but on the whole good-humoured. Simon and John pushed their way through the drinkers towards the benches in the corners but there was no sign of Carew. They made several attempts to attract the attention of the hostess, a plump woman of uncertain years boasting unnaturally red hair who was obviously being propositioned by a burly mariner, before she finally listened to what they had to say.

'We're looking for a young man of the name of Carew,' Simon told her. 'I understand he is staying here before voyaging to Virginia. Do you know where I might find him?'

'Don't know anyone of that name,' she replied. 'There's no Carew staying here. But then there's plenty who don't say who they are, particularly if they're going off in a hurry, if you know what I mean.'

So Simon patiently described Carew to her, adding untruthfully that the young man's family, with whom he had fallen out, had sent him to Deptford to beg Carew to change his mind before it was too late. At this she reluctantly agreed that the young gentleman who'd taken a chamber at the back for a few days might be the one they were looking for, 'But he calls himself Spenser – Master Spenser. A cut above my usual trade but, as I said, we get all sorts.'

'So he's still here then, he hasn't sailed yet?'

The hostess shrugged. 'Well, if he has he's left all his belongings behind. But I can't see that's possible. He's due to sail on the *Spirit of Venture* but I know she's been held up for some repairs.' She paused. 'It's funny though. Earlier today he asked me if I knew which ship was sailing to the New World on the dawn tide. I told him so far as I knew, there was none. Being in here with all the seamen coming in and out all the time I reckon I know as much as anyone and there's been no talk of another vessel bound for the Americas.'

'You're sure of that?' Simon insisted.

'As sure as I can be. Here,' she said, beckoning her would-be lover over, 'have you heard of there being any ship here bound for the Americas apart from the *Spirit of Venture*?'

The sailor wiped a sweaty hand across his mouth. 'Nah,' he replied, '*Venture*'s the only one. The next ship out's the *Alice* and she's off to Bordeaux about noon tomorrow to pick up a cargo of wine.'

Simon thanked him for this information, then asked the landlady if they could look in Spenser's chamber. 'You can check we aren't carrying anything off from there afterwards if you like,' he said. 'It's just that there might be something to indicate where he's gone.'

'Help yourself,' the hostess shrugged, 'but don't blame me if he comes back unexpected like and takes you for thieves. It's the middle room on the left.'

They climbed up the dilapidated wooden stairs to a rickety landing off which there were several chambers. They felt their way into the room with difficulty for it was almost completely dark. Fortunately, by the bed was a candle, flint and tinder and after a short struggle they had a light, but there was little to see. The bed had no sheets and was covered with rough blankets. Other than that, the only furniture was the chair on which they had found the candle. A large chest stood in the middle of the room, securely bound with ropes and beside it were two large bags. A quick inspection showed that they contained only clothing, though Carew's sword in its hanger lay propped against one of them.

'It hardly looks as if he's sailing at dawn,' said Simon, 'for surely by now both he and his goods and chattels would have been safely aboard.' He held up the candle and looked around then, having satisfied himself that there was nothing more to see, he led the way back downstairs.

'Any luck?' enquired the hostess who was now giving her attention to another seaman who, from his appearance, was somewhat better heeled than the previous one.

'Nothing,' Simon told her. 'We'll have a look round the other taverns and if we don't find him, we'll come back. He can't have gone far, he's left everything up there.'

'He'd two visitors though this afternoon,' she said. 'First a young fellow in a shabby doublet who he seemed to expect and who drank with him for an hour or so. I heard him say it was no bad thing to go adventuring in the New World, for there a man might make his fortune. The second gentleman came later and I don't think Master Spenser was expecting *him* for he looked really surprised. It was after speaking very seriously with this other older man that Master Spenser asked me about the other ship which was supposed to be going to the Americas.'

'What was this older man like?' Simon wanted to know.

'Not like those who usually drink here,' the woman said with a laugh. 'He was of middle years so far as I could see, though his face was mostly hidden by a big hat and he didn't take it off. He was rather grand in a long furred gown like City merchants wear and he'd fine leather gloves on too. I thought it might be young Spenser's dad, but from what you say it couldn't have been. They spoke soft and whispered together in the corner and then the man stood up and I heard him tell Master Spenser to mark what he'd said. Then he left and the young fellow asked about the ship.'

Simon thanked her and gave her a shilling to buy some of the canary wine she obviously enjoyed since she was constantly filling her cup with it. Then he and John went out into the night. As in any major port, taverns, inns and ordinaries jostled together and they went in all of them but there was no sign of Carew.

'Do you think he's made off already?' asked John. 'Perhaps this unknown man frighted him and he's wasted no more time.'

'But where could he have gone?' queried Simon. 'We know no large vessel's leaving port tonight and besides, he'd hardly go leaving all his goods behind. I suppose there's a slight chance he's changed his mind and picked up a small ship bound for Devon or Cornwall and intends sending for his chest and bags. Though I doubt he'd find much left in them of any value by the time he got them back, if that is the case.'

John agreed. 'So now what do we do, doctor?'

'Walk along the quay, look down both sets of steps to see if anyone's taken a boat anywhere in the last couple of hours, have another walk round the town then go back to the Red Bull. He's probably back there now, fully warned of our arrival.'

The two men began with the place where they had been landed

but there was no sign of life and they noticed Roger's boat had gone. They then made their way towards the Watergate. Once again there was nothing to be seen – no boats, no sign of life except for a discarded cloak. Simon picked it up. It must have been dropped carelessly for it was nearly new and made of good wool. He ran his hand along it. In one place, where there was a small tear, it was slightly sticky.

'I don't like this,' he said. 'Whoever was wearing this cloak didn't just throw it away and I think there's blood on it.' He looked down the steps. The tide had dropped sufficiently for there to be shingle at the foot of the steps. 'Let's go and see if the owner's down there. Perhaps he was attacked and thrown down the steps in the hope the river would take him away.'

They made their way carefully down the slippery steps but there was no one on the small piece of beach nor, so far as they could tell, anything floating in the water nearby. 'I suppose he could have been set on some time ago,' said Simon, 'if that is indeed what's happened. If so, then he could be on his way to the sea by now. We'd best go back, there's nothing here.' They had reached the top of the steps and were about to return to the Red Bull when they heard a faint moan from the dark corner of an alleyway. Simon stopped. 'What's that?'

'Be careful,' warned John. 'It could be there are fellows up there trying to lure us over so they can knock us on the head and take our purses. It's best we draw our daggers.'

At the entry to the alleyway they heard the noise again. It was pitch black and they had to feel their way along a wall, John in front. He stopped as his foot struck what seemed to be a heap of rags whereupon the moaning noise came from immediately below him. He bent down. 'Lord help us, reckon some poor fellow's been attacked just like I said.'

They regarded the body which lay face down. It was

impossible to see anything. 'Let's get him out of here and into some light, then we can see what we can do,' said Simon. 'You take his head and I'll take his feet.' They backed out of the alleyway and struggled with their burden towards a lantern hanging on a pole from a building on the quay. 'Fetch that cloak,' Simon told John. 'I dropped it at the entrance to the alleyway. It must be his anyway.'

John did so, spread it out on the stones and they laid the injured man gently down on it under the light. 'God's Blood!' exclaimed John. 'It's Carew.'

'And badly injured, it seems.' Simon knelt down beside the recumbent form and ripped his doublet open. 'Nothing here but, look, we've left a trail of blood.' He turned Carew on to his side. 'See there, the back of his doublet's soaked in it. He's been stabbed in the back. We'll have to try and get him back to the Red Bull. There's nothing I can do for him here.'

It took them a good ten minutes to reach the tavern and make their way in with Carew. Their appearance stopped all conversation dead. 'What you got there?' enquired the sailor nearest to the door.

'A badly injured man, close to death.' Simon looked across at the hostess. 'It seems we've found your guest. He was in an alleyway near the Watergate. He's in a bad way,' he added, 'he must have been bleeding for some time. Do you recall when he went out?'

The hostess replied that she didn't notice but one of the customers chimed in with the information that he reckoned it would have been just before eight o'clock. 'Not long before you came in yourselves,' he said.

So they'd missed him only by minutes, it seemed. 'Well, I wish we'd got here faster,' Simon replied. 'Now, can I have some help to get him up to his bed so I can tend to the damage? It seems he's been stabbed. We'll need some aqua vitae or brandy, please hostess.'

There was a mutter of conversation at this. 'He ain't the first and he won't be the last to feel a length of steel,' said the sailor nearest the door. 'There's too many round here who use knives first and think later, not to mention the cutpurses and runagates.' He came over to them. 'All right, I'll give you a hand up with him.'

They laid Carew down on the bed, partly on his side, and Simon got his jacket and shirt off. Blood still oozed from a small round wound just below his left shoulderblade.

'It's precious close to the heart,' commented the sailor.

Simon looked closer. 'Aye. I think he must have heard something or felt someone behind him and was beginning to turn so that luckily the knife entered him at an angle; however it's impossible to tell what other vital organ it might have pierced. It looks like a wound made by a poniard rather than a dagger.'

'He looks almost gone,' said John.

Simon felt Carew's pulse. 'No, he's still alive – just.'

'There's a barber surgeon a few doors down,' the sailor told them. 'Should I go fetch him or his man?'

'No, I'm a doctor myself,' Simon replied. 'Will you ask the hostess if she'll bring me water and some stuff for bandages and to make a pad, so that we can at least try to stop this bleeding and, if you will, bring the strong spirits for which I asked. Tell the mistress I'll pay her for her trouble.'

The sailor did as he was bid, reappearing a few minutes later with a bottle of brandy and a cup, the hostess following behind with a bowl of water and some cloths.

'Jack here says you're a doctor,' she said, setting the bowl down on the chair. 'It seems this young man has struck lucky.'

Simon wiped away the dried blood from around the wound,

made a pad of some of the cloth and bound it tightly round with the rest. 'He'll need all the luck he can get,' he told her. 'There, that'll have to do for now.' Carew moaned again. 'Can you hear me?' whispered Simon into his ear. 'Can you speak? You're all right, you're safe now.' He poured a little of the brandy into a cup and put it to his lips, but Carew had lapsed again into unconsciousness.

'I'd best stay with him,' he said to the hostess. 'Even if he survives the night he can't be moved until tomorrow.' She agreed that to be the case and even went so far as to offer to bring in a couple of straw mattresses for him and John, to which end she took away the sailor to help her carry them in.

Simon looked thoughtfully after them then turned to his man. 'As soon as there's any sign of life out there in the morning I want you to see if it's possible to hire a horse. If it is, I want you to ride like hell from here to Southwark, then over the Bridge to Blackfriars and from there to Sir Walter's house on the Strand and tell him what's happened. If you can't find a horse you'll have to take a boat straight upriver to the Strand. At first light I must also send someone from here to the nearest apothecary – Carew's bound to run a fever.' He gave John a grim look. 'He needs to be in a place of safety.'

'You think it was no ordinary footpad then?'

'There's always the possibility in a place like this but my heart misgives me. There have been too many coincidences. If I'm right, whoever did this might well return to make sure Carew's dead, and if he learns that not to be the case then there's every chance he'll make another attempt and this time succeed.'

'Do you reckon he'd an accomplice then and they fell out?'

Simon shook his head wearily. 'I don't know *what* to think. But if we're ever to get to the bottom of it all Carew must be kept alive at all costs.'

Chapter 12

A Visit from a Doctor

After an hour of watching, during which time Carew had still not shown any signs of recovering consciousness, Simon lay down on one of the two mattresses and tried to sleep. John Bradedge was already snoring away on the other. But although he was tired out he slept only fitfully, trying again and again in the intervals in between to make sense of events. Carew had felt it necessary to leave the country, had made arrangements to leave for the Americas on a certain ship. He had then been visited by a stranger after which he had enquired about a vessel which was supposedly leaving earlier. Come the evening he had gone out, leaving all his possessions behind him and someone had either come across him or followed him and stabbed him in the back.

Towards morning he fell into a doze and awoke suddenly to the sound of life stirring in the street outside. A clock chimed six. He shook John awake. 'Go now and see if you can hire a horse anywhere here.' He felt in his pocket and gave him some money.

'It's a long and winding way to the Bankside,' grumbled John. 'It's a bad road and it's still dark.'

'But probably quicker than taking a boat,' Simon told him. 'Look, if you find it impossible to get hold of a horse, then by all means take a wherry.' He did some brief calculations. 'It will soon start to get light. If you leave here by half six you should be at the Bankside sometime after eight and over to Sir Walter's house on the Strand by nine at the latest. Tell him we have to have a carriage to convey Carew back to London because of the state he's in, and that he must send for him straight away. Tell him I'm not happy it was a simple footpad attack and that whoever did this might well return to discover the outcome. Go now. With any luck you should be back again before noon.'

When John had left he went over to his patient again, raised him up and gingerly peered under the bandage. There was little further blood on the pad which suggested the wound itself had stopped bleeding though it was not possible to know whether or not there was any internally. He felt the young man's head which was quite definitely hotter. Young Carew needed something to help bring his fever down.

Simon went below and searched out the hostess in what passed for a kitchen. He asked if she knew of an apothecary locally and also if she could give him something to eat. She gave an unenthusiastic 'yes' to both questions. There was an apothecary next to a chandler's ten minutes away and she supposed she could wake the boy and send him. As to food – well, there was some bread and bacon, neither very fresh, but it was all she had. The production of a shilling sent her off to wake the boy who arrived some minutes later, rubbing his eyes and yawning.

'Ask the apothecary for feverfew and borage,' Simon told him. It was unlikely the man would have anything much better. 'I need sufficient to make a posset. Be as quick as you can.' The boy stumped off and he sat in the closed taproom which smelled unpleasantly of stale wine, ale and unwashed bodies in front of a smoky fire which made his eyes sting. The landlady came in and plonked down a wooden platter on which she had put a slice of dry bacon and two pieces of coarse bread.

'How is he then?' she enquired, jerking her head towards the stairs.

'Still much the same,' Simon told her.

'Will he live?'

Simon sighed. 'I don't know. It depends how much damage there is that I can't see. If the knife did not injure any vital part then, since he's young and robust, he has a chance. If it did . . .' He shrugged.

'He was running away, wasn't he.' It was more a statement than a question. Simon agreed that he was.

'Do you know why?' the woman persisted.

'I'm not sure,' Simon told her truthfully.

She went over and poked the fire into life. 'There's many such come here, running off to the Low Countries or France or some such, even to the Americas. But he was better off and better bred than most.' Simon thanked her and gave her another coin, assuring her that both he and his charge would soon be out of her way.

After some time the boy returned with the herbs. The apothecary had taken a good deal of waking and, being newly wed, had proved loath to leave his bed but had finally and with much grumbling stumbled about in his storeroom and produced the ingredients for which he had been asked. Simon went into the kitchen and infused the herbs in some of the hot water which was heating in a pot hung over the kitchen fire, poured the mixture into a cup and took it up to Carew.

'Come now,' he said, raising him on his arm, 'drink this. It will help to bring down your fever.' Carew stirred and moaned but did not open his eyes. However, after further prompting, he did take a few sips of the posset before slipping once again into torpor.

Simon laid him back on the pillow and again searched the room to see if he could find any clues as to what had driven

Carew to Deptford or to what had prompted his almost fatal visit to Watergate; once again it proved fruitless. He looked out of the small window to see if there was anyone standing around as if they were watching the premises, but there was nothing to be seen other than people going about their business, a wherry-man coming for a pint of ale before returning to the river, a woman carrying a basket of wet washing to hang on the nearest hedge. Alone with the sick man Simon felt cut off from everything, and it also occurred to him that if he waited in the taproom he might just hear something that would prove useful. As there was no way anyone could reach the bedchamber without walking through the taproom and up the stairs, he felt it safe to leave Carew for a while and so, having settled his patient again, he went back downstairs to await the arrival of John Bradedge bringing help.

It was a long time coming. The morning dragged on inter-minably and he was seriously considering finding a messenger to despatch to the Bankside to find out what was happening, if anything, when, a little after noon there was the bustle of arrival outside and John appeared at the door followed by two burly men and a sensible-looking middle-aged woman.

'Sir Walter's sent his carriage, doctor,' he said by way of explanation. 'We've come to take Carew back with us. This goodwife here is Sir Walter's housekeeper who, he says, is an excellent nurse. Oh, and he sent this,' he produced a purse from his pocket, 'to pay for the trouble caused.' Since the tavern was fairly full by this time the appearance of a grand carriage outside the Red Bull and a train of servants caused no little stir.

'Come upstairs then,' Simon told the men, 'and we'll get him away from here. And you, goodwife, come too and see how you think he fares before we take him to the carriage. I presume there are blankets and pillows in there?' The housekeeper assured him she had seen to them herself and they all trooped up to the bedchamber.

Carew's eyes were still closed but Simon thought he looked slightly less grey though he showed no reaction when they called his name. Simon showed the woman the dressing he had put on the wound and she agreed with him that the obvious bleeding seemed to have stopped. 'You must carry him down as gently and carefully as possible if we don't want it to start again,' Simon told the two servants. This was easier said than done as the stairs were steep and the headroom low, but they finally managed to get him down between them and placed him on one seat of the carriage, propped around with pillows.

'What about his things?' enquired John.

'Stow the two smaller bags and his sword in or on the carriage somewhere. I'll give the hostess something for storing the chest until later and tell her there will be more to come if all is exactly as it is now when it is sent for.'

Sir Walter's carriage was a roomy one and it was possible for Simon and John to sit on one seat and the housekeeper next to the sick man on the other, protecting him so far as was possible from jolts and ruts in the road; the two servants joined the driver outside. John had been able to hire a horse, he told Simon, and had returned it and paid for it out of the money Simon had given him for the purpose, though he grumbled that a wherry would have been quicker and easier.

Simon saw what he meant as they slowly negotiated the bumpy road back to London. From time to time Carew moaned and stirred though his eyes never opened. The housekeeper, who was keeping a critical eye on the bandage, told Simon that there was still, so far as she could see, no sign of any further bleeding. When they came to London Bridge, John Bradedge was set down to return home, leaving Simon to continue on to the Strand.

Finally, to his great relief, they arrived at their destination where Carew was at once carried in and placed in a prepared bedchamber.

'How is he?' asked Sir Walter anxiously, after seeing him safely bestowed.

'Very poorly,' replied Simon. 'He must have lost a great deal of blood and he has a fever. The next few days will be critical. If he survives them, then it should mean that the knife did not touch any vital spot and provided that is the case, then there's a good chance he will pull through.'

'You man tells me you doubt it was some ordinary cut-throat?'

Simon agreed. 'I could be wrong, cut-throats are common enough in those parts, but added to everything else it seems too pat an explanation,' and he told Ralegh of what he had learned of Carew's activities immediately before the attack.

'You say he had a another visitor then, apart from Matthew Roydon?'

'According to the hostess of the Red Bull, this man suddenly arrived from nowhere and it was clear Carew was not expecting him and that he was greatly troubled by his presence. She described the visitor as a serious-looking, well-dressed man of middle years who might be a wealthy merchant or man of letters. She could see little of his face for he wore a large hat which overshadowed it. She thought it might be Carew's father or a member of his family but I told her that could not be.'

Ralegh concurred, adding, 'It's possible some other person got wind of what Carew was planning, as did you yourself, some older and wiser family friend perhaps, who learned he was in trouble and what he proposed and so went down to Deptford to persuade him to give himself up whatever he might have done. That would explain why his visit proved so disturbing and why Carew wanted to leave the country even sooner.' He frowned. 'I wonder who it was? The description you give would fit any number of respectable gentlemen, including members of our own circle, and hardly suggests anyone coming with sinister intent.'

Seen in the cold light of day, Simon had to agree. 'It could be that there was someone else also lurking there in Deptford who wanted to see Carew safely off to the Americas before he landed them both in serious trouble. I've thought for some time that he must have had an accomplice to help him in his undertaking. This gentleman visitor, possibly a family friend as you suggest, learns Carew is in trouble, visits him in Deptford, remonstrates with him as to his behaviour and begs him to return to London. Possibly he threatens to return the next day to ensure he does so. Carew panics, tries to sail earlier, finds he cannot, tells his accomplice what has happened and the accomplice decides to silence him for good.'

Ralegh agreed that seemed the most likely explanation, adding, 'We must pray the lad survives and can finally tell us the truth though not, I hope, only to have to face the gallows. I have sent a further urgent message to his home,' he told Simon, 'this time informing his parents that he has met with a serious accident and they must needs come to London without delay, though even if they leave at once they are unlikely to be here before another week is out.'

Simon finally took his leave, having promised to return the next day to see to Carew's wound and with Ralegh assuring him that if the young man recovered sufficiently to be able to speak, he would send for him before then. He took a boat across the river and climbed wearily up the steps to his home. He would, he decided, take some food then go to sleep for an hour in an effort to clear his head; but when he opened his front door his heart sank for it was clear it was not to be. Sitting patiently waiting for him in his large, square hall was Lavinia Tapworth and, beside her, a well-dressed older man. Dear Lord, thought Simon, is this the younger Tapworth brother? He was soon disabused of this notion but quite unprepared for what was to come.

'This is Dr North, Dr Forman,' Lavinia informed him, 'the physician, if you remember, who came to our aid when James died. He tells me he is willing to support your view that my late husband died of an apoplexy and not poison. So, as you see, I have brought him to you as I thought it might be helpful if the College of Physicians make any moves to accuse you again.'

Simon greeted his colleague and shook him warmly by the hand. He could hardly believe his good luck. Once he had learned that North had removed to Lincoln, he had more or less given up any hope of finding him yet now, thanks to Lavinia, here he was on his own doorstep. He had to smile. Mistress Tapworth really was a most remarkable young woman and he was about to ask her how she had discovered North when she informed him that it was he who had sought her.

'Dr North happened to be visiting nearby, saw that he was close to our shop and so called to see how I did. I told him what had happened to you and he was most concerned. Indeed, it was his suggestion that we seek you out.'

North inclined his head in agreement. 'I trust this is not an inopportune moment, Dr Forman?'

Simon assured him it was not. North made quite an impressive figure. He was well into his middle years, not tall, shorter than Simon in fact, but broad-shouldered. He looked the epitome of the successful physician, his doublet and breeches of fine dark velvet, lace at his cuffs and wrists, and his fashionable hat boasted fine curled feathers. Simon at once took the visitors into his study, sat them down, and fetched wine and glasses. North took the glass offered to him in a finely gloved hand and looked round at the shelves which lined the walls.

'I see you have Cocke's *Treatise on Medicine*, Dr Forman,

something of a rarity. I consider it to be one of the best treatises on the subject.'

Simon smiled. 'I came across it by chance in Oxford many years ago at a time when it looked as if I might never fulfil my ambition to become a doctor.'

North raised his wine cup. 'To your good health, Dr Forman. Tell me one thing, though. You would appear to be well set up here, but why the Bankside? Why not Blackfriars or Billingsgate?'

Simon shrugged. 'When I first came to London I lodged in Billingsgate but I had little money to find myself a property there, whereas this house has plenty of room, a garden in which I can grow many of my own herbs and it is close both to London Bridge and to water steps for wherries. It suits me well and doesn't seem to deter people from crossing the water to see me. Also,' he added with a wry laugh, 'it keeps me from being under the feet of the Physicians in Knightrider Street.'

'I heard you'd been unfortunate there,' commented North, 'but I can assure you I had no hand in it. Once I had thought over the matter I was certain Master Tapworth died of an apoplexy rather than poison. Unhappily many people blame poison if they have stomach pains, whatever the real cause.'

'I'm relieved to hear it,' said Simon, 'and it was good of you to come. I did try to find you but was told you had removed to Lincoln.'

There was a fractional pause. 'That's right,' North agreed, 'but I like to visit London from time to time. One can become set in one's ways in the country. As to the College of Physicians, luckily I have never had to face their wrath and had no trouble being given their licence to practise.'

Simon smiled. 'So I would suppose. I understand you're a Fellow of the College and have also acted as a Censor in the past. You'll forgive me if I say I have few happy memories of being hauled up before your Committee nor do I enjoy hearing myself described as no better than a "hedge doctor".'

North shook his head gravely. He had, thought Simon, a somewhat self-important manner. Perhaps, after all, he had made great claims for himself. 'I'm sure you'll agree, Dr Forman, that it is necessary to be vigilant against those who claim skills they do not possess and I can assure you from my own experience that there are all too many of them.' He smiled to himself. 'I rather prided myself on being able to distinguish the wheat from the chaff; indeed, I was present when the greatest deceiver of them all, Edward Kelley, was brought before the Committee.'

'That's interesting,' said Simon. 'His name has been mentioned several times recently even though I understand he died some years ago.'

'He did indeed,' North agreed, 'but his name and reputation linger on. He was, in many ways, remarkable.'

'I'm told he had his ears cropped for necromancy,' observed Simon.

'He had, and was heavily branded on the hand at Tyburn as well,' said North. 'In fact, I was there at the time and saw it happen. However, we're not here to discuss the late Kelley and I'm sure you are as busy as I am. Now tell me if there's any way in which I might assist you.'

So Simon explained everything that had happened, starting with the visit by Tapworth with his problem (which caused his widow to have trouble quelling a smile), to Simon's being arrested on his return to London accused of poisoning the silversmith with candied sea holly. He spoke of the subsequent spell in gaol from which he was only released on the demand of the Countess of Pembroke.

North raised an eyebrow. 'Sidney's sister? A formidable woman. You appear to have friends in high places.'

'Not too many,' Simon told him, 'and most of those I've met through an association to which I belong, of which you might well have heard. We call ourselves the School of the Night, and devote ourselves to the study of the new learning and sciences.'

'Ah, the School of the Night! Yes, indeed.' The doctor smiled to himself as if at some secret joke. 'However, to business. Now James Tapworth . . .' He looked across at Lavinia. 'I trust you won't find this too distressing, Mistress Tapworth?' She shook her head. 'I think the young lady here told you how her husband and I first met by chance in a City tavern. When he realised I was a physician he complained of various symptoms and, looking at him, I discerned he was of an extremely choleric humour. From what I saw myself, he ate and drank heavily and was obviously overfleshed. However, he seemed well enough as we rode out to Chelsea together and showed no signs of illness when we parted so I was somewhat surprised to find myself sent for later that evening.

'When I arrived at his house he was indeed showing every symptom of apoplexy; his face was dark and congested and he was breathing with difficulty. If the question of what he had eaten had not been raised by others, then I would certainly never have considered poison.' He then went into more medical detail which showed he had an excellent grasp of the subject, before ending, 'I therefore agree with you that he died as a result of an apoplexy suffered, in my opinion, as a result of too much food and wine, exacerbated by temper and frustration over his inability to perform as a husband should, and I am fully prepared to support that view.'

Simon experienced an immense feeling of relief. 'You know the College far better than I do. Do you think I should pay them a visit now and inform them that Dr North, the doctor who actually treated Tapworth and a Member of their own College, supports my diagnosis if they wish to take it any further?'

'Most certainly,' North assured him. 'It would be as well to do so in case they come up with some other pretext to have you confined. I fear they do not like being thwarted.'

'Presumably they know your direction?'

North smiled. 'Of course. Both at home and when I am in London.' He stood up and proffered his hand to Simon who took it, then he turned to Lavinia. 'Come, Mistress Tapworth. I will see you home.'

'Don't worry on my account,' she returned. 'I want Dr Forman to cast a horoscope for me, and I am quite capable of finding my own way back unharmed.'

'If I'm to go to Knightrider Street, then I can see you safe myself,' Simon reassured her, 'for while I don't want to lose any time informing the College of Dr North's support, it will wait while I do what I can to answer any questions you have, Mistress Tapworth. Though, if you will bear with me, I must have something to eat first.' He saw North to the door and watched him rather grandly descend the watersteps to hail a wherry, then returned to his study. He thanked Lavinia for her intervention, asking her if she had already dined. She told him she had already done so and that he could safely leave her to her own devices while he ate. After quickly disposing of a piece of pie and downing a tankard of ale, Simon returned to find her immersed in the *Treatise on Medicine*.

'Will women ever be able to become physicians?' she said wistfully. 'I think I would find it most fascinating.'

'Maybe,' he commented, 'but I doubt we'll live to see it. But I must thank you most sincerely for bringing Dr North to see me.'

'I thought it the least I could do,' she told him, then settled back in her seat. 'Now, will you tell me some of my fortune? I find that even though James is scarce coffined, would-be husbands are gathering around me like bees about a honeypot, and while

I'm still firm in my purpose not to rush again into marriage, I would appreciate knowing if any of these present suitors for my hand might eventually prove suitable.'

She gave him the information he required as to her age and, as nearly as possible, the exact time, as well as the date, of her birth and watched closely as he drew a careful figure based on the calculations he had made. 'I think you are right in pursuing the course you have set for yourself,' he told her, 'nor do I see any proper man about you at present. I am sure, though, that you will eventually remarry but in your own time. I suspect your husband will appear from some unexpected quarter and that when he does, you will recognise he is the one for you.' He smiled at her. 'You are very fortunately placed. Few girls of your age have so much independence and choice.'

She grinned. 'Don't think I don't appreciate it. But set against that, think what I first had to do to obtain it: marriage to a gross old man followed by an accusation of murder.'

In spite of himself Simon yawned and swiftly apologised to her. 'Forgive me, I was up most of the night nursing a badly wounded man.'

'Why was that?' she enquired.

'My man and I found him lying in an alleyway in Deptford last night. He had been stabbed in the back and I did what I could for him until further help came this morning. Indeed, when I came in and found you here I had only just come from delivering him safely to the house of Sir Walter Ralegh who knows his family.'

'He lived, then?'

'Just about,' Simon informed her. 'Though he is very sick for he lost much blood before we discovered him.'

'Why was he in Deptford?' she persisted.

Simon hesitated. 'He was there to take ship for the New World.'

Her eyes sparkled. 'Oh, how I would like that! To visit a whole New World.'

He smiled at her enthusiasm. 'Perhaps you will one day.'

They walked together across London Bridge and parted at the end of the street where she lived. She thanked him then, unexpectedly, put her hands to his face, drew it down and kissed him on the lips. He had to admit he found it pleasant and was considering whether to return it when he glanced over her shoulder to see Avisa, rooted to the spot on the opposite side of the street. She gave him one speaking look and walked quickly away. Dear God, he thought, releasing Lavinia, is there no end to my misfortune?

Lavinia looked up at him enquiringly. 'I must be about my business,' he told her gently and thanked her once again for her help. He watched her depart to her table of books and ledgers and wondered what to do next. His every instinct was to follow Avisa home and attempt an explanation, but reason told him it was impractical. What if her husband opened the door to him? Or she herself refused him entry? He decided therefore to go to the College of Physicians then send word to her when he returned home begging her either to come to him there or suggesting a discreet place where they might meet.

The Clerk who let him into the College building in Knightrider Street gave him a frosty reception. The Committee members present were busy about their own affairs, he intoned, and he could not promise that anyone would be available but he would see what he could do. However, after Simon had kicked his heels for half an hour or so in the hallway, the Clerk returned bringing with him one of the Censors who had been present at his hearing when he was sentenced to imprisonment in the Counter Gaol.

He gave Simon a disparaging look. 'Well, Forman, what is it now? I would have thought you would have kept away from us in the circumstances. I might add that left to me you would still be in gaol, countess or no countess.'

Simon reined in his temper. 'I am here because I was sent to the Counter accused of murdering a patient. Today one of your own Fellows, a physician who was actually present when James Tapworth died, called on me offering to support my view that the most likely cause of death was apoplexy and that there was no question of his being poisoned by eating the *eringo* I prescribed for him.'

The Censor was obviously taken aback. 'I find this hard to believe. Which of our Fellowship are you claiming as an ally?'

'A Dr North,' replied Simon confidently. 'Surely support from such a source must convince you, for he is not only a Fellow but was one of your Censors.'

The Censor looked at him incredulously. 'Do I understand you are speaking of Dr Henry North of Lincoln? Have you run mad that you stand there wasting my time?'

'Am I never to have anything but insults from this place?' shouted Simon, throwing caution to the winds, 'You obviously know of Dr North and that he now lives in Lincoln, though whether or not his name is Henry I have no idea. What I'm saying is that Dr North is willing to defend my diagnosis. God's Blood, man, he was sitting in my very study only an hour since!'

The Censor turned to the Clerk. 'Fetch me the copy of the letter that I left on my desk to show this fool here.' The Clerk disappeared but returned almost at once with a paper in his hand. The Censor thrust it at Simon and instructed him to read it.

Simon did so. 'But I don't understand!' he said, baffled. 'This is a letter from the College to the University in Leyden asking them if they will give Dr North every assistance in his researches while he is with them.'

'I'm relieved to know you can read,' sneered the Censor. 'So Dr

North was sitting in your study an hour ago, was he? Then tell me how it was I myself saw him on to a vessel bound for the Low Countries two days ago. He did not stop over in London for he was delayed on his journey from Lincoln and arrived only just in time to catch the tide.'

'But a gentleman who was certainly knowledgeable in medicine, claiming to be Dr North, came to my house today, brought to me by Tapworth's widow who herself had called him in when her husband was taken ill. She heard everything he said to me.'

'Then you have been gulled, sir,' snapped the Censor, turning on his heel. 'Clerk, throw him out! Ask for help if necessary.'

Simon blundered back across London Bridge, unaware of the crowds jostling around him, even Avisa forgotten. He no longer knew what to think. He entered his house, went straight to his study and began pacing up and down trying to make some sense of it all. There was a tentative tap at the door and Anna came in bearing a small packet.

'This came for you yesterday morning, doctor, and in all the bustle of your going off to Deptford I forgot to give it to you. Forgive me. I hope it's not urgent.'

He took it from her and felt a chill of recognition as he did so. He opened it and shook out the Tarot card from within. It was the card of the Magician.

Chapter 13

More Trouble

Simon slumped back in his chair then sought out the explanatory pamphlet he had purchased along with his own set of Tarot cards after discussing their meaning with the shopkeeper. As was the case with all the Greater Trumps, the Magician had a variety of different meanings. Those attributed to that image were particularly ambiguous: it could represent either a man in search of knowledge or the elusive source of that knowledge. He wondered if in this particular case it might mean both. Not only did he feel tired but thoroughly disheartened. Two days ago he was convinced he had almost solved the mystery and that Spenser Carew had been the instigator of most, if not all, of the chain of events.

Here was a young man with an arrogant and vindictive disposition who had been spoiled from youth. Possibly he had been made to feel immature and unimportant in the deliberations of the School of the Night and, whether or not this was actually the case, had decided to show its more distinguished members that he was more than capable of causing trouble for them, gaining much satisfaction as he learned of their discomfort. He had then turned his attention to Simon in particular, because he believed the sea holly had poisoned him and that it was Simon's fault. After that the picture became more blurred but it was beyond doubt that Carew had had the opportunity to murder the printer and subsequently was sufficiently desperate to attempt to flee the country.

The notion of an accomplice was a convincing one, not least in that it offered an explanation for what had happened in Deptford. But as he sat staring into space, Simon became aware of a more chilling possibility. Suppose he had been wrong after all? Suppose it wasn't *Carew* who had an accomplice, but Carew himself who was the accomplice of another? Of a sudden he recalled what the Countess had said, that she had not thought Carew bright enough, that she feared there was a darker, subtler intelligence at work. Had he then been wrong all along?

And where did the so-called Dr North fit into the picture, if at all? He was evidently not what he had claimed to be, but he was hardly the first doctor to have passed himself off in such a way. Many competent men had been prevented from practising because they had not attended either of the universities of Oxford or Cambridge or were sufficiently well in with a Bishop or other notable allowed to grant licences to favoured practitioners. As he knew to his cost, being granted a licence even by an organisation or person accepted as being highly responsible, still did not guarantee full recognition by the College of Physicians. Presumably this 'North' was good at his work, but he was taking a very real risk by assuming the name of a physician who was still alive and practising.

Whatever the man's motives might be, Simon was sure Lavinia Tapworth had brought 'North' to see him in good faith. Therefore, what he needed to do now and urgently was to find the man as soon as possible in order to assure himself he had no connection with any of the recent happenings other than that, doctor or not, he had attended Tapworth on his deathbed. But why, if that was the case, had 'North' encouraged him to go to the College?

Presumably because he was certain the real Dr North was safe in Leyden. It was a daunting task and Simon's heart sank as he wondered where to start. As to the part played by Carew, very possibly by tomorrow he would have recovered sufficiently to be able to speak to them; in his weakened state and knowing he had been so close to death, he might feel a real need to unburden himself whatever the consequences. In the meantime life must go on and he finally wrote his letter to Avisa, despatching John Bradedge to deliver it there and then.

She arrived in person the following morning. She looked better than when he had seen her last, but had none of the bloom so often seen on women when they are with child. She allowed a chaste kiss on her cheek as he sat her down but looked at him with none of the old passion or tenderness.

He began with an explanation as to who Lavinia was and why she had come to see him, assuring Avisa that, although a widow, Mistress Tapworth was still only an impulsive young girl and had acted as she had out of gratitude, embracing him as she might an uncle or even her father. Not surprisingly, Avisa did not appear completely convinced of this but seemed prepared to accept what he had to say at least for the time being. He then told her as briefly as he could of the predicament in which he found himself, but she seemed to be only half listening, remote in some world of her own. Finally he stopped, unable to go on any further in view of her silence and lack of response.

'Are you feeling unwell?' he queried. 'Or is it that you're worried for the safety of the child?'

'I'm well enough,' she told him. 'At least, the sickness is past and as for the child, it moves and seems lively enough. It is in my mind and heart that I feel bleak.'

It was only too apparent that her weeks in the country had changed nothing. His heart sank. While she had held him off for a considerable time, when she had finally become his mistress they had both been aware of the possible consequences.

'Are you telling me that you still feel racked by guilt?'

She clenched her hands. 'This monstrous deception of William, it goes against every tenet of my religion and I have nowhere to turn. There is no priest of my faith to whom I can confess and who could advise me, possibly even shrive me, for they dare not practise now on pain of death. Nor is there any friend or family in whom I dare confide, not even my mother who is now in London spending a few days with us. I have to bear my burden and my secret alone.'

Her words hit him hard for they posed a real dilemma. He had always known that the woman who had brought her up was not her real mother but her aunt. Indeed, he and Avisa had first met at the graveside of Avisa's *real* mother who had been one of his patients and who had confessed to him, when dying, that she had given birth to a child which was not her husband's while he had been away at sea and that her sister had agreed to take the baby and bring her up as her own child. The dying woman too had been a recusant and had pleaded with Simon to hear her confession since there was no Mass priest able to do so. He had promised then, and kept that promise, never to break her confidence.

Now he wished there was some way around an undertaking he had made so easily, never imagining it would come back to haunt him. Surely the woman who had been such a loving mother to Avisa in every way, excepting that of giving her life, would show understanding and find a way of helping her.

'Why don't you say anything?' Avisa demanded.

'What do you want me to say?' Simon replied in frustration. 'We have been through this over and over again. We are virtually certain the child is mine, both from its likely date of conception and because, throughout fifteen years of marriage during which you have always played your part as a wife, you have hitherto been childless; you have not even miscarried. To all intents and purposes therefore you were a barren wife. You have never really told me what passes between you and your husband in the privacy of the bedchamber but if, as I suspect, you were still having congress with him while also allowing me to make love to you at the same time, then there is still the remote possibility that it is, after all, his child. So let him think so. It's what he's always wanted.'

He came and stood over her. 'You are not the only one to suffer,' he said savagely. 'It gives me no pleasure to be unable to acknowledge that I have fathered a child on the woman I love. Do you think I'm not racked with jealousy? That I won't worry myself to death about you when I hear you are in labour? Have to smile and grit my teeth when told of the grand christening and all the celebrations following the birth of an heir to the family business, particularly if the child should be a boy.'

She got up from her seat and burst into tears, pulling away from him. 'You don't understand,' she sobbed. 'You don't care.'

Exhausted and worried as he was, for the first time in the two years of their relationship he lost his temper with her. 'And neither do you. Have you even taken in what I've been saying to you? You are burdening me with all this when I'm being hunted down by a mischief-maker intent on my destruction. I thought I'd discovered his identity but now no longer know what to think. Already there have been deaths and near-deaths: possibly some poisonings, a man hanged from his own beam and he I'd thought to be at the root of the trouble stabbed in the back by some unknown assailant.

'Yet still you go on and on about your child, the baby you told me so often you desperately wanted and now have every prospect, God willing, of holding in your arms at long last. God's Blood, woman, think of your child for a change! It needs a healthy mother, calm in her mind, to welcome it into this hard world. Whatever sins you want to heap upon yourself, this child is innocent of them.'

She looked at him open-mouthed. She had never seen him like this. Hitherto he was always the one who begged for favours, pleaded with her for her love, had done everything in his power to please her. She could never have believed he would speak to her in such a fashion.

'I hate you!' she cried, sweeping up her cloak. 'I never want to see you again.'

'That's for you to decide,' he shouted at her. 'But before you do so, talk to your mother, will you? Do this one last thing for me – for *us*. Tell her the situation and how you feel and ask her if there is anything you should know.'

'What now?' she enquired, through her tears. 'Are you maligning my mother too? Like mother, like daughter, is that it? Are you daring to suggest I am not my father's child?'

He almost pushed her through the door and out of the house. 'No,' he said as he did so, 'rather the reverse. She is a woman I greatly admire and respect.' He gripped Avisa by the arms. 'Let her talk some sense into you, after which we'll meet again.'

She freed one of her hands and slapped him hard across the face, leaving him reeling, not only from the blow but from the intention behind it. 'Never!' she declared, and walked away in the direction of the Bridge.

He must, he really must put this to one side, he told himself, whatever the cost. He dare not even think about it until the other matter was resolved. At one time he would have run after her begging her to forgive him, to return with him and mend matters. Now all he could see was the impossibility of there ever being a resolution to his loving another man's wife.

Meanwhile the morning was getting on and he had still heard

nothing from Ralegh. Since there were no patients requiring his attention and he felt trapped inside his four walls, he determined to discover how his patient was faring and so took a boat across to the Strand and presented himself at Ralegh's house. Sir Walter appeared almost at once and took him into a small dayroom where they could not be overheard.

The news was reassuring. 'He's certainly better than he was. The fever appears to have broken and the wound is clean.'

'May I see him then?'

Ralegh hesitated. 'There is a difficulty. He has spoken a little . . . God save me, to put it bluntly he says he will not see you or have you anywhere near him.'

Simon looked aghast. 'I don't understand. If it hadn't been for John and me he would have died. Surely he knows that?'

Ralegh sighed. 'I don't know what maggots he has in his brain. All I know is that when he came to he was rambling about you, indeed worse than that, blaming you for the attack on him.'

'Then it is even more important I see him straight away,' said Simon, 'not only to put his mind at rest regarding my own part in the affair but to see if he has any other ideas as to who might have wanted him dead. Not to mention all the other business, though I'm now having some serious doubts about that,' and he told Ralegh of his growing suspicion that Carew might have been an accomplice to whoever was at the back of their troubles, rather than it being the other way around.

Ralegh looked unhappy. 'There is a further development about which you should know. His parents are here. No,' he added, seeing Simon's surprise, 'my messages did not reach them, neither the first one telling them he was planning to leave the country, nor the more urgent one informing them that he was wounded, perhaps mortally. As it happens they came seeking him of their own accord to haul him back to Devon for he is in trouble of quite a different sort to anything we imagined – and it certainly explains his sudden decision to leave the country.

'His father tells me he was contracted to marry the daughter of a neighbouring landowner of great wealth, and now I come to think of it I seem to recall having heard as much some years ago. The match had been planned since their childhoods. The contract was properly witnessed, the settlements drawn up and signed and plans were in the final stages for the wedding. Then, just before our meeting at Sherborne, they discovered that he went through some form of marriage with the slut he brought down to visit him there. A young woman from God alone knows where who has been passed from hand to hand around half the men at Court! You can imagine the uproar this caused. Not only has the legal contract between the two families been broken and the prospective bride insulted and jilted shortly before the wedding day, he has disgraced his entire family. No wonder he saw flight as the only means of escape from the situation he has brought about.'

It certainly was reason enough but Simon was still sure Carew had played his own part in the affair, if only a minor one. It further confirmed his growing belief that he was not the main protagonist. Mary Herbert was right. He should have kept an open mind.

'You're quite sure I can't see him?' he asked Ralegh again.

'Not today, certainly. I've called in my own man and I promise I'll do my best to change his mind. His parents only arrived late last night and I've had little chance to talk with them properly, but I will assure them not only that you had no part in his attack but that you had every reason for preventing it. I have already stressed to them that you saved his life and that he is rambling.'

There was obviously nothing further to be gained. 'What did he say about me?' enquired Simon as they made their way toward the door.

Ralegh frowned. 'It was somewhat disjointed as you might imagine. When I said you would be coming this morning to see how he did he became very distressed, indeed to the point of crying out, "Don't let him near me!" and "Surely you know he tried to kill me?". I told him he raved but he wouldn't have it, tossing about and muttering that you would not rest until he was dead.'

Simon was about to take his leave when he was suddenly seized by a monstrous idea. 'Can you recall his exact words? Did he actually say that you must keep the doctor away from him? Or that *Dr Forman* meant to kill him?'

Ralegh was obviously puzzled. 'I don't understand.'

'I'm not sure I do – yet,' Simon told him. 'Can you remember his exact words?'

Ralegh thought for a minute. 'Now you mention it, I believe he simply raved on about a doctor so I assumed it must be you.'

'From the very beginning of this affair I have been haunted by mysterious doctors,' declared Simon. 'When I was in the Counter Gaol, one of the prisoners, now released, spoke of a physician who lodged above the shop of that very printer we found hanged, a man who claimed to be "the cleverest doctor in London" or even the world. He was the first. Then, before I was released, I was asked to attend on a man who was seriously ill and who, like Carew, took fright. He started crying out about a doctor with some kind of mark on his hand. Then I discover that yet another physician, a "Dr North", was called in to attend the man I was supposed to have poisoned when he was dying. So I make enquiries about him and find that he is a respected doctor who now lives in Lincoln.

'But it does not end there, for yesterday Tapworth's widow brings me a man claiming to be this very Dr North! He is most friendly, agrees with me that the man most likely died of an apoplexy, assures me he will support me if I am arraigned in any way again and claims to be a Fellow of the College of Physicians and a past Censor.

'So, I go immediately to Knightrider Street to inform the College that one of their very own Fellows is prepared to give me his support and defend my diagnosis if need be – and what happens? They show me a copy of a letter that Dr North is taking with him to the University of Leyden, and the Censor to whom I spoke swore he had seen Dr North on to a boat bound for the Low Countries two days earlier.'

'You did not take the man who visited you for a quack or a charlatan then?' Ralegh's eyes gleamed with interest at Forman's story.

'Not at the time – he seemed most knowledgeable. And even after I had seen for myself that the real Dr North was not in the country, at first I merely thought it amounted to no more than the fellow claiming qualifications he did not in fact possess. I could not altogether blame him, for I know only too well the attitude of the College to those they consider to be unworthy of a licence, however skilled and experienced they might be. I did think he had taken a considerable risk by passing himself off as a real doctor, and obviously I felt angry at having exposed myself to the ridicule of the College, but now I am beginning to think there is something more sinister about this plethora of "doctors".'

Ralegh looked sombre. 'This is a dark business but I'm not sure what it is you are suggesting.'

'I think it could be that there is not a host of unknown "doctors" but one alone. And it's essential that I find him, whoever he is, before there is even more mayhem.'

'Do you have any idea at all as to his true identity?'

'I think he is the Magician,' said Simon and left.

He walked back along the north bank looking down at every

flight of water steps to see if he could see Roger Warren, finally discovering him jostling with the rest at Blackfriars.

'You certainly get yourself into trouble, Dr Forman,' Roger commented as he pulled away from the bank. 'I went back to Deptford with a fare yesterday and was told you'd found your man half dead in an alleyway, stabbed in the back. Did he live?'

'Oh, he's alive all right and I think he'll survive,' Simon assured him, 'but that's not the end of the matter. Now, when we get to the other side I want you to come in with me, for there are things I need to discuss with you. I'll pay you the cost of another river crossing and if you'd like to bring your woman in to see me I'll cast her horoscope for nothing.'

Roger beamed. 'She'll be really pleased. We're to be wed next week. She says she's quickened but I tell her it's just the wind!'

He tied up his boat at the Bankside and followed Simon into the house. Simon took him through to the kitchen and asked Anna for ale for them both. 'Now,' he said, 'I'm sorry to have to go through all this again but I want you to describe for me once more the doctor who treated your eyes, the "cleverest doctor in the world". I want to know *exactly* what he looked like – the shape of his face, his features or as much as you could see of them, for I recall you said he wore a close-fitting hat. Tell me again how tall he was, how he was dressed, how he spoke. Everything.'

Roger looked at him thoughtfully. 'Well, doctor, it's a funny thing but I could swear I've seen him again.'

'When?' demanded Simon. 'Where?'

'Yesterday – close by the Rose Theatre. I tried to attract his attention but there was a great crowd going in and he was among them and he didn't see me though I shouted and waved.'

'He's not changed much, then?'

Roger shook his head. 'A bit older, but aren't we all? As to his looks, I told you true when I said there was not much to tell. A little shorter than yourself, still, well, *distinguished-looking*, I think they call it. The very picture of a piss-prophet and figure caster, dark blue velvet doublet and breeches, great hat with a plume . . .'

He had described 'Dr North'. 'Listen,' Simon told him, 'I want you to look out for him for me most urgently. The best thing possible would be for you to have him in your boat.'

'I can hardly bring him to you if he wants to go somewhere else,' objected Roger. 'He could say I'd abducted him, and then where would I be? What's the word of a professional gentleman against an old runagate and copesman?'

'If this particular "professional gentleman" has done what I think he has,' returned Simon, 'then you are a very paragon of virtue by comparison.' He paid Roger for his time, then sent him away and went in search of John Bradedge, to bring him up-to-date with the latest development.

John listened to what he had to say about Carew then threw up his hands. 'Here we go, doctor, blamed for everything as usual. The ungrateful coxcomb! Surely he must be made to realise that we saved his life? Didn't I ride all that way on that apology for a nag (my backside is still sore) to fetch help for him? And you sit up half the night tending his wound? So he's running away because he's married a common slut and upset his folks – is that it? Are you now telling me the young swine's got nothing to do with your troubles?'

'No, I still think he was responsible for them in some part but that he was, possibly unknowingly, only a puppet for another. Behind all this I now begin to see the shadowy figure of a doctor or a man who calls himself one. Could it not be that the fellow who lodged over the print shop, about whom I had you enquire what seems like half a year ago, is the very same man who came here yesterday calling himself Dr North and falsely claiming he was a Fellow of the College of Physicians?'

John scratched his head. 'So what do we do now?'

'I want you to go first to Lavinia Tapworth. Say you come on my behalf as I am busy with patients, and that after visiting the College of Physicians I wanted to thank Dr North and speak to him again, but the College were unable to tell me his direction in London. Try and find out if she has any idea where he lodges. Then, whether or not she is able to tell you anything useful, enquire around in the City and see if he's known there, either under the name of North or any other. You know how to set about it, you're becoming something of an expert!'

'You don't think he's really a doctor then?'

'I'm not saying that,' replied Simon. 'He might be. Like me he might have studied abroad and is licensed to practise by some body other than the College. But if he is truly a physician then I fear he might well be a disgrace to our profession.'

'So, you reckon this man could be behind it all?' John looked thoughtful. 'What you're saying is that he's both "the cleverest doctor in the world" who shared a house with the printer, *and* "Dr North" *and* . . . God's Breath!' He stopped suddenly and looked at Simon as the same idea occurred to them both.

'And,' continued Simon, 'that grave and professional-looking gentleman, to use the description afforded by the landlady of the Red Bull, who visited Carew on that fateful afternoon. It has to be!'

Chapter 14

The Search for the Magician

John walked briskly across London Bridge, happy in his task. Apart from the misunderstanding over the forged letter and a much earlier occasion when he had been persuaded to dispense medicine by a dominating young woman against the doctor's orders, his relationship with his master had been an excellent one and he saw no reason why it should not continue. More than that, on two occasions he had actually saved the doctor's life. On the first of their adventures he'd arrived in time to preventing his being drowned in the Thames by two villains (in spite of his master having told him he didn't need any help) and on the second he had helped rescue him from the Edinburgh gallows.

The trouble with these professional folk with all their book-learning was that they often lacked basic common sense and as to the doctor, well he really was a one for rushing into things without any thought of the dangers he might get himself into. He needed a fellow with his head on his shoulders to put him right. Just think what might have happened that first time if he'd done as he was told and left his master to his own devices. All right, so he'd thought he was going off for a bit of bedwork with a fancy piece who gave herself airs but it had looked suspicious to him from the start.

As to what had happened in Scotland . . . he shivered. Savages, that's what they were, up there on the Borders. They even spoke a foreign language. But mighty fighters, he had to give them that. There was a girl there too, he recalled, a young redhead who wielded a sword like a man. Ah well, the doctor was always weak where women were concerned. What he needed now was to find himself a bride, not go carrying on with another man's wife.

He was so deep in thought he almost passed by the Tapworths' door. He was shown in to see Lavinia immediately he presented himself. She looked eagerly up from her ledgers and an expression of profound disappointment crossed her face.

'Oh,' she said. 'So *you* are the real Master Bradedge.'

He looked at her nonplussed. 'Why, mistress. Did you expect someone else?'

'Dr Forman called himself Master Bradedge when he came to see me first,' she informed him. 'I think it was for fear my brother-in-law was here. I thought he might have done so again.'

She was a very pretty and tempting young lady, John thought. Possibly even a hot piece . . . He pulled himself together and cleared his throat. 'The doctor's sent me on his behalf, since he is much occupied with patients, to ask if you know where he might find Dr North. He wishes to thank him for his help and would also like to talk over certain other matters.' He thought he put that rather well.

She shook her head. 'I'm sorry, but I don't know. I believe he said that he'd lodgings in the City somewhere near Cheapside but I thought he told Dr Forman that the College authorities would know where to find him. Didn't your master ask them?'

It was a good question and John considered how best to answer it. 'I believe the person to whom he spoke at the College did not know,' he told her mendaciously, adding, 'I think he said it was because the doctor had recently changed his direction, but it could be that he was just putting him off because of the disagreement my master has with the College.'

'I see.' Lavinia did not seem inclined to continue the conversation. 'Is there anything else?' she enquired, making obvious play with adding up columns of figures.

'My master found Dr North most interesting,' John continued, determined to carry out his mission to the letter, 'and also wondered what else you might know of him.'

Again she looked blank. 'Very little. I met him for the first time when he was called to James, although my late husband had told me of their previous meeting. Then, as I told Dr Forman, he arrived on my doorstep of his own accord the other day to see how I was, which I thought most kind of him. We took some wine together and chatted a little but I did not learn much from it. No doubt like most men he considers that his work and the mysteries of medicine are far above the heads of women, especially young women.' She frowned in concentration. 'I had the feeling – it was no more – that he had studied on the Continent and had connections there, but I might well be wrong.' She then made it quite evident that she intended getting on with her work and so he thanked her for her trouble and left her to her books. Well, he had learned little or nothing there.

An hour and many enquiries later he was no further on. By this time he had reached Cheapside with its shops and stalls and, gritting his teeth, had asked the owner of each of them, along with their customers, if they knew of the whereabouts of a doctor called North. Soon he was overloaded with the names and directions of doctors, barber-surgeons and apothecaries by whom his various informants swore, some even recommending a Dr Simon Forman who lived on the Bankside but no one had heard of a Dr North. Finally he reached a group of stallholders who were busily shutting up shop and asked his question of the nearest of them. The man shook his head but called out noisily to a colleague across the road who, in turn, shouted at the stallholder beside him.

In no time a number of customers had joined in and the name 'Dr North' was bandied from side to side of the street until a casement was opened above them and a head, swathed in a nightcap, poked out and asked what all the hue and cry was about.

'Forgot to get up did you, Grandad?' chuckled one of the men.

'Hardly worth bothering now, it'll soon be night again,' quipped another.

'Got some hot whore up there teaching you tricks?' suggested another.

The elderly face at the window scowled. 'If you must know I played cards and dice all night and went to bed this morning with a foul head which still plagues me. Your yelling doesn't help. What's this "Dr North" done that he's wanted so urgently?'

'Dunno,' said the man who'd first spoken, pointing at John. 'It's him who's asking after him.'

'Well, if it'll shut you up, there's a doctor who's been drinking in the Cock tavern in Fleet Street – I think he calls himself North. Try there and leave me in peace,' and with that the man in the nightcap snapped the window to and pulled his hangings across to shut out the light.

Very well, thought John, I'll try just once more and anyway, I could do with a quart or so of ale. And with that he retraced his steps towards Ludgate and from there to the Cock tavern. His enquiries of the landlord bore little fruit, however. The name meant nothing and the description of a well-dressed, professional-looking man of middle age was greeted with the information that it might fit any number of customers since the tavern was so near both to the Inns of Court and the City merchants. 'Though most folk like that drink in one of the private rooms,' he concluded.

John was just considering whether or not to order a second quart of ale when a rough-looking fellow entered, looked around at the drinkers and asked loudly if the cove was about who'd been asking after Dr North. Somewhat surprised, John made himself known. The man grinned through blackened teeth then came over and seated himself beside him. He was extremely dirty and gave off such an unpleasant smell that John swiftly moved a foot or so away. 'You aren't proposing to gull me that *you* are Dr North?' he demanded.

'Nah. Tannin', leather goods, that's me. Obadiah Smith's the name. Ask anyone up the hill – they all know me. That's why I came down here looking for the fellow who was asking after Dr North, for it seems everyone in the Cheap knew you was wanting him. What's up then? Wife with child? Daughter with the green-sickness? Got the pox?'

'I don't see why I should tell you,' John retorted.

'Suit yourself,' the man replied. 'But if you'll stand me a quart of ale I'll take you to where North lives. 'E's got lodgings just roun' the corner from me.'

Still unsure as to whether he was about to be cheated by a rogue into buying him a drink, he called the tapster over and ordered a quart for Smith and a pint for himself. The ale duly arrived and the trader picked up his tankard and drained half of it in one mighty swallow. 'Phwor, that's better,' he said, setting it down. There was a dirty bandage round his hand that had almost come adrift, its ends dangling over the tankard.

'Watch out,' warned John, 'or you'll have that in your drink.'

Smith looked down and smartly tightened it with his teeth. 'I was going to see old North about this when I got 'ome. Knife slipped, the one what I cuts the skins with. I bound it up best I could but now it's gone bad on me. Thought he might be able to give me somethin' to put on it. Can be nasty, you know. Knew an old fellow cut his thumb with the same knife he cut up skins and he were dead within the week.' He downed the rest of the ale then stood up. 'You comin' or not?'

John wondered what to do for the best. The doctor had given him no instructions about actually visiting North but he had also given him a free hand. He came to a decision. He would go along with Smith and find out where North lived and then make some excuse to go back home.

'How is it that you know about Dr North when no one else in the City seems to have heard of him?' he asked the tanner.

'Easy,' replied his odorous companion. 'He's only been in his lodgings a week or two and from what he was saying I take it he's not staying long since he doesn't live in London.'

'Do you live far?' asked John as they set off in a north-westerly direction.

'Far enough. Up almost to Holbourne right by the dirty old Fleet. I brings the cart when there's lots to carry.'

John grimaced. 'By the Fleet? It's no better than a sewer. How do you stand it?' Even as he asked he thought it was a foolish question since the man himself smelled so foul and did not appear to notice it.

'Oh, you gets used to it. It's not that bad all the time and in my trade you're used to smells.'

Half an hour later they were standing outside a dismal row of ramshackle buildings and warehouses, and the stench from the Fleet was such that John decided he would never get used to it if he lived there for half a century. It was getting dark and beginning to rain. 'Is this it?' demanded John. 'What have you brought me here for? Surely you aren't going to make me believe that a doctor, a professional man, lives in a place like this.'

'Not smart enough for you, eh?' the man rejoined. 'See that archway? Go through there and there's three or four fine timber houses. The doctor lodges in the second one on the right, upstairs on the first floor. If he's in, the door'll be open.'

This was the time to turn back, thought John, now that he had found out what he had been sent to discover, but he was intrigued to take a look at this Dr North for himself. When he'd visited his master Anna had let him in and Simon had shown him out so he'd had no chance to see the man for himself. It would be easy enough to come up with some mild complaint that would not require an astrological casting. He felt in his pocket. He should have just about enough to pay the man. He looked round. Smith had disappeared, presumably into a rat hole of his own.

He walked through the archway. The trader was right. There were several substantial dwellings inside although they looked as if they had fallen on hard times. The second on the right . . . a light glimmered in an upstairs window. The doctor must be in then. He pushed at the front door which opened and swung inward on creaking hinges. The hallway inside was very dark.

'Anyone there?' he called out.

There was no reply. Tentatively he made his way up the staircase and called again. Still nothing. He carried on upwards, carefully holding on to the rail at the side. In the gloom he could see that the door at the top was ajar, the light, stronger now, clearly visible. He went over to the doorway. There appeared to be no one there but dimly he could see shelves on which were books, jars and glass phials, not unlike the doctor's study at home. A mystical figure was painted on the floor.

He suddenly felt uneasy. He had seen enough, he'd go home now and report to his master. He was turning to do so when the blow caught him on the back of the head and he fell forwards into a pit of darkness.

* * *

It had been an eventful day, thought Simon, first the quarrel with Avisa, then the visit to Ralegh and now sending John Bradedge off in search of Dr North. He was thankful he had no patients for he was in need of both peace and quiet. But it seemed there was to be more excitement yet, for within half an hour of John tramping off towards London Bridge he heard the sound of wheels outside the door and voices, followed by a peremptory bang on the knocker.

Oh no, he thought, not the College! Surely the physicians haven't decided already to put me back in gaol? Anna almost ran to open the door, stood and gaped at what she saw then came back in a flutter to tell him that there was a grand lady outside proposing to visit him. He went at once to see who it was, to find no lesser person than Mary Herbert, Countess of Pembroke, on his doorstep. He greeted her formally then looked past her to the carriage and the maid waiting outside.

'Oh, I've told George to bring the carriage back at the end of the afternoon,' she told him. 'I'm sure he and my maid can find somewhere to wait and the groom can walk the horses if necessary,' and with an airy wave of her hand she dismissed them. He swept her inside while Anna, her eyes like saucers, took her cloak. The Countess was, he noticed, more plainly dressed than usual and without her entourage could well have been taken for a merchant's wife. Possibly that was her intention. He showed her into his study and sent for refreshments.

Once inside she gave him a mischievous smile. 'Well, Simon, I told you I'd call on you one day unexpectedly. I trust the visit is not inconvenient?'

He assured her that it was not, wondering the while what had prompted it today of all days.

'I first visited your actor friend, Tom Pope and his family. He has two fine boys, has he not? I hope I reassured Mistress Pope that I had no designs on her husband after the gossip I'm sure arose following our private meeting on your behalf. Not that he isn't a most handsome man and an excellent actor.' She glanced round Simon's study at the books, the crowded shelves, the mortars and pestles, jars of salves, phials and flasks. Sheets of paper covered with calculations for horoscopes lay scattered across his desk.

'You are obviously a very busy man,' she commented. 'What occupies you most? Your medical practice or the casting of horoscopes?'

'Probably the former,' he told her, 'though as you know most physicians also use the planets to help us forecast the outcome of illness or injury. But mostly I am applied to for horoscopes by those wanting to know such mundane matters as whether their argosy will come safe home to port, if there is a handsome husband on the horizon or if their wives are faithful to them!'

The countess began walking round the room, picking up and examining objects as her fancy took her for all the world as if they were old friends and she a frequent visitor. She stopped in front of his small library of books, then turned and smiled. 'I've often thought I'd have liked to be a physician,' she said. 'I am fascinated by scientific matters as you know, and it would be such a challenge to try and discover what ailed people and then seek to cure them.'

Simon laughed. 'You're the second woman who has said that to me in as many days.'

'Dear me, how dull,' she retorted. 'And there was I thinking I was quite an original. Might one ask who the other lady was?'

'A brisk young woman of but sixteen years. The widow of that very man I was accused of poisoning.' He gave a rueful smile. 'Pretty she may be but she has a mind like a steel trap and is about as soft. I marvel at how her next husband or lover will fare and she still hardly more than a maid. But delectable as she is, I have no wish to find out for myself.'

'And you? Have you at present no mistress?'

'I thought I had. Now I'm not so sure.'

She smiled thoughtfully then changed the subject and came back and sat opposite to him. 'I visited Ralegh today, you must only just have left. He told me of your recent adventures in Deptford and some of your thoughts on our pressing matter.'

'I should have listened to you,' he told her, 'rather than rush off as I did, so sure that I had the answers and that Carew was at the back of it all. You were right, of course.'

She made a gesture of dismissal. 'As it turns out I was, but there was no real proof either way. I merely found Carew a shallow young man with what I considered insufficient intellect to carry out so diverse a campaign. One or two things, yes. Posting bills all round the town, printing slanderous pamphlets about me, writing letters to the authorities accusing Hariot of blasphemy, but as for the rest . . . I understand you've come round to my way of thinking, that we have here a far subtler and more ruthless intelligence.'

He agreed and explained how he had arrived at his opinion and the possible link between the mysterious doctor who had once lived over the print shop and 'Dr North'. 'Not only was he the doctor who so fortuitously, it seems, met up with Tapworth the day before he died but also attended on him when he did. Mind you, he seemed plausible enough when we discussed the case and I believed him when he said he'd been a Fellow of the College as well as a Censor before I discovered there was indeed such a Dr North but that he was not the man.'

'So you are now seeking him out?'

'Even as we speak my servant, John Bradedge, is combing the City for him.'

'You think he will succeed in his quest?'

Simon smiled. 'He's done so many times in the past and is now adept at being my eyes and ears and gathering information.' Suddenly he recalled the second Tarot card. 'I also received this,' he said, producing the Magician. 'Even if I didn't now know that Carew was escaping from a jilted bride and two angry families rather than the might of the law, I can't see him sending it to me.'

She took it up and examined it. 'It is from the same pack as the other, obviously. I sent to Dr Dee as I promised but have heard nothing in return so far; it could be that he is not well. I must try and pay him a visit. Do you know its meaning?'

'I think so, though I'm not sure. I understand the figure can mean either a searcher after knowledge or its source. Since we met I bought a pack of my own and with them some notes as to patterns of the cards and their meanings but I've had no time to study them.'

'Then let us see if they can tell us anything,' returned the countess and Simon took the pack out of a drawer, put them on his desk in front of her and she took out the Greater Trumps. She gave him an impish look. 'Now, I will choose the card I think suitable for you and we will make some patterns and see if we can learn anything.'

'What card's that?' he asked, intrigued in spite of himself.

'Wait and see.' She spread the cards out in several different ways, pursing her lips and shaking her head from time to time. 'I think you too could be the Magician, the seeker of truth, but that is not what I've chosen for you. Can you guess your card?'

He bent forward and picked up the one she had placed in the centre. 'My thanks, lady,' he said with irony. 'I should have guessed I was the Fool. Here I am in this picture blithely going on my way, staring up at the stars and about to step over a precipice.'

'But in my own pack,' she told him, 'the Fool is made to look a giant among men, and in another I have seen he appears in the guise of the god Mercury who is also related to the Magician, which is highly apposite in your case. I think it says that you are prepared to go where others fear to tread, but that does not necessarily mean you are a fool. They also say the Fool makes things happen, that he does not of himself set events in train but they occur because of him and that he concludes them. That seems to me very apt.'

She became more serious. 'But I don't need the cards to tell me that you are now in no small danger. This doctor, magician, whoever he is will want to put an end to you and so finish the business. Once you are gone I doubt he will continue causing trouble for the rest of us.' She looked round the room again, then stretched her arms above her head. 'Have you any other plans for this afternoon, Simon?'

'No,' he answered in some surprise. 'Why do you ask?'

'I don't expect my carriage to return for me for at least an hour and therefore we need to find a way of entertaining ourselves.' Her meaning was obvious.

He thought of Avisa, of how they had parted and how she had refused to let him near her for weeks. It was, quite possibly, the end of the affair. It was a rare offer. Mary Herbert was very attractive and as he knew from his one previous experience, both generous and skilled in the art of love.

'You hesitate,' she mocked. 'Still fearful of a jealous mistress?'

He made up his mind. 'Next door there is a small sitting room in which there is a daybed. Shall we adjourn? I'm sure there is much more you can teach me about Tarot cards.'

It was dusk; they both heard a clock chime six as the countess's carriage returned. Simon handed her into it. 'We must meet again,' she said affectionately. 'Sometime I would like to hear of your adventures in Scotland.'

He was suddenly brought back to earth and the old suspicions. *Did* she also sleep with Robert Cecil? Was it possible Cecil had set her on this course for his own ends? Mary Herbert looked at the shadow crossing his face and uncannily read his mind.

'Are you thinking of Cecil? Don't be afraid I'll reveal any of your confidences to him. He and I have a strange relationship; we both respect each other's intelligence and share some of the same interests, even desires. I enjoy the spice of danger it gives me to dally with him a little. But I would not trust him with my life or that of anyone else for whom I cared.'

Simon went back into the house. Two almost sleepless nights, a tiring chain of events and an hour or so of sport with the countess had left him quite exhausted. He was behind with writing up his case notes and he determined he would spend some time on them then go early to bed. It grew dark and he lit the candles. After some time it occurred to him that John Bradedge must have returned by now and wondered why he had not been in to tell him what, if anything, he had been able to discover. But possibly there'd been nothing to report and he'd decided not to interrupt his master while he was closeted with his illustrious visitor in the small sitting room.

Half an hour later he went into the kitchen to find Anna trying to persuade her small son to go to bed. She looked up at him anxiously. 'Where did you send John, doctor? I'd expected him home well before now.'

Simon looked at her in surprise. 'He's still not back then? I assumed he must have returned a while ago. I didn't send him far afield, only to Mistress Tapworth's and then to make some enquiries for me in the City.' He frowned. 'He must have been told something that made him decide to pursue his task elsewhere.

I'm sure you've no need to worry. We both know how well he can look after himself.' She nodded and began to wash the child's face, somewhat reassured.

It was odd though, he thought as he left her. John was usually so reliable. He was not the kind of servant who would drink the night away or romp in brothels when let out of the household. He was diligent and, unless prevented by unforeseen circumstances, punctual. Simon yawned, overcome with weariness. There was nothing for it: he had to go to bed. No doubt by the time he awoke John would be sitting eating his breakfast at the kitchen table with a perfectly good explanation for his prolonged disappearance.

As was often the case when he had a good deal on his mind he was subject to uneasy dreams. In the longest one he was pursuing a shadowy figure down long corridors that twisted back on themselves and flights of stairs which led upwards only to go down again then, just when he thought he had his hand on the object of his pursuit, it turned and began to chase him so that he laboured back up the stairs, slipping on them and bruising his limbs before tumbling headlong down the next flight. Next he was seated again with Lavinia Tapworth and North, in his plumed hat, who was laughing and holding up a chalice full of red wine between his gloved hands as if it were the Eucharist.

Finally he was in some dark place, part refuge, part prison, while outside unknown people were banging at the door trying to get in. He struggled awake but the knocking continued and would not stop. He blinked in the half-light and called out to whoever it was to come in.

It was Anna, white-faced and distraught. 'It's John, doctor. He never came back. What do you think has happened to him?'

Chapter 15

The Tyburn Brand

He dressed rapidly and as soon as it was decently possible raced over to Lavinia's house and banged on the door. It was opened to him by a surprised servant who informed him coolly that the mistress was at breakfast and not receiving visitors. Simon made no attempt to argue but pushed past him and strode into the house. He found Lavinia, prettily dishevelled and dressed in a plain gown, seated at the table in her parlour. She looked at him in some surprise.

'He rushed in, I couldn't stop him,' explained the servant who had panted in behind.

She waved him away and motioned to Simon to join her, offering him some bread and honey. 'I'm flattered that you are so desperate to see me, Dr Forman, but I think this must be something more important than a social call.'

Simon agreed that it was. 'It's about my servant, John Bradedge. I presume he did come to see you yesterday afternoon?'

'Yes,' she replied, obviously curious. 'At first I thought it might be you since you gave yourself that name when you came here first. He explained that you were busy then told me you wanted to know more of Dr North, also his direction. I'm afraid I wasn't very helpful as I know so little myself, since I met him for the first time when James died and it was he who sought me out some days ago, not I that sent for him. As to his direction, I thought the College of Physicians could have told you that. Why do you ask?'

'Because John never returned last night.'

She shrugged. 'So? A servant sent out by his master does what he's asked to do then, loath to return to his work, drinks in the taverns, perhaps seeks out some old friends or takes a whore, who knows? Surely it's common enough? No doubt he'll arrive back this morning, if he hasn't already done so, with a thick head and you can dress him down or beat him as your fancy takes you.'

'But it's not like that,' he told her. 'John is more than an ordinary servant, he's my trusted right-hand man and he doesn't behave in such a manner. I sent him to ask about North because I now know for certain that he's not who he says he is: more than that, I believe he's dangerous.'

Lavinia's eyes widened. 'I see. No doubt you have your reasons for concluding that, but I must say I'm surprised.'

He told her briefly of his visit to the College of Physicians and its result. 'But if that were all I'd think no more of it. However, being put in gaol for poisoning your husband is only one of many mishaps I have suffered at someone's hands these past weeks. There is more I could tell you, but there is no time now. Please don't think me importunate, but before I leave you is there anything, anything at all you told John that might throw some light on why he hasn't come home?'

She considered this gravely then shook her head. 'Truly, there's nothing more I can tell you. He too asked if I knew where North had lodgings and I told him what I have just told you.' She paused. 'The doctor seemed quite plausible to me. Are you suggesting that it was he who caused James's death?'

'I believe no one was responsible for it,' he reassured her. 'It was the natural consequence of over-indulgence. But I think this "North" made use of it for his own ends.' He looked at her. 'Was there nothing at all that struck you in any way strange about him?'

She thought again. 'One thing I thought a little odd. When he and I took wine together he kept his gloves on which seemed an odd thing to do – but then we all have our little quirks. It can't be important.'

For a reason he could not explain Simon thought to himself that she was wrong. It *was* important, but why? Now she drew attention to it he realised the same had happened when North had sat drinking wine in his own house. Her comment reminded him of his dream, of North holding up a chalice of red wine in his gloved hands. He racked his brain for the connection but nothing came. Finally he thanked Lavinia and said he must leave.

'Don't be so downcast,' she told him. 'You might still find you've worried over nothing and that John Bradedge is already there, waiting for you on the Bankside.'

'I sincerely hope so,' he replied, and left her to finish her breakfast. Outside in the street he pondered on whether or not to try any of the taverns to see if he could learn anything, but there were dozens of them. It was quite possible John had been in several in his effort to discover the whereabouts of North – but which ones? He could waste the whole morning, indeed the whole day, trying to find out if anyone recalled seeing him and when.

He walked briskly back across the river, flung open the door and shouted for Anna. She came to him at once and he had no need to question her, for her face told him that there was still no sign of her husband. As he closed the door he saw that a packet had been pushed under it and picked it up, expecting another Tarot card but this one was different. He opened it and saw inside a scrawled letter while at the bottom there was something heavier.

'Did you know this letter was here, Anna?' he asked.

'No,' she said. 'I've been in the kitchen this while and heard nothing.'

From behind her he heard the child whimper. 'Go back to him and find me a glass of brandy. I'll be with you when I've read this.'

He removed the letter. *This for you, Forman,* he read. *I'm as weary of this charade as I'm sure are you. If you value your servant's life you will meet me this evening at the place I have marked on the map I have drawn below. Should you attempt to bring anyone with you or it later transpires that you have told anyone of your visit, I shall cut his throat. I am sure you will believe me capable of it. Have I not, after all, recently hanged a man? And, but for your interference, would certainly have caused the death of another. To prove to you this is no hoax I enclose your servant's wedding ring.*

He shook the packet and the ring rolled out into his hand. He went cold. How could he face Anna? Reluctantly he made his way into the kitchen to where she sat, her little boy on her knee. The lad had tears running down his cheeks. 'He can't understand why his father isn't here,' she said. 'He always plays with the boy when he rises in the morning.' Then she saw Simon's face. 'You have something bad to tell me.' She put little Simon down and rose to her feet. 'Is he dead? Is that what you've come to tell me? Was he killed in a tavern brawl or on the streets?'

He did his best to comfort her. 'He's still alive and, so far as I know, unharmed. But he's been taken by a wicked man, the same who has been causing us all so much trouble. He has written asking me to meet him tonight otherwise harm *will* come to John. In evidence of which . . .' He handed the ring to her. 'I presume it is his?'

She nodded, at first unable to speak. Then she whispered, 'We bought the two together in Holland. See, mine is exactly the same.'

Simon put his arm round her. 'I know it is almost impossible, but try not to think the worst. I will go and see what this devil wants of me and I promise you I'll do all in my power to bring John home safely.'

'Then you must take men to help you,' she warned. 'Alert the Constable.'

'If I do that he threatens he will . . . well, let's just say it's best if I go alone. But I'm not a complete fool. I will write a letter explaining what has happened, with a copy of the map the man has drawn for me. It looks as if our rendezvous is in a house close to Holbourne near to the Fleet. When I leave to keep the appointment, give me an hour then take the letter to Tom Pope and tell him what's happened, see if he has any ideas as to what to do next. In the meantime I must think this through; somehow I have to outwit this villain.'

Simon went into his study, took a piece of paper and began to list everything he knew about his antagonist. The latter had spent time in London some years previously and had openly bragged of his cleverness and skill, after which he had disappeared. Next had come a string of unpleasant incidents all involving members of the School of the Night, following which the emergence of 'Dr North' on the scene had coincided with murder, attempted murder and now blackmail. Yet all he knew about him, apart from the fact that he was utterly ruthless, was that he was not who he claimed to be. Simon paced up and down the room, thinking hard, as the germ of an idea began to form in his mind.

He must talk to Mary Herbert at once. He went into the kitchen and told Anna that he had to go out urgently but that he would be back again long before it was necessary to keep his assignation by the Fleet. If anyone came to the door asking for him, she was to say that he had been called out to attend a patient some miles away in the south. Although he rarely rode on horseback in London, on this occasion he collected his mare from the stables where he kept her and was soon trotting briskly over the Bridge, ignoring the protests of shoppers and pedestrians complaining of dangerous rakehells prepared to mow folk down as they went about their lawful business. Once he reached the other side he pressed on faster, finally clattering into the yard behind the Pembrokes' house, scattering a group of grooms who had been standing chatting together beside the countess's carriage. He dismounted, flung the reins to one of them and demanded to know from a servant who had come running to see what the fuss was, if the Countess was at home as Dr Forman needed to see her urgently on a matter of life or death.

She came at once and seeing his expression made no attempt at a joke. 'Good day, Simon, and from the early hour of your visit I imagine you meant what you said.'

Without preamble he told her what had happened then showed her the letter.

'Will you go?' she asked.

'What alternative have I? I can only hope I'm not being watched and that this villain doesn't know or suspect why I'm here or I might find myself hazarding my own life only to discover that John's already dead.' He paused.

'I understand,' she said, 'but if that is the case, why have you come to me and how do you think I can help you?'

'Because I think I might have the beginnings of an explanation, although when I make known to you what it is you may well consider I'm fit only for Bedlam. Tell me, if you will, everything you know of Edward Kelley.'

She was shocked. 'Edward Kelley? Surely you aren't suggesting

226

he's the man we've been seeking? He's been dead these last five or six years.'

'But is it absolutely certain that he's dead? Is there not the remotest possibility of a mistake? I remember at Sherborne being told he'd died abroad then later you told me he'd been executed. Are you sure that's true?'

'At first there was a rumour that he was secretly garotted in some Bohemian dungeon but later we had news that he had been publicly executed before a great crowd.'

'Do you know of any witness to the execution?'

She looked at him then slowly shook her head. 'No, now you put it to me, I know of no one here that actually saw it, but that is hardly surprising since so few Englishmen travel to Bohemia. However, there were those who described the event to Dr Dee while he was still on the Continent.'

'Do you know the nature of the charge which brought him to the scaffold?'

'I never heard what it was. It might have been serious but could easily have been nothing. No doubt he'd done everything he could to ingratiate himself with those in high places there but princelings in such realms are often fickle and can easily turn against their one-time favourites. All I'm certain of, for Dr Dee told me this himself, is that someone warned Dr Dee of what was toward and helped him escape. Dr Dee never speaks of Kelley now and out of respect for my old tutor I would be loath to raise the matter with him. He is deeply ashamed of the connection.'

'But suppose Kelley wasn't killed after all,' Simon said quietly. 'Suppose he got away and returned to England. He could hardly appear as himself, could he since, as I understand it, he was wanted for murder.'

'He killed a man, certainly,' she agreed, 'but again I know nothing of the circumstances other than he alleged it was in self-defence though it was obvious he wasn't prepared to put it to the test. No,' she said definitely, 'I'm sure you're wrong. Even if he had survived, a branded felon with cropped ears could hardly remain unnoticed.'

She was right, of course, thought Simon. Yet he still felt sure there was some connection, however tenuous. 'Did he have any pupils, disciples, call them what you will? A man with powerful influence often has such. If so, maybe one of them is determined to make everyone who had anything to do with him pay for their actions, though that would not explain what has happened to me. But then,' he admitted, 'that would rule out Kelley as well, for I never met him and was not even in London when he was in his prime.'

This time the Countess looked more convinced. 'I see what you mean. Yes, he did have a coterie of admirers, eager to learn more of the Black Arts, particularly necromancy.' She shuddered. 'The Wizard Earl told me Kelley lost his ears when he was in the service of Lord Strange and was found digging up graves to make use of the bodies for strange obscene practices such as the raising of demons and spirits. It was even said he'd taken unbaptised babies for use in the Black Mass but that I find more doubtful. But that he had an extraordinary effect on people is without argument. Ferdinand, Lord Strange, is an example for there he was, a superstitious recusant, frightened of his own shadow, yet he wouldn't hear a word against Kelley, gave him his patronage, believed he had supernatural powers.' She nodded. 'I think you might have a point. There is no doubt he was evil through and through; it is hard to imagine what makes men like that.'

'I was responsible once,' Simon told her sombrely, 'for the hanging of a young man, a player who had every gift. He was handsome, very talented – indeed, I believe he could have been one of the greatest actors of the age – intelligent and charming, and yet he murdered a fellow actor then did everything to ensure his greatest friend swung for it. He also, but for the grace of God, would have killed a child who adored him. I asked a priest what he made of such a smiling villain and he said he was like to one of the Dark Angels who fell with Lucifer.'

'Such a one as Kelley,' said the Countess grimly, 'never even fell from grace for I believe he never knew the light! But I think you could be right about this supposed disciple of his, one who has festered in his mind ever since Kelley died. No doubt Kelley had told him how he had been mocked by the learned men who now belong to the School of the Night and how he had also angered them by bringing the New Sciences into disrepute. Yes, I see why such a fellow has been determined to exact vengeance ever since on behalf of his great master. It seems you've found yourself a formidable adversary. Perhaps we should risk going together now to ask Ralegh's advice.'

But Simon was adamantly against it. 'I'm fearful enough as it is, and it would be all too easy for him to pay a fellow to watch my movements and report back to him – or even find ways of watching me himself. He seems uncannily aware of every move I make.'

'So what will you do?' she demanded. 'Whoever this man is, he means to kill you, of that I'm sure, and might well do so if you put yourself in his hands by meeting him alone and on his terms.'

'If I take anyone with me and he realises that I've done so, then I believe he will cut John's throat,' Simon said flatly. 'I've promised his wife to do all in my power to save his life, but I've also told her to give me an hour then take the note I have left with her to Tom Pope saying where I've gone, since by that time, God willing, John will have been released. If anyone is able to think up a plan to save me, then Tom Pope can; he's one of the most resourceful men I know. That's the best I can do.'

229

She went over to him and grasped his hands. 'Then I cannot see what I can do immediately to help you. So I will also allow you the time you say you need, after which I will take steps to have this criminal hunted down without mercy.'

John Bradedge blinked into consciousness sometime during the night and was, at first, completely unable to account for where he was. His head was thumping and when he tried to move he realised that his wrists and ankles were securely bound. He moved slightly and discovered that he was lying on the floor of what seemed to be a closet, the door open on a room in which a light was shining. Suddenly and painfully it all came back to him. He'd been sitting in the Cock tavern having been told Dr North had been seen drinking there, when he'd been approached by some tanner or leather-worker who'd dragged him off on a wild-goose chase, leading him to the supposed residence of the doctor. He'd walked up some stairs and then suffered a crashing blow to the head. From whom? Thieves lying in wait? As his mind cleared further an awful thought struck him regarding that helpful tanner. Obviously the man had been in league with them, but why bring him all this way? An attack in a dark alley near to the Cock would have been far easier.

He cursed himself for a fool. Why hadn't he thought it strange that the man had gone to such lengths to seek him out merely because he had heard him enquiring about a Dr North? Then he had an even worse thought. Suppose he was an accomplice to this supposed doctor. But why bring me here? he asked himself. Why not get rid of me and have done?

A movement in the room beyond drew his eyes which were now becoming accustomed to the gloom. He was also aware of a strange aromatic smell. Then the figure of a man in a long gown wearing a strange hat came into his line of vision. So far as John could tell he was standing in the middle of the figure painted on the floor, setting round its edge small lights floating in saucers. Then he turned to face where John lay and to his astonishment he saw it was the supposed tanner, though he hardly recognised him in this garb. And not only that . . . of a sudden he recalled the strange cut-off head of the night-capped man in the window who had sent him to the Cock in search of Dr North. As if aware of his gaze, the man stopped what he was doing and made his way towards him. John promptly closed his eyes, trying to breathe as regularly as he could.

The man grabbed him by the hair, almost making him cry out – then, seeing no apparent sign of life, let his head fall back with a thump on the wooden floor, bringing tears to John's eyes. Satisfied that he was still unconscious, the man returned to his work. Once again John opened a cautious eye. A small brazier stood just outside the circle and the man threw some powder on it, causing it to flare up with a lurid green glow. Then he took up a staff, returned to the middle of the circle, and banged the staff down hard on the floor.

'Come!' he intoned. 'Come, Astaroth and Aziel, Beelzebub and Mephisto, and come to me, all you spirits of the dead.'

'God save me,' muttered John, 'God protect me. Sweet Jesu, I'll go to church every single Sunday from now on without fail. I'll fast, I'll spend a week on my knees but don't let me see him raise any spirits!'

The man threw more powder on the brazier and this time it flamed red. John's mouth went dry. Some months back he'd been persuaded to go to the Rose playhouse to see a piece by the notorious Master Marlowe, a performance in which a crazed doctor had raised a demon and sold his soul to the Devil in return for power and forbidden knowledge. He had found much of the play hard going, it was short on humour and long on philosophy, and the masque of the Seven Deadly Sins which had tempted him along in the first place and the appearance of Helen of Troy 'the face that launched a thousand ships' was deeply disappointing. It would have been different, had the part been played by a sprightly young piece in flimsy garments but the boy must have been nearly fifteen and looked absurd in a long blonde wig and farthingale. He'd enjoyed the end, however, when a troop of red-clad devils had spilled out of a wooden hellmouth from which billowed red smoke and dragged Dr Faustus screaming down to Hell. However hitherto he had considered it to be only a story but now he shook in his bonds as he faced the prospect of seeing the real thing.

The man ended with a stream of Latin, which John could not understand. He stopped shaking and lay rigid with fright, waiting for the thunderclap and lightning which must herald the appearance of a disgusting demon from the pit or a band of walking corpses. That's what had happened at the Rose Theatre. There'd been a huge roll of thunder followed by a flash of light and great puffs of red smoke (the Lord Admiral's Men were noted for their special effects) and out of the trapdoor there had emerged the servant of Lucifer, his face a ghastly white, on his mission to catch the soul of Dr Faustus.

However, this present occasion proved to be an anti-climax. A silence of about five minutes was followed by nothing at all. No bangs, no flashes, no demons. The instigator seemed disappointed and after a few more calls to spirits from the mighty deep, he gave up, dowsed his lights and began to clear away his paraphernalia. So at least he was only mortal, thought John, with a return of his old determination. What he was dealing with was a flesh and blood villain. He *had* to escape.

But in spite of himself he was overcome by weakness and drifted off again. He came to with a start when he felt himself being turned over some time later and realised, though his eyes were still closed, that it was now light. This time he thought it best to feign a very slight recovery and so moaned a little before apparently again becoming comatose.

'God's Blood,' the man muttered. 'I must have hit the fellow harder than I thought, that he should still be senseless.' He felt Johns' bonds and satisfied himself that they were secure then to his amazement John felt him trying to wrench off his wedding ring. What now? he thought. Surely he isn't a common thief as well as a mincing wizard? After a few minutes during which time the man discovered it to be impossible to remove the ring while his victim's wrists were tied, he sighed and began methodically unpicking the knot. John wondered if he should try and attack him there and then, but could see the impracticality of it with his legs tied. Besides, the man was probably armed. It seemed his assailant was in a hurry for he then swiftly loosened the bonds, removed the ring and held it up to the light before taking it into the other room.

John had learned a thing or two in his chequered career. Using all his strength he did everything he could, without alerting the fellow to the fact he was awake, to hold his wrists in such a way that they could not be tied as tightly as they had been previously. He was in luck. The closet was gloomy, the man in haste and when he had done John could tell that there was now some slack in the rope. He had also noticed something else. Looking out from under one of his eyelids he'd caught sight of the man's thumb. Clearly marked on it was the letter T. So that was the reason for the bandage. The villain had been branded at Tyburn.

After a little while his captor went over to a window in the next room, opened it and called out to someone passing below. It must be his accomplice, thought John. Are they going to drag me down between them now and throw me in the Fleet? But when the person entered the room John saw it was only a scruffy young lad.

'Take this letter,' he heard the man say, 'and go with it at once to the house of Dr Simon Forman on the Bankside. It's close by the water steps and anyone will tell you its direction if you can't find it. Make sure there's no one about then push this under the door. Here's sixpence.'

'Thank you, sir,' replied the boy.

'And if you tell anyone of it or say who gave it to you I will cut out your tongue,' the man promised, 'wherever you might be.'

Time passed. Hours of time. John thought of Anna; she must by now be distraught. He recalled only too well his self-importance and conceit as he crossed London Bridge, how he had felt so superior to the doctor, so sure that his hard head would never lead him into trouble. Yet at the end of the day he had been guilty of the very stupidities of which he had accused the doctor. He had gone further than asked in his search for Dr North, he'd been gulled by what he should have realised to be a disguised villain, allowed himself to be taken halfway across the City without either informing his master or sending word of his intention, and had then walked like a silly sheep into a dark house when every instinct should have screamed danger at him. It would serve him right if this madman, who practised the Black Arts, killed him. Dismally he realised that he might actually have found the elusive Dr North.

Finally, he heard the sound of his gaoler's feet again. This time he came only as far as the door of the closet, satisfied himself there was still no sign of life then, to John's great relief, he left the main chamber, banged the door shut and descended the creaking stairs to the floor below. Immediately John started trying to wriggle out of his bonds. Although there was indeed some slack there was barely enough and he soon rubbed his wrists raw. There was no saying when the man would return and the game would be up if he discovered by the marks on his wrists that his supposedly unconscious victim had been awake for some time. Time was of the essence, he had to hurry.

Finally and very painfully, he slid first one, then the other, hand out of the bonds and began to attack the rope binding his feet. He was stiff and aching from lying in one position on the floor for so long and his head still throbbed. His fingers kept slipping on the rope, hindering his progress but eventually his legs too were free.

There was still no sign of life from the room outside. With no small difficulty he rose to his feet, his head spinning. He felt the back of his head and found a large lump and a little blood. He limped through to the main door and tentatively tried it, only to find it had been locked on the outside. Now what? He went over to the window through which his gaoler had called to the boy and opened it. He was well above ground level, but although it would be a squeeze he was almost sure it was big enough to allow him to climb out. He looked down. Between him and the filthy Fleet there was only a narrow pathway but there was no other exit.

He went swiftly back into the room. The fellow must need to sleep, there had to be sheets or a blanket somewhere. He found two grubby linen sheets on a pallet bed, seized them, tore them into strips and began knotting them together. The house was an old one and the window frames were very solid. In this case there were two of them divided by a stout piece of oak, one of which opened and another which did not. He seized a candlestick from the floor beside the painted circle and smashed the fixed one, tying one end of the sheet rope round the wooden strut that divided them. He found himself sweating with the effort, his hands shaking.

Finally he heaved himself out of the window and began making his way hand below hand down the improvised rope. It felt most unsafe, and in spite of his care he kept swinging out away from the wall of the house and back again, bruising his knees in the process. When it came to the last few feet he let go and dropped, praying he would hit the path and not the river. He landed with a jolt on the very edge but managed to keep his balance though for a few seconds he feared he was about to disappear under the revolting stream of sewage and other foul things he could see slowly floating down towards the Thames.

He looked both ways. There was no sign of the man nor of anyone else. He wondered what the time was and whether or not the doctor was searching for him. He made his way along the path and stumbled off, not even sure, in his muddled state, of the direction in which he was going and it was not until he reached Holbourne that he realised he had been walking the wrong way.

It took him a long time to reach London Bridge for he kept being overcome with dizziness and as he reached the Bridge he realised just how much time had passed; he must have been in his prison all night and for most of the day for it was now getting dark again. He stopped for another few minutes' rest then took the final few steps which brought him home and made his way round to the back of the house, letting himself in through the kitchen door. Anna was seated at the table feeding their son, her face creased with anxiety. At his step she looked up then rubbed her eyes in disbelief.

'John,' she cried. 'Oh, John,' and threw herself at him, bursting into tears.

'Hush now,' he told her, 'it's all right. I'm back safe and sound . . . or safe at any rate. I've a rare lump on my head, see for yourself.'

She let go of him and he bent his head for her to examine it. 'It needs cleaning,' she told him, 'and some of the doctor's salve.'

'That's what I thought,' said John, 'and you must bring him here straight away for I've a great deal to tell him.'

She looked surprised. 'Is he not with you then? Haven't you come back together?'

He was mystified. 'What are you talking about, woman? I'm here on my own, having escaped the clutches of a true villain.'

'Sweet Jesu,' she said. 'The Holy Saints preserve us! The doctor had a letter this morning with your wedding ring inside it, telling him he must be in a certain place at a certain time and that he must tell no one of it if he was to find you alive.' She sat down suddenly, her eyes staring. 'He left half an hour ago to keep the assignation.'

Chapter 16

Death in the Sewer

By half-past six, Simon could stand it no longer. He would go and meet his antagonist earlier than expected and take his chance. Before leaving he repeated his instructions to Anna yet again, that she must wait until she heard the church clock strike seven then go at once to Tom Pope and enlist his help. 'I don't want to make you even more anxious, Anna, but there's no doubt we are dealing with a very dangerous man. However, it's me he wants, not John. Tom's resourceful and if anyone can help, then he can.'

If there had ever been a time when he needed John with him then it was now, he thought, as he crossed the river, recalling the various occasions on which his loyal servant had come to his aid when he'd run into trouble but at least he now had a chance to try and repay the debt.

It was a fair walk to his destination and as the light was fading rapidly he missed his way once or twice for he was largely unacquainted with that part of London. Finally he decided it was best to aim first for Holbourne where he would be able to cross the Fleet. Its smell assailed him long before he reached it. As he crossed the river at the bridge, the flare of a link attached to a tavern wall briefly lit up the scene below. The bloated corpse of a dead dog floated by on the oily flood, caught up in a mass of other detritus and he recalled Roger's vivid description of the contents of a river which was now no more than an open sewer. He wondered how much longer boatmen would still be prepared to ply their trade up and down between the Thames and Holbourne.

Uncertain in spite of the roughly-drawn map where to go next, he moved nearer to the light from the link and saw there was a narrow lane running parallel to the Fleet on its west side which was marked on the paper in his hand. He was now full of apprehension as to what might await him, fearful that his antagonist had already carried out his threat and that the letter and ring had been sent merely to ensure he kept the appointment. Finally, and after several false turns, he found himself as had John before him outside an archway to a courtyard, inside which he could dimly make out several semi-derelict houses, one of which had a light in the window. So far as he could tell after so much twisting and turning, the Fleet must run down the back of them before curving slightly towards the south-east. For a little while he stood outside trying to decide on the best way of dealing with a situation where all the odds were stacked against him.

Unbeknown to him, the man awaiting his arrival was similarly exercised. Satisfied that his victim could not possibly escape, he had been driven out of the house by the need to find something to eat, after which he had sat at the window of a derelict building next door which gave him a better view of the archway which was the only approach to the house. There was always the possibility that Forman would ignore his instructions, decide his servant was expendable and alert the authorities to go in and seize him.

So far everything, or almost everything, had gone his way and he congratulated himself on having lost none of his old skills. It had given him the most intense pleasure to set to work on that smug coterie of scientists, mathematicians and alchemists who so grandly called themselves the School of the Night, the very same elite who had not only refused Dr Kelley entry to their circle but had openly mocked him into the bargain. *He* was no charlatan, his gifts of prophesy and spirit raising were real – which is why Dee had offered him his patronage and had so much faith in him. By rights he should now have been acclaimed and respected throughout the land.

The child of a poverty-stricken North Country mother, with no known father, he had raised himself out of the dirt by sheer willpower, natural intelligence and that gift which was something apart from the rest. As a young lad they had said he could persuade folk black was white then, as he grew older, he had found he could convince the credulous that there was nothing he could not do, from turning base metal into gold to curing the incurable, not to mention the scrying when he gazed into a mirror or a pool of black ink and saw visions of the future. Though sometimes there had been occasions when he could see nothing and had to invent it. He had to believe in his powers for without that surety he was nothing. This reminded him of the last occasion on which he had sought to discover his own future. The experience had left him shaken, for as he gazed into the ink at first he saw nothing, only blackness, but then the blackness had grown wider and deeper until it had engulfed him.

He had come to London all those years ago with such high hopes, bolstered by the patronage of Lord Strange only to find he would never be accepted by those who mattered. He had survived his earlier brushes with the law, the cropping of his ears readily disguised by a hat, the branding on the hand taking place among a crowd of others. How he had laughed inwardly when he told Forman truthfully that not only had he been present when the College Censors sentenced 'Kelley' to imprisonment but also when he had been branded at Tyburn.

But a charge of murder was not to be so lightly shrugged off though Dee had believed in his innocence and had swept him off to Europe. Fame and adulation had followed them both until Bohemia when disaster struck. Two years he'd spent in a filthy dungeon for upsetting the prince as well as being put to the question on two occasions. He still had the scars. Yet even then his skills had not deserted him; a mixture of bribes and threats of dreadful curses falling on his gaolers had resulted in another prisoner, dressed in his clothes, going to the scaffold in his place. Oh yes, there had been plenty of time to brood on his ills and plan his revenge on his supposed betters. As for Forman . . .

Time passed uneventfully and no one came near. He was safe then. Finally, a little before the time he had set for the assignation, he strolled back to the empty house, the first floor of which he was renting, unlocked the front door, went upstairs and felt in his pocket for the key to unlock the door which opened on to his living quarters.

He had already decided how he would set the scene for what was to come. All would be in darkness except for branches of candles illuminating him as he sat at the end of the room on a high-backed chair. He would have Bradedge, still firmly bound of course, on the floor beside him, a knife at his throat, ready for use if Forman did not obey his every instruction or made any attempt to escape. He was not as yet sure what to do with Bradedge once he had dealt with Forman but on the whole it would seem sensible to dispose of him as well. Then he would be off elsewhere, where a new identity already awaited him. All his plans were complete.

He pushed open the door and a gust of air, redolent of the Fleet, met him in the face from the open window. The end of a sheet tied to the window frame told the story all too well. He ran over to it and looked down in the hope that the man might have broken his neck or injured himself in his flight but there was no sign of anything on the narrow pathway outside except a few pieces of bottle glass. How long had Bradedge been gone? Long enough to get back home and so prevent Forman from coming?

Feverishly he untied the knotted sheets, rolled them up and threw them into a corner. Inside the closet the ropes with which he thought he'd secured Bradedge lay abandoned. How could he have been so careless? Obviously the fellow had been fooling him that he was still comatose after so many hours. Not for the first time he wished he had all those skills of a physician that he so often claimed. He should never have left the room. But time was running out now and he would have to do as best he could. It might well be that Forman had left the Bankside without knowing his servant to be safe, and if that was the case then he could be convinced Bradedge was still held hostage. Mechanically he began setting the scene for what he had imagined would be an easy, as well as an enjoyable, triumph. He set up his chair, lit the candles then, placing a dagger and a primed flintlock pistol in an obvious position, he sat down to wait. Ten minutes later he sighed with relief as he heard footsteps on the staircase: the trap had worked, Forman did not know his servant had escaped.

Simon pushed open the door and walked into an impressive scene. The man he knew as Dr North was seated on a high-backed, elaborately-carved chair flanked by candelabra containing fine wax candles, dressed much as he had been before but now without the plumed hat or gloves. Simon noted the sword and the pistol, aware he himself was unarmed except for a dagger tucked down in his boot. He looked again at his adversary, noting at once the lack of ears and the brand on the hand. So, he had been right after all: Kelley had not died years ago in Bohemia. What a poseur, thought Simon, what a trickster! So this is how he acquired his reputation as a magus, by cheap theatrical tricks to impress the credulous with scene-setting, lights and, no doubt, incense and coloured smoke for good measure when the need arose.

The man on the chair smiled unpleasantly. 'Pray come in, Dr Forman. You're a little before time.'

'I didn't want to keep you waiting, Kelley,' returned Simon, his eyes travelling over the man's head and hand.

This Kelley had not expected and it took him a moment or two to recover himself. 'So you know who I am? How very astute of you. I had thought my secret entirely safe. It seems I underrated you.'

'Before we continue with this fascinating conversation, may I see my servant and make sure he's safe?' Simon enquired. Kelley made obvious play of looking across at the door of what looked like a closet. Simon followed his gaze. So that's where John was imprisoned.

'All in good time,' countered Kelley. 'He suffered a blow on the head and his bonds are no doubt uncomfortable but he is alive and in one piece. You may see him shortly. In the meantime, do sit down. After all this time I feel we must have much to say to each other.'

Simon was about to reply that it was highly unlikely and that he preferred to stand, then thought better of it, glancing again at Kelley with his weapons within easy reach. I must keep him talking, he thought. The longer I allow him to prate on, the better chance I have of reaching John before he does or of us both being rescued. Then it dawned on him that there was something else that was odd about the situation. Why was John confined in the closet? Surely the obvious way for Kelley to make his point was to have him there in the room with them, threatened with instant death if he did the wrong thing. Or was this, after all, an elaborate charade and John already dead? He walked over to the chair Kelley had set opposite to him and sat down, doing his utmost to appear unconcerned.

'Why not?' he agreed. 'We have plenty of time.' He settled back into the chair. 'I think I have pieced most things together but there are one or two questions I would like answered. First of all, was it you who sent me the box of sea holly?'

Kelley smiled broadly. 'I have been remarkably lucky or possibly the spirits have been with me. Under the name of Dr North (who I know scarcely ever moves out of Lincolnshire) I have been going to and from the Low Countries about my business for several years, and it so happened that I was in Harwich, having just returned from such a visit, and was at the shop of an apothecary when one of his colleagues arrived post haste from Colchester. He said he was searching urgently for a supply of *eringo* for a Dr Forman of London who lived on the Bankside and was wanting to use it in an experiment to be conducted by a circle of scientific gentlemen in London. Finding it hard to obtain at the present time and not wanting to disappoint a valued customer, he had come to Harwich in the hope his friend could help him.

'I never heard the outcome as I left the shop at once. I couldn't believe my good fortune for I had been racking my brain for some time as to the best way of starting to make trouble for you. So I made a diligent search myself and discovered a source and bought a box. I realised that even if the apothecary succeeded and you received two boxes of *eringo* you would think only that your man had sent you two in error.'

'But why me?' demanded Simon, baffled. 'What have you got against me? I've never harmed you – we've never even met.'

'I knew only too well of your growing reputation as a physician, of your dabbling in mysteries, and that you had set up in practice in the very place where I had once been considered by the simple fools who lived there as . . .'

'. . . the cleverest doctor in the world,' Simon completed for him. 'How modest.'

'But that's exactly what I am,' blazed Kelley. 'I'm cleverer than all the rest of you put together, for not only do I have my own wit and learning but the power of many deadly demons and spirits at my beck and call.'

The man's raving mad, thought Simon. He must always have been on the edge and now his mind has thoroughly turned. He needs chains and a dark room. Meanwhile, time was getting on. Anna must have spoken to Tom by now. How much longer would it take him and others to reach them? 'I still don't understand,' he said, affecting puzzlement, 'since to all intents and purposes you are dead, executed in Bohemia years ago. You couldn't possibly set up in practice in London again under your own name without fear of discovery and being sent to the gallows. You have no Dr Dee to protect you now. So what can it possibly matter to you if I practise as a physician either on the Bankside or anywhere else?'

But Kelley, hardly listening, ignored him. 'So I delivered the sea holly at your house in person – disguised, of course – and sat back to await what would happen.'

'I take it you did tamper with it,' stated Simon, since it was clear he was not going to get any answer to his previous question.

'A subtle poison made from a recipe I came across in Italy. I used it on only a few pieces and that in different strengths otherwise it would have been too obvious. It was not difficult to deduce that the circle of "scientific gentlemen" was your famed School of the Night and its members my mortal enemies. Then the spirits came to my aid again for I kept close watch on your comings and goings and heard you telling some player fellow that you would ride down to Sherborne with him where the School of the Night was to meet. I also saw Tapworth visit you and was sufficiently intrigued to follow him across the river and make his acquaintance where I learned, to my delight, that you had actually prescribed *eringo* for him. It suited me very well. I could travel to

Chelsea with him and see if he ate one of the pieces of poisoned sea holly after which, whether he did or not, I would take the road west to see the results of your experiment.

'However, if it gives you any pleasure, Forman, I still believe the man died of an apoplexy but it wasn't difficult to encourage his brother to think otherwise and to ensure he sat down and wrote in complaint to the College of Physicians. After that everything was simple. I bided my time in Sherborne, certain that I would not be recognised, since everyone thought me dead, and awaited results. Such a gathering is bound to cause gossip in the nearby taverns; rumours abounded of secret meetings where blasphemous matters were discussed, of diabolical experiments and the taking of strange potions, and news of the poisonings soon got out. After most of you had left I found young Carew drinking in a nearby inn, damning you to hell and wanting revenge before he left the country. The rest was simple.

'He and I rode to London together, you went to gaol and if it hadn't been for the intervention of that interfering witch, Mary Herbert, you'd still be there. Believe me, by the time you had come out you would have had no practice or reputation left. Carew had an example of your writing, a poor scholar's hand like my own and so easy to forge. Where I went wrong was to assume you would be in the Counter for weeks, even months. I did not take into account your being released so soon and searching out the printer as you did, so it was necessary to silence him since he was clearly untrustworthy.' He laughed to himself. 'Carew and I found much amusement in publishing the handbills.' Then he stopped laughing. 'No, Forman, there's no place here for both of us. You have usurped my position. The situation can't be allowed to continue.'

Simon glanced across at the closet door and debated if now was the time to risk making a dash for it. If John was still alive and he could somehow manage to free him, they would be two against one. 'But I haven't "usurped" you in any way,' he said. 'I practise medicine and astrology but not the Black Arts. I am no necromancer, though at one time the College of Physicians put it about that I was such a one.'

Kelley looked at him with loathing. 'I was cleverer and more powerful than all of them: the College of Physicians and all those licensed by it, the little astrologers and alchemists who now strut the City in their fine robes so sure of themselves, arrogant Hariot with his telescopes and philosophy of figures, Hues with his books on navigation and geology, the whole pack of them. None of them have my powers.'

He became completely carried away. 'I can cause graves to open and give up their dead, raise tempests and move the stars in their spheres. Yet you, the puny son of a Wiltshire labourer with your little skills, you were admitted to their company, made a member of their School of the Night, when it was denied to me . . .'

God's Blood, the demented fellow must at last be bringing matters to the end, thought Simon. He sprang to his feet and made for the closet, wrenching open the door before Kelley could stop him. It was empty. 'Where is he?' he shouted. 'Where's my servant? The bargain was that he would remain unharmed if I came here as you demanded.'

Kelley smiled a slow smile as he stood up, picking up the flintlock pistol as he did so. 'You're not really very clever at all, are you, Forman? Surely you didn't think I would risk him remaining alive? *Or you.*'

'God's Blood!' swore John Bradedge, sitting down on a kitchen bench. 'Did the doctor tell you to fetch help for him?'

'He told me to give him some time then, when I heard th

clock strike seven, to go and find the actor, Thomas Pope, with this paper here. I don't know what it says.' Anna held it out to him and her husband snatched it off her.

'He's gone to meet this necromancer because he thinks my life's at stake,' cried John, 'and now he's put himself in jeopardy. There's no time to be lost. I'll be off to Master Pope's.'

'You look in no fit state to go anywhere,' replied his wife. 'At least let me clean up your head for you.'

John gingerly felt his head. 'Very well, and bring me a cup of brandy and a piece of bread. My stomach's empty as a drum.'

Ten minutes later, still a trifle unsteady on his feet, he made his way to Tom Pope's house to find the actor sitting studying lines while his sons played at being privateers at the other end of the room with two splendid toy vessels. Tom greeted John in his usual friendly fashion and one of the boys at once came over to show him his new plaything, which John duly admired.

'The lady who came to visit us and who Father says is a countess brought us these model ships,' he said proudly. 'Aren't they splendid? You can join in our game if you like.'

'They're very fine,' agreed John, 'and it's kind of you to ask me, but right now I have urgent business with your father.'

'Go back to your game, boys,' Tom told them, then looked closely at John. 'Heavens, man, you look rough! What is it? Are you all right?'

John shrugged his shoulders then winced. 'I've felt better. I've had a blow on the head, that's all, and been tied up in a closet for hours.'

The actor smiled wryly. 'Now let me guess . . . could it just be that your plight has something to do with that wretch Simon Forman? You'd better start at the beginning, I think.' So John told him as much of the situation as he was able then handed over Simon's note, adding that the doctor thought this man to be the villain who had been behind all the troubles that had recently befallen him.

'If it is,' he continued, 'then he's already got one death on his hands and would have had a second had we not prevented it, and from the way he threatened me, he'll not lose sleep over half a dozen more.'

'What kind of a man is he?' enquired Tom. 'As an actor, would I play him as rough and threatening, or smooth and sinister?'

'A very evil one and both in turn,' replied John. 'He also practises the Black Arts and necromancy. While I was there with him and he thought me still out of my senses I saw him calling on the spirits with oaths and Latin words, using coloured fire and incense.'

'And did they come?' Tom asked cynically.

John shivered. 'No, God be thanked, they did not. I'll tell you another thing about him too. He has the Tyburn brand on his hand.'

'Then we must waste no more time,' said Tom. 'Do you think we should find others to come with us, or can we take care of this fellow between us – that is, if you feel fit enough to come with me.'

'Don't worry about me,' John told him. 'I think the two of us should be able to manage it. Unless, that is, he really can call up devils to aid him,' he added, still a little doubtful.

Tom laughed. 'I don't think we need fear that for a moment. The man's obviously no more than a charlatan and is a branded felon to boot.'

With no further ado he sought out his wife, telling her briefly what was toward, explaining the need for haste. Jenny was obviously somewhat uneasy but made no attempt to dissuade him for Simon had proved a good friend to both of them over the years; that being so, she could not bring herself to argue against her husband's determination to fetch him back safely. Tom unhooked his sword from where he kept it, strapped it on to his belt and took up his cloak asking as he did so if John was armed.

'I have my dagger as always,' John confirmed, 'and, standing outside your door, there's a stout cudgel.'

Tom kissed his wife, ruffled the hair on his sons' heads, bidding them behave themselves while he was gone and led the way out into the street and towards London Bridge. 'I assume you can remember how to get there,' he said as they walked quickly past the water steps.

'Pretty well,' declared John, 'though I was so confused in my head when I left, I nearly fell into the Fleet . . .' A sudden thought struck him and he stopped in his tracks. 'Why don't we go by boat? This Dr North or whoever he is would be unlikely to expect an attempted rescue by water.'

'By *boat* right up the Fleet?' queried Tom. 'Are wherrymen still prepared to ply that far?'

'It seems some do. The boatman who rowed us to Deptford and was in the Counter at the same time as the doctor, told him he'd recently taken a fare from the Mermaid tavern right up to Holbourne and pretty foul it was, which is true enough; but it proves it's still just about possible. Why don't we try and find him?'

They turned back as one and made for the water steps. By now it was nearly dark and there were only a handful of boatmen at the bottom hoping for fares. John shouted down to them, asking if Roger Warren was among them, to be told there was no one there of that name. 'Though,' said one large fellow as he took a swig from a leather bottle, 'if you mean the newcomer with his uncle's boat then I saw him in the Anchor tavern not ten minutes ago.'

Tom thanked him and they set off at a run for the Anchor. 'If he's not here,' he panted, 'we'll find the first wherryman that can take us regardless of cost.'

They were in luck for Roger was finishing his ale having decided to give up for the night and was somewhat startled to find himself in such demand. As quickly and quietly as he could, Tom explained that Dr Forman was in great danger and that they needed a boat to get them up the Fleet straight away; would Roger be prepared to take them? He agreed at once. 'You can tell me all about it as we go,' he said, snatching up his jacket, 'but if it's as bad as you say, we'd best not waste any more time. The boat's further on, past the Rose.'

Five minutes later they were in the wherry. Roger pulled strongly on the oars and soon they were making good progress towards the opposite bank. Before they had even reached the entrance to the Fleet, the rubbish coming from it met them in a steady stream on its way to the sea.

'You'd best hold your noses,' said Roger as he turned the boat expertly into the smaller river. 'Disturbing the water with the oars will raise a stench rare enough to turn your stomachs!'

'What have you done with him?' shouted Simon. 'If you've killed him, then where's the body?'

Kelley walked over to the window and pulled aside the curtain revealing the gaping hole. 'In the Fleet. Or most likely out in the Thames by now on its way to the Channel. I killed him and disposed of him hours ago.'

It made sense but, inexplicably, Simon did not believe him. The ring he'd received definitely belonged to his servant and he was prepared to accept that Kelley had been holding John hostage. He also had no doubt that Kelley would be quite capable of murdering John once he had served his purpose as bait, but the broken window might have another meaning. Suppose this too was but playacting and John had somehow managed to escape? He was tired and his head ached. If John was no longer there then he must now do his best to escape, but to reach the door to the outside world he would have to cross the room and if he attempted to do so, Kelley wouldn't hesitate to shoot him. He felt in his boot. A small dagger was hardly a match for a firearm but it was better than nothing.

In the event Kelley made his mind up for him. 'I'm bored with you, Simon Forman,' he said, 'I've spent enough time on you these last weeks. I haven't finished with the School of the Night, however. I have written to Sir Robert Cecil in the guise of a Dutch academic visiting this country, informing him that I was invited to attend meetings of a circle calling itself the School of the Night, meetings which I had understood to be of a religious and learned nature, only to find myself in the company of a crew of blasphemers and atheists who deny the existence of God and want to spread their deadly doctrine throughout the land. Knowing his nature, I think he will act upon it. They can look to see themselves arrested and brought before the Star Chamber charged with blasphemy and atheism, the penalty for which, as I'm sure you know, is burning at the stake.'

There was no help for it. Simon threw caution to the winds and made for the door as Kelly levelled the flintlock and fired. Simon ducked as the ball whistled past him so close that he felt its wind. Mercifully the door was still unlocked and he pushed it open easily, then raced down the stairs, Kelley closing fast behind him. He ran across the courtyard, out under the archway, turned down first one alleyway then another, only to find that the second ended on the narrow path beside the Fleet. As he hesitated, unsure what to do next, Kelley flung himself at his legs from behind and brought him to the ground, his head only inches away from the river.

Although Kelley was the older man, he was fit and stronger than he looked and Simon, even as a lad, had never had much skill in this kind of fighting. They rolled over almost into the water until Kelley emerged on top and, kneeling on Simon's stomach, tried to force his thumbs into his eyes and blind him. Choking for breath, Simon, using all that was left of his strength, heaved himself out from under him, rolled over again and found himself in the sewer that was the Fleet River.

He floundered about in the stinking water, struggling not to swallow any, drawn inexorably towards the middle of the river by the outgoing tide which was now running strongly back into the Thames. He had never been much of a swimmer. Should he let himself go with the current then? If he didn't drown, he doubted he would survive anyway if he gulped down water putrid with God alone knew what. A wall came down to the water on the other bank so it was impossible to climb out there. Time seemed to have stopped. It was now too dark to see his assailant and he was getting tired with treading water while his mouth felt vile with the water he had already swallowed.

Then, unbelievably, he heard the sound of oars. He tried to call out though he doubted he could be heard, but spurred on now by hope he made once again for the bank from which he had fallen, only to find Kelley waiting for him. As he struggled to climb out, Kelley set on him yet again, knocking him back into the water then, grabbing him by the hair, he forced Simon's head down beneath the poisonous brew.

'Look,' shouted Tom, 'look there.' He unhooked the lantern from its pole and held it up. 'There's someone struggling on the bank.' Roger bent to his oars with redoubled energy as they came closer, while John peered along the dim beam of light. 'It's the scoundrel who took me prisoner,' he told them, 'and who's that in the water?'

Gasping, Simon rose again to the surface and as Kelley, suddenly aware of the boat and the light, turned to see what was happening, he made one last mighty effort to heave himself on to the bank. Again Kelley tried to prevent him, but this time Simon hung on to the grasping hands and jerked backwards and with a cry Kelley slipped and himself fell into the Fleet. As he did so Simon reached the bank and, now quite exhausted, hung on as well as he could, meanwhile calling out to them.

'It's the doctor there,' yelled John, as Roger began to back the boat up to the struggling figures. 'Make for him as quick as you can!'

'Where's the other fellow?' Tom called out as they came close.

'In the water,' gasped Simon. 'For God's sake get me out before he drags me under again. You'll have to haul me in, I haven't the strength.'

Together Tom and John heaved Simon on board while Roger steadied the boat which rocked dangerously under them. 'God preserve us, man,' said Tom, averting his face. 'You smell like a sewer.'

'So would you if you'd spent as long as I have in this one,' croaked Simon. He looked across the murky water into darkness. 'Hold the light up, Kelley must be here somewhere. He can't have drowned.'

'Kelley?' queried John. 'Who's Kelley?'

'The villain of the piece, alias Dr North,' Simon choked out. 'He mustn't be allowed to escape.' But all was silent except for the lapping of the water against the banks as the tide ran ever swifter towards the Thames. Suddenly the boat lurched over as a pair of slimy hands grasped the side. 'Watch out!' cried Simon. 'He'll have us in. He'll drown us all if he has the chance.'

'Not if I know anything about it,' Roger retorted, and hauling in one of the oars, he brought it down on the man's hands as

Kelley again attempted to capsize the boat. His head rose from the Fleet, his face eerily lit by the lantern. Eyes, rinsed of humanity, met theirs for an instant as once more he tried to sink them. Without any compunction, Roger lifted the oar and this time brought it down with all his strength on the man's head then, as Kelley's body rose to the surface, to make sure, he held it down with the oar until it sank beneath the surface.

'Sorry, gents,' he said, panting slightly, 'but I was trained in a rough school. It was him or us, and if what you say is true he's killed many times before and was prepared to kill again.'

'He's been wanted for murder for at least five years,' Simon confirmed through chattering teeth, 'and has recently murdered again, nor would he have had any qualms if he had added John and me to his tally. He'd turned completely mad.'

'We must get you home,' said Tom. 'Look at the state you're in! You'll need to soak for hours to get the smell off you and as for your clothes, I imagine the only thing to do is to burn them.'

'And purge myself as well,' said Simon, 'to try and rid myself of what I must have swallowed.'

Roger rowed steadily towards the Thames through the flotsam and other rubbish until they reached the larger river where, thankfully, they were greeted by the fresher smell from the wind blowing up from the sea. Tom looked back up the Fleet. 'What will happen to him?'

Roger shrugged. 'The tide's still flowing down the Fleet into the Thames and it'll carry him with it unless he's washed up somewhere along the way and the foxes and rats get him.'

Tom Pope shuddered. 'What a terrible end,' he said, 'to die like a dog in a stinking ditch. Will there be any trouble over it? Should we tell the authorities?'

'Leave things be,' said Simon. 'Kelley was already dead, he's been officially dead these last five years, "executed" in far

Bohemia no less. What point is there in proclaiming the death of a dead man?'

'Death of a Dead Man,' said Tom. 'It will do for his epitaph.'

Chapter 17

'Oh my America, my
New-Found-Land!'

It took Simon several days to recover. Whether it was the purge that made him sick or his immersion in the Fleet he did not know, but whichever it was he had great difficulty keeping food down. He dosed himself, lay in of a morning and refused to see any patients. On the second day he sent a brief note to Ralegh by John Bradedge, receiving in return a letter informing him that Carew was now making steady progress and that although he had said little of the events of the past few weeks, even to his parents, he had made it known that 'the doctor' of whom he had been afraid was not Dr Forman.

We trust you will soon feel better from your ordeal, Ralegh wrote. *When you do I will call the School of the Night together so that you can explain everything. Who would have thought it to be Edward Kelley! It seemed so certain that he was dead. Mary Herbert, who is here dining with us today, also sends you her best regards and says to tell you that the Fool conquered all in the end. I assume it has some meaning for you!*

A little while later Simon asked John if he could find Roger so that he could thank the wherryman. 'Not only do I need to express my gratitude, but I also promised his woman a casting. Find him if you can and ask him to bring her here and I'll do my best for her.' John returned within the hour with the information that Roger would bring his Betty round that very afternoon if it was convenient to the doctor as they had a special appointment to keep that morning.

He had also picked up another piece of news which explained another puzzle, if a minor one. During the time John had spent imprisoned in Kelley's closet an enraged leatherworker of the name of Clem Wilkins had been found, tied up and stripped to his breeches, in a yard close to St Paul's. He remembered nothing after taking a short cut on his way home, except that he had been knocked on the head. The reason for the assault was a complete mystery for he still had his purse in his pocket with the day's takings and it seemed beyond all reason that anyone would want to steal his old, worn and smelly work-clothes.

When Roger and his Betty arrived, the nature of their previous appointment was obvious. Roger looked unusually clean and sported a nosegay in his buttonhole while Betty, now very obviously rounding to the child, was wearing a gown which, although it had clearly seen better days, had been refurbished along with a white cap newly trimmed with ribbons. They had come straight from church where they had just been married.

'My uncle has loaned me the boat indefinitely,' Roger told Simon. 'He says he's too old for it now, there are far too many boatmen plying for hire and cutting each other's throats these days and no respect like there used to be. He's also going to see if I can be admitted to the Honourable Company of Watermen.' He put his arm round his bride. 'There'll be no more cross-biting now, will there, girl? Nor the Counter or Bridewell.'

Simon cast Betty's horoscope and made his calculations,

informing the young woman that she should carry to full term and that the child would be healthy. 'I don't see great riches for you,' he told her, 'but nor do I find poverty either. I think you will do well enough from now on.'

They thanked him and left to join a party in the Anchor which had gathered to drink their health. Simon looked after them with no little envy. He was beginning to think that he alone among men was unable to find lasting happiness with a loving woman, even though he was able to find willing partners for casual bedding. He smiled a little at the thought of the Countess but he was under no illusions that their dalliance would be a regular occurrence. Mary Herbert took her pleasure where and when it suited her, but she had been born into a great family and married into another and knew well where her duty and responsibilities lay. She would keep her part of the bargain and there would be no real scandal.

The meeting of the School of the Night in Ralegh's Tower Room some days later was a sombre one. They heard Simon out in silence as he told his story, explaining how eventually he had begun to consider the possibility that Kelley had not, after all, died long ago in Bohemia although it was more likely that they were dealing with one of his disciples.

'I am to blame for not accepting that you might be right,' the Countess broke in, 'but I had heard, time and time again, of his supposed public execution and after our conversation I wrote to Dr Dee most urgently asking him if he was absolutely sure that Kelley died in Bohemia. I received his answer yesterday.' She handed it to him.

So far as I am aware that is so and wonder why you feel the need to ask me, Dee had written. *He had been behaving most strangely and had spent much time closeted with the prince on matters outside my knowledge. There was a deal of talk at the*

Court of raising spirits and communicating with the dead and I warned him to stop whatever it was he was engaged in; indeed, I told him in no uncertain manner that if what was said of him was true then we should leave while we were able. But he would not listen. By this time he did not feel he had any need of my patronage nor felt any obligation towards me.

One night I was woken by a friendly courtier who told me he had horses waiting below and that if I wanted to escape with my life I must rise and go with him at once. I immediately saw the truth of this and he proved a staunch friend, riding with me day and night until he saw me safe over the border. On our way he told me Kelley had mortally offended the prince and had been thrown into a dungeon and was to be executed. Later, in Germany, I heard that this was so and witnessed by many hundreds of people.

As to the Tarot card about which you wrote earlier, it is similar to those that are commonly sold in Bohemia and might well have been brought back by a visitor to that country – but then such packs can change hands many times or be copied by card makers elsewhere. He ended by assuring his 'old pupil' of his undying affection, trusting that he would see her again before too long.

'So it certainly does not look as if Dr Dee knew that Kelley had survived and was back in the country, let alone that he was aiding him,' commented Henry Percy.

'Rather the reverse,' declared the Countess. 'Whatever it was Kelley did in Bohemia it might easily have cost Dee his life.'

Hariot agreed. 'So we now find we also have Kelley to thank for setting the Privy Council on to enquire into our activities,'

'I'm sure he isn't the only one wanting to make trouble for us,' Ralegh commented. 'There are others who are deeply suspicious of our activities. Kit Marlowe was muttering as much to me the other day, warning against informers and intelligencers. I'd hoped to ask him further as to what he meant, but he's sent word that he was unable to come having taken himself off to Tom Walsingham's at Scadbury as he's still wrestling with his poem of *Hero and Leander*.'

'You are quite certain that Kelley *is* dead this time, Dr Forman?' enquired Hues.

'So far as it's possible to be,' replied Simon. He had deliberately said very little about what had happened during his rescue but considered the time had now come to offer an edited version. 'After trying to shoot me as I attempted to escape, he followed me out of the building and set about me on the pathway beside the Fleet. He was possessed with all the strength of a madman.

'I struggled with him as best I could but finally he pushed me into the river but in so doing fell in himself. I don't know what happened to him for I was floundering about myself in that vile brew. It was then my friends arrived in a wherry and hauled me into it. Although it was dark, they had a lantern, and we sought for him for some time but he never surfaced; had he done so, I'm sure we would have heard him.' He paused. Suppose, he thought, the body did finally surface and it was clear there had been a massive blow to the head?

'It could be that he hit his head on something,' he added quickly, 'or was caught by the feet in the slime and rubbish on the bed of the Fleet.' He shuddered at the remembrance of it. 'It is a disgrace to our great city,' he said. 'It's no longer a waterway but an open sewer of filth and disease. The City fathers should cover it over and have done.'

The meeting broke up with no plans by its members to meet again in the immediate future. In view of the circumstances it was felt that caution should prevail though Hariot voiced the thoughts of all of them when he said that it was a sad time when honest Christian men could not meet to discuss new discoveries in science and philosophy without being considered atheists and blasphemers.

'God gave us our intellect in order that we might use it to gain even more knowledge of His wondrous universe. It is only little petty men who are frightened to learn more. Every new discovery is a marvel.'

Before he left, Ralegh asked Simon if he would visit his patient. 'I think it would help his recovery if you gave him the opportunity to apologise,' he said. 'I think he is now most contrite over the part he played.'

Ralegh took him into a small dayroom and Simon saw before him what appeared at first glance to be a charming domestic scene. Carew, still somewhat pale, was sitting beside the fire, his mother opposite him working at some sewing. Beside him sat the young woman Simon had last seen in his bedchamber at Sherborne crying noisily and wearing only her shift. She was now attired in a respectable dark stuff gown and a married woman's cap, trimmed with lace; this then must be the new bride. A closer look at the group revealed a truer picture. Mistress Carew senior was very obviously ignoring her unwanted daughter-in-law, looking through her as if she were not there whenever she turned her head in that direction. The younger woman, a rebellious and determined expression on her face, was doing everything except hang on her husband's arm to claim her ownership of him. Given the circumstances it was not surprising that Carew looked relieved to see Simon and out of courtesy tried to stand up, but Simon motioned the young man to sit down, asking him how he was feeling now.

'Very much better, thanks to you, Dr Forman. I'm only too well aware I owe you my life. I can only say how sorry I am and beg your forgiveness. I do believe I was mad at the time. I'd offended my family . . .' he looked at his wife '. . . jilted the girl who for years had expected to marry me, and caused untold trouble. I fear I wasn't rational when I came to Sherborne and so became convinced you'd poisoned me.'

'But you really *were* poisoned,' Simon informed him. 'In that you were right. It was the man we now know to be Edward Kelley who actually sent me the sea holly in the first place and tampered with some of the pieces in order to make as much mischief as possible. But I could not possibly have known that when you became sick.'

'He took me in completely,' said Carew bitterly. 'He posed as a grave doctor who had been badly treated by his colleagues in general and you in particular. He persuaded me that we could both revenge ourselves and in the crazed mood I was in, I believed him. He persuaded me into finding him an example of your handwriting, which was not difficult since I'd seen you making notes after our meetings, though I found it somewhat hard to decipher.'

Simon said nothing. His handwriting was something of a sore point with him for he was aware it was only legible when he took the time and care to make it so.

'I gave it to him,' Carew continued, 'and he told me he was going to amuse himself by writing letters as if they came from you. He told me . . .' he hesitated '. . . he told me he'd discovered you had a mistress in the City and that he would send one to her. Then later, in London, he had the idea of posting up handbills saying you were giving up your practice and others he knew to be against the law.

'So it was he persuaded me to help him. By the time it came to putting the plan into practice, however, I had other matters of far more importance to contend with and was no longer so set on revenge though, God pardon me, I still thought it a joke to distribute the slanderous bills. But as God is my witness, I never intended it should go any further.'

He swallowed. 'When I met up with you in the printer's shop I already knew that Holt was dead. I'd found him hanging there from the beam earlier, shortly after I left the . . .' he glanced across at his mother and then at his wife.

'The ordinary,' suggested Simon.

Carew looked at him gratefully. 'Yes, the ordinary. I was panic-stricken and walked about in a daze before going back again, heard voices and so came upon you. I realised at once that you might think I was to blame. Only then did I perceive the true nature of the man with whom I'd become involved, my apprehension confirmed when I went to him to tell him what had happened. His reaction was such that I feared he would betray me to the authorities and tell them that *I* was responsible for the man's death. It was then I decided to sail for Virginia, for I have an uncle there. Dr North, as I thought he was, told me I must do so at once.' He shuddered. 'He didn't actually go so far as an open threat but his meaning was clear: either I leave the country or risk suffering the same fate as the printer.

'But the ship on which I was to sail for Virginia was delayed and somehow Kelley learned I was still in the country and so came to Deptford, insisting that he'd found another vessel and I must leave at once if I was to save my skin.' He turned to his mother, putting his arm round the girl. 'I hadn't even told my wife of my plans. Whatever you say, Mother, or think of us both, she deserves better of me.'

He turned back again to Simon. 'So, like a fool, I arranged to meet him later on the quayside and the rest you know. He'd obviously intended from the first to make away with me once I'd served his turn. Please tell me you believe me and accept my apologies.'

Simon reassured him, promised to look in on him again in a few days, and made his way home. Before he left, Carew's mother informed him stiffly that her son and his *wife* (she spat out the word) would now sail for Virginia in April where an uncle had a sizeable plantation. Ah well, thought Simon, Carew wasn't the first young hothead who had mindlessly got himself into deep waters and he wouldn't be the last. Hopefully he'd at least learned something from it.

To his surprise, Simon found Avisa waiting for him on his return home. They greeted each other awkwardly, unsure what to say after so bitter a parting, then he took her through into his small sitting-room, apprehensive as to what she had come to tell him.

'You knew, didn't you?' she began without any preamble. 'You knew all the time that the woman I've always thought to be my mother is really my aunt.'

'I discovered it only by chance,' he averred. 'I knew your real mother and attended her when she was dying. She told me then of the child she had borne for, desperate to confess and with no one to turn to, she confided in me and I comforted her as best I could, telling her that if she considered what she'd done a sin, then most of us had far heavier ones to bear. At the time I had no idea we would ever meet. Then her husband begged me to attend her burial.' He stopped. 'Do you now blame me for that too?'

She shook her head. 'No. I realise you were put in an impossible situation. I wish though it had come out in some other way and not now. My "mother", as I will always think of her, told me that for some years she had wanted to tell me the truth, but was prevented for fear that I would turn against her if she did. I trust I've reassured her on that score for no one could have been a better or more loving parent. I hardly remember the . . . the other. I think she had a market stall, did she not?'

'She sold fruit and salad from a stall close to Rose Alley,' Simon told her gently. 'She was a gallant soul and had a hard ending. Her husband, your uncle, was devoted to her right until the end of her life. It was a good marriage.'

'And my real father? Did you know him too?'

'No. I understand he was a wanderer who came into her life when she was lonely and sad, her husband having been away for a long time. He brought with him joy and laughter – and love. Whatever passed between them during the brief time they were together mattered to both of them a great deal.' He looked at her levelly. 'I presume you also thought your late uncle was your father?'

'That too,' she agreed. 'So, I was the child of neither my uncle nor my mother's husband. How ironic!'

'Yet you are you,' he said. 'Whatever the sin, if so you think it to be, it has in no way affected you. You are a good daughter and will be a good mother, of that I'm certain.'

She came over to him and put her arms round his neck. 'I'm sorry. I said some very harsh things to you when we parted. I still cannot pretend I'm happy at the situation I find myself in but I am now, I think, reconciled to it. You tell me I am what I am, whatever my making, and that is also true of the coming child.'

He put his arms round her. 'No day passes but I wish we could be together,' he told her huskily. 'It might still be.' But even as he said it, he could see no such positive outcome. 'Let us then still show our love for each other and remain true friends. I may be a caster of horoscopes but I do not wish to look too closely into what the future might bring.'

After a little while she left, promising to return in the near future. 'Do you remember the time when we went to see Drake's ship at Deptford?' she said. 'I'd so much like to go again. To stand on its deck and imagine that it is sailing us to a new life halfway across the world.'

'Then I shall take you,' he promised her. He had an idea. 'A young man who's played a part in my affairs of late is sailing to the Americas shortly. I will send you word when it will be and we can both take refreshment on *The Golden Hind* and see Carew off on his adventure.'

Two weeks later on a breezy April day they alighted at the same watersteps at the top of which Simon and John had found the half-dead Carew. The ship bound for Virginia was anchored in the middle of the river and there was a constant procession of small boats ferrying passengers and goods aboard. Carew, his wife, and parents were on the quayside looking across the water at the vessel that was to take them so far away. It was plain the Carews were still far from reconciled to the match, standing apart from the couple and making no effort to engage the girl in conversation when they spoke to their son but, given the circumstances, Simon considered Carew might have fared far worse. Apart from anything else the girl looked strong and sturdy, attributes which would be useful in a pioneer's wife.

As he and Avisa watched the busy scene from a little way away, Ralegh appeared on horseback accompanied by Matthew Roydon. They hailed Simon as they dismounted and, after waving a greeting at the Carew family, Ralegh came over to him. 'I thought I'd see the lad off,' he said.

'I take it the family were not prepared to have him back in Devon?' commented Simon. 'There was no last-minute change of heart, in spite of his having been so near to death?'

'No,' replied Ralegh, looking across at the Carews. 'I'm told there are endless problems and arguments regarding the contracted match. No doubt the lawyers will grow fat on it, they always do. I think it was felt best by all concerned that he should go ahead with his planned voyage and remain in the Americas at least until matters have improved somewhat. It might be a truism but time *is* the great healer.' His eyes glowed for a moment. 'When I see that brave vessel out there, I could wish myself twenty and adventuring again!'

Simon introduced his friend, Mistress Allen, to Ralegh and they walked over to the Carews. Mistress Carew thanked Simon again profusely for all that he had done for her son then turned to Avisa. 'Ah, I see you are to become a mother,' she said, then, to Simon, 'and you a father. Your wife looks blooming.'

In spite of himself, Simon coloured and Avisa blushed to the roots of her hair. 'You are mistaken, mistress,' he declared. 'This is an old friend, Mistress Avisa Allen, who has kindly agreed to accompany me to Deptford.' There was a general laugh at the mistake and Simon was wondering if he should say anything further when a carriage appeared on the quay and clattered to a swift halt.

'Some latecomer,' Ralegh noted as servants began rapidly unloading luggage. 'I trust most of their goods are already stowed aboard. There's little time left if the ship's to leave on the flood tide. I wonder who it is?'

They were soon to find out. The door of the carriage opened and a motherly-looking maid descended then helped out her mistress.

'God's Blood!' swore Simon. 'She really is the most amazing young woman.'

'I take it you know the lady?' commented Ralegh.

'I would say most certainly,' said Avisa, looking closer. 'Was she not the young woman I saw you . . .'

'I do indeed,' Simon broke in hastily. 'It's the young Tapworth widow – she whose husband I was accused of poisoning. I never thought when she confessed to me how much she desired to see the New World that she had any intention of doing so!' He excused himself and went quickly over to her.

Lavinia greeted him with a beaming smile. 'How very fortunate. I'd no idea you would be here to wish me well.'

He explained that he had come to see off an acquaintance. 'When did you decide on this?' he asked in wonderment.

'Only a week or two ago,' she told him. 'The captain of the ship is an old friend of my father's. I told him how much I'd love to see the Americas and he suggested I travel with him and do so. So here I am.' She did not look in the least daunted at the prospect.

'Do you intend to remain there?' asked Simon.

She laughed. 'Who knows? I haven't made up my mind yet. They say there are great opportunities for trade and business in the New World and I'm very good at both, as you know. In the meantime my father sits in the counting-house and looks after my affairs. William Tapworth will find little escapes him.'

What it was to be so young and so utterly confident, mused Simon. While the Americas might have much to offer her he was quite sure she would also have a great deal to offer the Americas. Perhaps she would find some stout fellow out there in Virginia who would take her fancy and so found a great dynasty. A group of less distinguished passengers was discharging from a boat and making their way on to the waiting vessel. One fellow seemed to be having trouble, as if he was suffering from some injury and had to be helped aboard. As Simon watched he turned and looked towards the shore.

It couldn't be . . . thought Simon. Surely he couldn't have survived the Fleet! He stared again. The build was like, very like but then there was nothing unusual about it. The hairs rose on the back of his neck. If Kelley had survived then maybe, after all, he truly did possess demonic powers. The man disappeared below deck and Simon shook himself. No, it had to be his imagination.

The boats were coming back from the ship to pick up the last passengers. Carew shook Simon's hand, said goodbye to Ralegh and Roydon and made his final farewells to his family, his mother crying copiously throughout. Then he took the hand of his new wife and helped her into the boat. Lavinia Tapworth and her maid swiftly followed.

Those gathered on the quay looked across the water as they were all helped aboard. The ship hummed with activity. Figures raced here and there, hauling on ropes and the sound of a shanty reached them as men climbed up aloft and began to unfurl the sails. The anchor was hauled aboard and pennants broke out on the mastheads along with a flag bearing the royal arms and a Tudor rose. Almost imperceptibly the vessel began to glide downriver on the tide, seagulls wheeling behind it, bound for America, that newfound land.

Simon was suddenly consumed with envy. Why should he not throw caution to the winds, pack up his goods and chattels, persuade Avisa to leave her husband, and sail off into the west? They would be new people starting a new life, leaving the old behind them and no one need ever know they were not truly man and wife. But even as the thought came to him he knew it could never be. They both had too many responsibilities. Their roots in their homeland went deep and Avisa would not leave her burden of guilt behind in England; indeed, it might well become heavier still abroad. Nor would it be sensible for a woman in her condition to make such a long and hazardous voyage.

He put his arm gently around her. 'Come, my dear heart. Let's make our way to *The Golden Hind* and drink a toast to our brave venturers.'

Author's Note

THE REAL DOCTOR SIMON FORMAN

Almost the only knowledge we had of him for a long time was the note in the *National Dictionary of Biography*, written by Sir Sydney Lee in the late 1870s, which is full of inaccuracies and describes him as a charlatan and a quack, a view taken presumably after reading of the clashes Simon Forman had with the College of Physicians when he was accused of being both. Later research, however, reveals a very different story. Contrary to what the Physicians recorded – that he had no medical books and practised medicine purely by the use of astrology – this is provably not true, for his most frequently used medical sources, along with 150 pages of his medical notes and diagnoses, are now known to exist in King's College Library, Cambridge. Nor did the fact that he practised astrology and cast horoscopes, sometimes using the latter for diagnosis, make him a quack as all doctors of his day did the same.

Simon Forman was born in Wiltshire in 1558, the youngest of five children. His father, a small tenant farmer, died when he was a child. He achieved a place at a grammar school in Salisbury where he was fascinated by the New Sciences and wanted to study medicine. His teachers were anxious he should go to Oxford but his mother refused to support him. After time spent as an apprentice, he went to Oxford as servant to a young man of good family and studied, when he was able, at Magdalen College for two years; however, he was unable to keep it up owing to the demands of his employer. On his return to Wiltshire he combined schoolteaching with basic medical practice but fell foul of a local landowner and lawyer who had him sent to prison for a year.

There is then a great blank in Forman's life, after which we find him working briefly as a physician in Salisbury (during which time he fathered an illegitimate child), spending some time in London, then in Holland (where it seems he might well have acquired more medical knowledge) and possibly elsewhere before finally setting up as a physician in London, first in Billingsgate and then in Lambeth. For many years, even after he received a licence to practice and medical qualification from Cambridge University, he had constant trouble with the College of Physicians who kept refusing to license him, not least because they considered him a low-class upstart who practised the Black Arts.

Dr A. L. Rowse did an invaluable service by publishing edited extracts from Dr Forman's *Casebooks* and diary, which are in the Bodleian Library, Oxford, though he was apparently unaware of the material in Cambridge. He dated Simon Forman's setting up in London as around 1593, but it was at least two years earlier. Interestingly enough, during one clash with the College of Physicians, when Forman was sent to prison for defying them, no lesser person than the Lord Privy Seal, Sir Robert Cecil, Elizabeth's spymaster and Acting Secretary to the Privy Council, intervened on his behalf.

Eventually he acquired a substantial house at the Lambeth end of the Bankside with an orchard and garden in which he grew herbs for his own medicines. He treated patients both at home and by visiting them and, uniquely, he crossed the entire social spectrum from the publicans, actors, dramatists and whores of the Bankside, through wealthy City merchants, privateers and the great seafarers, to the aristocrats at Court. He enjoyed the theatre and gave us our first accounts of Shakespeare's plays.

In real life he spent a good deal of time out of London and there are diary entries of him visiting the West Country, the Midlands, the Welsh marches, Ipswich and Suffolk and many other places, including one unexplained medical note which begins, *When I was in Scotland . . .*

Simon Forman had a tremendous appetite for women and was candid about sex. He used a code word (*halek*) to describe the activity he entered into with those women he fancied or who paid him in kind. This led to a reputation for curing sterility in women. He had a brief and stormy affair with Emilia Lanier, who was possibly Shakespeare's Dark Lady, but the love of his life was undoubtedly Avisa Allen, the Catholic wife of a City merchant and venturer by whom he had a child which did not survive. She also 'distilled', that is, made up herbal medicines. Divorce was, of course, out of the question but Avisa became Simon's long-term mistress until she died five years later. He finally married Anne or Jane Baker, a girl half his age, the daughter of a knight from Kent.

Forman was considered an expert on poisons, so much so that he would have been a witness in the trial of Frances Howard, Countess of Essex, for the murder of Sir Thomas Overbury but he died beforehand, most probably of appendicitis or a burst stomach ulcer. During the trial he was blamed for providing the countess's accomplice with the poison used and, since he was unable to defend his reputation, this added to his undeserved posthumous notoriety.

Like some doctors of his age, including Shakespeare's son-in-law, John Hall, he kept case notes of his patients, their maladies, the outcome of his treatments and their horoscopes and only now are his *Casebooks* considered to be models of good practice for their time. He also wrote 'books' on, among other things, medicine, astrology and the need to find a method of calculating longitude. While my portrayal of him owes much to poetic licence, the original was lively, questioning, energetic and a true Renaissance Man.

THE SCHOOL OF THE NIGHT

It really did exist. Its loose membership, drawn together by Sir Walter Ralegh, included some of the finest scientific and creative minds of the day, such as the astronomer and mathematician Thomas Hariot; Henry Percy, Earl of Northumberland ('the Wizard Earl'); Robert Hues, the geographer; Emery Molyneux, globemaker and friend of the real Simon Forman; Christopher Marlowe; George Chapman (translator of Homer); Matthew Roydon (poet) and others. It cannot be proved either way whether or not the real Simon Forman met up with the rest in Ralegh's Tower Room or at his country estate in Sherborne, but it is quite likely that he did, given his wide-ranging interests and the fact that he knew many of its members.

The School of the Night was looked on with great suspicion. Rumours abounded that its members were atheists and blasphemers practising strange rites and experiments, but in actual fact they discussed such subjects as the real (rather than the Biblical) age of the world, the truth of Old Testament stories, the place of the earth in relation to the universe, now that it was known that we circled the sun, and the 'new' sciences and mathematics. The reason we know this is from accusations made against Marlowe immediately before he was killed in Deptford while on bail awaiting a trial on blasphemy charges (among others). Following his murder, Sir Robert Cecil set up an Inquisition into the School which met and took evidence over several months but then, for some unknown reason, the whole matter was dropped.

THE TAROT

The use of the Tarot cards in this story is purely a fictional device, for the meanings of cards, including the Greater Trumps, depends on their place in the spreads and patterns used. For more information see *The Tarot* by Brian Inglis (Orbis Books, 1977) and *The Tarot* by Alfred Douglas (Gollancz, 1973)

OTHER PEOPLE IN THIS STORY

Mary Herbert, Countess of Pembroke was a very lively lady, much as described herein. She had been tutored, among others, by Dr Dee and was highly intelligent with an enquiring mind, had her own laboratory in which she conducted experiments, and met and discussed scientific matters with her male counterparts on equal terms. She was a companion to the Queen, suggested the subject of *Arcadia* to her brother, Sir Philip Sidney, and revised and added to it after his death. She also collected and edited his poetry. She was a patron to many men of letters of her day, including Edmund Spenser, Ben Jonson and John Donne. John Aubrey describes her as 'a beautifull ladie of an excellent witt . . . shee had a pritty sharpe-ovall face. Her haire was of the reddish yellowe.' He also credits her with a number of lovers including Sir Robert Cecil.

Edward Kelley appeared almost from nowhere in the early 1580s, claiming a wide variety of occult skills including necromancy (the raising of spirits) and 'scrying'. He had indeed had his ears cropped in Lancaster for digging up corpses and was branded on the thumb at Tyburn for forging. In spite of this, he had sufficient charisma and confidence to fool a large number of people, among them Ferdinand, Lord Strange, Earl of Derby (who may possibly have been murdered later) and, notoriously, Dr Dee who became his patron. Finally, after killing a man, Kelley was taken abroad by Dee and, we are told, had a triumphal progress round the courts of Europe. However, at some stage Kelley offended a prince, either in Germany or Bohemia, and is said variously to have been publicly executed, privately strangled or to have broken his neck climbing down a wall trying to escape. His arrival in this story is history of the 'what if?' variety.

The Carew Family were prominent landowners in Devon and Cornwall at the time of this story. Their descendants still own and live in the great house at Antony, near Saltash, to this day. However Spenser Carew is fictional.

John Bradedge is based on a real character of that name who was born in Cheapside, then was briefly apprenticed to a silversmith. An idle lad, only interested in drink, girls and card-playing, he and his Dutch wife Anna were eventually taken in by Simon as his manservant and housekeeper.

THE FLEET RIVER

If anyone doubts the horrors of the Fleet at the end of the sixteenth century, they need only read Ben Jonson's poem *The Voyage* in which he describes a trip he made by wherry from the Mermaid tavern to Holbourne. It is far more stomach-churning than anything described here. Eventually the Fleet was covered over, it finally having been accepted that it had become nothing more than a sewer.

If you enjoyed this book here is a selection of other bestselling titles from Headline

THE DEMON ARCHER	Paul Doherty	£5.99	☐
JANE AND THE GENIUS OF THE PLACE	Stephanie Barron	£5.99	☐
PAST POISONS	Ed. Maxim Jakubowski	£5.99	☐
SQUIRE THROWLEIGH'S HEIR	Michael Jecks	£5.99	☐
THE COMPLAINT OF THE DOVE	Hannah March	£5.99	☐
THE FOXES OF WARWICK	Edward Marston	£5.99	☐
BEDFORD SQUARE	Anne Perry	£5.99	☐
THE GERMANICUS MOSAIC	Rosemary Rowe	£5.99	☐
THE CONCUBINE'S TATTOO	Laura Joh Rowland	£5.99	☐
THE WEAVER'S INHERITANCE	Kate Sedley	£5.99	☐
SEARCH THE DARK	Charles Todd	£5.99	☐
THE MONK WHO VANISHED	Peter Tremayne	£5.99	☐

Headline books are available at your local bookshop or newsagent. Alternatively, books can be ordered direct from the publisher. Just tick the titles you want and fill in the form below. Prices and availability subject to change without notice.

Buy four books from the selection above and get free postage and packaging and delivery within 48 hours. Just send a cheque or postal order made payable to Bookpoint Ltd to the value of the total cover price of the four books. Alternatively, if you wish to buy fewer than four books the following postage and packaging applies:

UK and BFPO £4.30 for one book; £6.30 for two books; £8.30 for three books.

Overseas and Eire: £4.80 for one book; £7.10 for 2 or 3 books (surface mail).

Please enclose a cheque or postal order made payable to *Bookpoint Limited*, and send to: Headline Publishing Ltd, 39 Milton Park, Abingdon, OXON OX14 4TD, UK.
Email Address: orders@bookpoint.co.uk

If you would prefer to pay by credit card, our call team would be delighted to take your order by telephone. Our direct line is 01235 400 414 (lines open 9.00 am–6.00 pm Monday to Saturday 24 hour message answering service). Alternatively you can send a fax on 01235 400 454.

Name ....

Address ....

....

....

If you would prefer to pay by credit card, please complete:
Please debit my Visa/Access/Diner's Card/American Express (delete as applicable) card number:

Signature .... Expiry Date ....